Derek sat ne[xt] ... turned to him ... surrendered. ... kissed him, li[ngering at] the feel of his lips against hers. She inhaled the expensive cologne mixed with his own scent to seal his signature fragrance for the days when he would no longer be around.

"I want to stay," she whispered.

He didn't move, simply stared down at her. "One sec."

He went down a hallway and came back with a damp washcloth. Then he dimmed the room.

"I love how you made yourself look like a supermodel on a photo shoot. But I like you with a more natural look. You are so beautiful without makeup." He wiped her face, slowly and gently as if revealing a work of art.

Toni saw the bronze foundation mixed with black eyeliner and streaks of copper lipcolor on the washcloth like a painter's palette. When Derek had finished, he reached behind Toni's head and unfastened the ponytail clip. He ran his fingers through her hair, fluffing it out to frame her face.

"You're so damned beautiful."

"I hear that all the time." Toni bit her lip.

"You know we're supposed to be eating crème brûlée."

"Let's do that later."

"At sunrise?"

ISLAND
Rendezvous

MICHELLE MONKOU

ARABESQUE®

ISLAND RENDEZVOUS

An Arabesque novel

ISBN 1-58314-613-X

© 2006 by Michelle Monkou

www.kimanipress.com

Printed in U.S.A.

Big thanks to my support groups:
Cosmo Ladies—Julia Canchola, Yvonne,
Marjanna Bogan, Kathryn Anderson, Lisa Arlt,
Deborah Barnhart, Julie Halperson and
Kim Feldmiller. Celebrity Café—Celeste Norfleet,
Candice Poarch, Shirley Hailstock.

Chapter 1

Toni Kimball stretched her neck and rotated her shoulders to ease the stiffness. She wished that there was a similar exercise that could perform the same wonders on her brain. Maybe then the decision would be easier.

She sighed. If only the right answer would pop into her head. The thought of going anywhere on her own scared her. Fear had sunk in, anchoring its way into her mind. How could she decide when only negative thoughts came to mind?

Her mission this week was to make sure her furniture arrived at the storage facility in Glen Knolls, Maryland. Then she had to go to her new job, sign paperwork, have her photo ID taken, and participate in her company's standard drug test. Her job as an engineer started in three weeks.

Later, she'd have to check on her condo. She'd be moving into her new home in the next few weeks. This meant that she'd stay with her cousin for a week. Living with Donna, even for one week, would test her patience and temper.

But all of that faded to the back of her mind.

Nicole had waited until she came back to Glen Knolls, with an invitation to stay in her B&B, before hitting Toni with one of her crazy ideas.

Toni sat cross-legged on the bed with a pillow hugged to her chest, looking at her best friend. Nicole sat sideways in the armchair across the room, with her long brown legs dangling over the side. The scene reminded Toni of their college days when they shared an apartment, along with the joys and heartbreaks of dating.

"Oh, come on, Toni. You'd think that I was asking you to do a monumental task. It's a simple yes or no," Nicole insisted.

"You know it's not that simple. I can't just up and leave and go traipsing out of the country. To the Bahamas, none-theless." Toni shook her head. "I have things to do."

Nicole sucked her teeth. "Name one thing."

"I'm helping my mother with painting the bathroom. My father can't mow the lawn like he used to, and instead of paying an expensive fee, I'm helping with that chore. Plus my parents are empty nesters. They need the company."

"It's been six months that you've been living there," Nicole reminded her gently. "I think they got along without you and they are in no way as dependent as you're making them sound. Your father did the 10k race two months ago, and your mother's never home because she is a social butterfly. It's time—"

"To move on with my life. There. I've said it for you." Toni finished with an emotional lump in her voice. Her eyes prickled with ready tears. Her throat closed painfully over a sob as she avoided Nicole's perceptive gaze.

"I didn't say that or mean that. I'm concerned that you're trying to bury yourself under what's important to other people."

"Oh, here we go with the psychobabble." Toni rolled her eyes. She wished Nicole would quit badgering her.

"For example, you hate yard work. And painting? Please. You don't even paint your toenails, much less a room."

"Maybe I've changed."

"Or not. I'm looking for my old friend Toni. I'm looking for that woman who could chew you up and spit you out with a look or that sharp tongue. I want to see that cute, sassy woman with the big butt and a smile."

"And it's gotten bigger." Toni ran her hands over her hips.

In the old days, she enjoyed the simple things. Her exercise regimen began in the mornings with a jog before work. Now that was a thing in the past. Twice a month, she'd volunteer at the neighborhood library. Once her world imploded, she didn't care to do anything or be around anyone.

She had a reputation of being a savvy shopper who could sniff a bargain. At the end of each season, she went after stores with overstocked inventory and discontinued items. Now the reclining chair in the family room was the only thing that garnered her attention. The chair, remote, and TV became her world, safe and undemanding.

"It'll get better. Give yourself a chance. You're too tough on yourself."

"I feel worn out." Toni fell back onto the bed, looking up at the ceiling.

She hadn't wanted to intrude on Brad and Nicole. Getting Toni to agree to stay with them while in town took their combined effort. She hated to intrude on the newlyweds.

When Nicole'd shown her the blue colonial, she'd envied her friend's keen eye for its potential. The farmhouse had an expansive property. For the weary traveler, the house provided a retreat from urban sprawl and noisy neighbors while rejuvenating the spirit.

The Montgomery B&B had more than hospitality. Originally, Nicole discovered the house's history quite by accident when she came upon an old newspaper article. She had successfully registered the property with the historical society. Old houses have character and personality that are part of history and past owners. The B&B played an integral role in the Underground Railroad during slavery more than a hundred years ago; its role was to shelter and protect the human spirit.

Toni stared up at the thick solid beams crisscrossing the roof, supporting the structure. It had been a temporary haven for those seeking refuge. She, too, was in need of such a haven, but lately she felt as if life was weighing her down emotionally and even physically.

"I get to be a statistic. One divorced woman sitting in your sights. I should've never married Clayton Boyd." She punched the pillow. "He doesn't deserve to be called a man. Nicole, he told so many lies." She'd wanted to hear how much he cared for her. She was disgusted with herself for thinking that getting married was the only solution.

Once they married, she played at being the perfect wife, making him the center of her universe. Over time, she ignored the niggling doubts. Instead she focused on creating a happy home for their child. No matter how hard she tried, all her good thoughts and energy couldn't produce what wasn't there.

"I know it hurts." Nicole sat on the bed with her, stroking her friend's hair away from her face.

How would you know? Toni didn't say the words, but she thought them. None of her family or friends knew how deep her pain ran. They didn't understand the drowning pool of anger she had stepped in and couldn't seem to break out of. And they certainly didn't comprehend why she would want to fall into a stupor so that she didn't have to feel anything.

"You feel betrayed. I was there in that hellish place when I had breast cancer. I know about feeling the bitter rage. Your mind and body are stronger than you think. But even when you were ready to give up, I was here for you during your heartbreak. It's time for a little good luck to come your way."

"Marrying Clayton had to be my biggest mistake. He didn't love me. I suppose that he was trying to save face with a child on the way. What did my baby do to anyone? Why did I lose my child?" Toni buried her face in the pillow. Her shoulders shook as the tears flowed. The bed shifted under her, and she felt Nicole's hand touch her back.

"Nature. God's plans. We don't always have all the answers. But you still have to take care of yourself. You have to decide if you're going to remain stuck or move ahead."

"You're not giving me any credit for landing a new job."

"I'm very proud of you. But I know you will struggle and you don't have to undergo that turmoil."

"I'm still in the anger phase. I still have depression to look forward to before I get to acceptance." Toni laughed, but there was no humor in the sound. Her doctor had suggested therapy, a support group, even seminars. She usually would try one or two sessions then retreat. She was never one to pour her emotions out like running water, while people waded through them, leaving their impressions on her inner thoughts and experiences.

Nicole took Toni's hand and held it between her own. "I know my request sounds bizarre, especially at this time in your life. But I think that you do need a change of scenery. No parents to hover over you. No friends to pester you about what you should or shouldn't do. No daily reminders of what you've lost to sap your energy." Nicole held eye contact with her. Toni felt her friend's calming reassurance that she was there for her. "I'm asking you to take this trip for selfish reasons too. I want you to do this for me and Brad."

"Brad?"

"I think I found his brother. All I need you to do is to confirm it while you have a glorious vacation."

Toni had to admit that Nicole always managed to deliver her news with a one-two punch. "What part of my background says private investigator? And I thought that I was the one on the verge of a breakdown." She pointed at Nicole. "Mine is emotional. Yours is mental." Despite her words, her curiosity had been ignited.

"Two years ago when Brad learned he had another brother, I was thrilled. He had spent some time trying to find the missing pieces in his life. This was a major breakthrough." Nicole readjusted herself on the bed to tell her story. "Once he knew he had a brother, he gathered as much information as he could, which wasn't much. But he also learned that his father raised his brother and never looked back, he never came back for him. Brad's feelings of abandonment have turned into anger and, if you ask him, hatred. He's stopped looking for his brother. He doesn't even want to hear any mention of him or his father."

"Where is the brother?"

"Bahamas."

"Bahamas? How does he get from Baltimore to the Bahamas? Both places start with the letter B, but that's about it."

"That's what I keep wondering. This is what you need to find out."

"Me?"

"This is a busy time of the year. I can't leave here."

"Yeah, right." Bahamas appealed to her a great deal, but this wasn't a quick jaunt to the next city. For heaven's sake, this was going out of the country; albeit a beautiful, tropical paradise.

"Why not write to him? Tell him that you're trying to reunite him with family," Toni asked. "By the way, isn't your sister living there?"

"I don't think this is the type of news you deliver in a letter. What if he's got issues too? I can barely deal with Brad's stubbornness over the whole thing. Hopefully his brother hasn't been warped by the experience. But once you find him, I'll hop on a plane, meet him, stay overnight, party, drink, drink, party, and then fly home. Plus, Vicky lives in Eleuthera and I don't want to get her involved. She's only met Brad once and doesn't know everything that's going on."

Toni nodded, knowing that the sisters shared a comfortable relationship, although not a close one.

"I suppose you're going to tuck Brad in bed, kiss him on the cheek and tell him that you're going to the Bahamas for a day and he won't care."

"I've checked his schedule. He's got to get his travel story into his editor in the next couple of weeks. He's not going to be thinking about me or anything else. As long as I keep the guests away from him, he'll be fine," Nicole explained. "I'll tell him that I'm with you at one of our slumber parties. Three nights or more and I'd have to come up with a more elaborate excuse. And I don't want to lie more than necessary to arrange a reunion."

"I realize that it's important for Brad to know his brother, but aren't you forcing this on him? What if he doesn't want to meet him, even after you've set it up? You're being overly optimistic about this entire situation. His brother could be a deadbeat and you'd be bringing him into your lives to create chaos."

"Whoa, Miss Sunshine." Nicole shot her an exasperated look. "I'll deal with telling him the truth after we find him."

"Be careful. Trust is a fragile commodity in a relationship. It's like Humpty Dumpty, it can be broken beyond repair."

"Humpty Dumpty shouldn't have sat so high off the ground. You'd think an egg would know better. Please stop lecturing me, and just say yes."

"Only if you'll stop lecturing me."

"In the space of a year, you have experienced more in life than any of us. Although it may not feel like it, you're stronger for it. Use this opportunity to heal. How often do you think I would pay for you to take a trip?"

Toni chuckled. "You ain't lying."

"And you're B-R-O-K-E, so when will you be able to take a fabulous vacation like this?" They shared a laugh. "It's time for the fighter in you to surface and get that mop on your head that you call a hairstyle, trimmed and hot-curled."

Toni swung her pillow at Nicole who rolled off the bed and headed for the bedroom door.

Part of the pain that cut deep was the humiliation. It had not been an easy decision to get married. But with a baby on the way, she didn't want to disappoint her parents by being an unwed mother. Plus, why bring her child into the world without a father, she'd reasoned.

Six months into the pregnancy she miscarried. Instead of dealing with her grief with the reassurance of her husband's care and love, she was alone. He'd used the miscarriage as a reason to end their marriage. Commitment had always been his weakness and in the face of adversity, it became evident that he had no intention of changing.

At her lowest point, when the world seemed to have turned on her, Clayton messengered the divorce papers to her work. In stark black letters against the crisp white paper, she read that he'd filed for divorce. The messenger who didn't know the contents wished her a good weekend.

She'd lost a baby that she desperately wanted. She'd lost a man who was never really a husband. Yet, both losses had taken their toll, sending her to the brink. Scared that she would lose control, she took an extended leave of absence and moved back home.

"By the way, your mother said that you could go."

"What? You asked my mother?" Toni stared at Nicole as if she'd grown another head. "Like I'm sixteen years old."

"You're the one acting as if you can't leave your parents' house without permission."

"What did she say?"

"I'd lie to get my way, but she said that it's up to you. She doesn't want to push you."

"It's not every day that I am offered an expense-paid trip to the Bahamas."

"Don't get carried away. Your expenses are enough for you to get a couple small meals daily to keep you alive, okay? I used Brad's travel connections to get a bargain on the airfare and hotel."

Toni still wasn't ready to jump on board. It all sounded like the perfect vacation except for the slight twist of having to find Nicole's brother-in-law. The timing couldn't be better since she wasn't due to move into her condo for a few weeks. She had moved her things out of her parents' home and put them in the storage facility where she put most of her furniture.

"Tomorrow, I'm going back home. Let me think about it. When did you need me to leave?"

"Like yesterday. The ticket is good for two weeks. You've got to confirm at least twenty-four hours before the date you want to fly."

Toni loved sitting in her mother's kitchen. The country décor reminded her of a 1950s television sitcom set. Everything matched down to the hand towels, oven mitts, and place mats on the four-seater dining table set off in an alcove near the kitchen. Pine wood cabinets and furniture smelled of lemon polish. Chrome appliances, along with the kitchen faucet, gleamed under the fluorescent lighting. Frilly curtains framed the windows that overlooked a small herb garden.

Being an only child, growing up amid such neatness and order was all she knew. As an adult returning home for holidays and other special occasions, the house struck her as old-fashioned, stuck in a time warp. Yet it was this familiarity and everything in its place and her parents' solid family values that provided comfort when she hurt the most.

The daily routine hadn't changed much with her mother making homemade bread for the next day's breakfast. Underlying the smell of baking bread, was the aroma of dinner. Sitting on the warming plate was roasted chicken, russet potatoes and carrots. The most inviting garden salad with fresh green leaves, accented with yellow and red peppers, along with crisp cucumbers was under cellophane ready to accompany them.

Breakfast and dinner required everyone at the table. If her father was late, they didn't eat until he came home or until he called and said that her mother could begin serving. Toni had learned to sneak her snacks when he was running late. Her mother wouldn't break the rule and let her eat or ruin her appetite with a quick bite. By the time she was in high school, she daydreamed about the freedom that she would enjoy in college. Her goal was to go to a campus that required a plane ride to get there. She couldn't wait to get away from her family and the confounded rules.

Her father had barely talked to her during her difficult teen years, so any important conversations were her mother's domain. He never asked her what she would like to be when she grew up. She felt he underestimated her. Getting an engineering degree was designed to prove him wrong. She could go toe-to-toe with any man.

Her father breathed old-fashioned traditional values. Her mother, well, she'd never quite figured out what her mother's motivation was, except to please her father. Toni hadn't followed in their footsteps regarding marrying young and settling down.

"Toni, sweetheart, I'm heading upstairs. Make sure you lock up when you finish up?"

Toni looked up at the clock. She'd lost track of the time.

"Going out tonight?" her mother asked.

Toni shook her head.

"Honey, you need to go out. Actually I thought that you would've stayed in Glen Knolls a little longer."

"I was only going for the two days. Plus I had gotten used to eating dinner with you and Dad on Fridays. I'll miss that when I leave at the end of the month." Even to her ears she sounded whiney and pathetic.

Her mother continued up the stairs.

"Mom, Nicole said that she talked to you about me going to the Bahamas." Toni waited for her mother to respond.

"Yes, but I'm leaving the decision up to you. Are you at least considering it?"

Toni nodded. She detected the hopefulness in her mother's voice.

"Good, so when are you leaving?"

"Geez, Mom, slow down."

"Honey, life will be difficult at times. Just when you think you have it all under control, something else will pop up. You can't change the past."

Toni tried to read her mother's expression. Was it regret

that she saw? Her mother was so prim that the thought of asking her outright died in her throat.

"Linda, you coming up?"

"In a minute, Wesley."

"Your husband is summoning you. Go. I'll be fine. I told Nicole that I would give her my decision in the morning." Toni motioned for her mother to leave.

Her mother nodded, mouthed good night and headed upstairs. Toni did her rounds of checking locks and windows before turning off the lights. A few minutes later, she followed her mother's lead and headed upstairs to her own room.

Like the house, her bedroom seemed like it had been plucked from a time capsule. The Pepto Bismal-pink walls and white furniture had been her favorite colors as a child. Nothing had been altered. Her mother kept the room intact. Once she moved back home, there was no way that she'd stay in this cotton candy world. She had gone the opposite route and purchased bright blue, yellow and green colors. No pastels allowed.

Her phone on the bedside table rang.

"I've been waiting for your call," Nicole prompted.

"Sorry, girl. I had to clean up the kitchen." Toni rearranged the pillows behind her, adjusting her body against the headboard until she found a comfortable position.

"She's quite the domestic soul," Shirley teased.

Toni not only looked forward to the weekly calls, but enjoyed the banter with her girlfriends. Heck, they were more than girlfriends. She much preferred the term soul-sisters to describe their foursome.

The four had gone to the same college. Toni and Nicole were childhood friends before Donna, Toni's cousin, came into the picture. Later, they all met Shirley, another student. Over the years their bond of friendship grew stronger.

So what if other women thought of them as a clique? They were closer than any sisters.

Shirley was the peacemaker. She had a generous heart that made her the target of deadbeat boyfriends. Her full-figured shape sometimes got her down, but she always thought of others before herself.

Donna was irritating enough to be anybody's real sister. Toni and her cousin Donna got into heated arguments about anything and everything, which often ended with them spewing venom at each other. But, no one outside their close-knit circle dared talk to Toni about her cousin.

Without intending to, they had somehow all ended up in Glen Knolls outside of Annapolis, Maryland. After they graduated, Nicole went to work in Washington, D.C. as a lobbyist. The other women followed and within two years they were living in the Glen Knolls suburb, enjoying the social amenities in Baltimore, Annapolis, and Washington, D.C.

"How are you doing?" Shirley asked, a question that was more obligatory than sincere.

"Fine," Toni answered.

"I'm glad you accepted the job."

"It was good money, so why not?"

"That's never stopped you from turning down a job," Donna reminded.

"Yeah, well I'm happy to change that."

"Ladies, don't start," Nicole warned.

"Lucky you. Wish I could land a job that pays the big bucks," Shirley piped in.

"When are you coming home?" her cousin asked.

"Donna, cut the girl some slack?"

"It's okay, Nicole. You know, Donna's got to act like she's my second mother," Toni teased.

"Whatever. Like I said, when are you coming home? You've been living up in your mother's house going on a year. You're a grown woman with grown-up responsibilities. It's time to get back on your own two feet and handle your affairs."

"Don't lecture me, Donna. And I've told you that I'm moving in with you in a few weeks." Toni allowed the sharpness in her tone to highlight her irritation. Her cousin knew how to turn the screws to piss her off.

"This was a call to show Toni that we are all here for her," Shirley prompted.

"Nice way of showing it, ladies," Toni mumbled.

"Donna, apologize," Nicole ordered.

"No."

"Then, I'm hanging up." Toni settled back against the pillows. It was only a matter of time before the others forced Donna to apologize.

A few seconds of silence and then an almost whispered apology was offered.

"Awesome," Shirley cheered. "Any news from you, Nicole?"

"What news?" Toni hated being left out of the loop.

"Nicole may be pregnant," Donna blurted.

"Get out of here."

"You all have the biggest mouths," Nicole said, clearly distressed.

"I hope you're not worried about me hearing such news?"

Toni asked. "Don't walk around on eggsshells with me. Yes, it hurts sometimes, but I can handle good news."

"Well, everyone is celebrating a bit prematurely. I thought that I was pregnant because I was late. But I did a test and it's a false alarm. Anyway, when I told Brad, he looked relieved."

"*You* don't sound relieved." Toni sensed the connection between the baby issue and the trip to the Bahamas.

"Brad isn't sure that he's ready, or even if he will ever make a good father. I reminded him how much the boys he mentored at the recreation center depended on him, using him as their role model. He's kind, gentle, but stubborn like you wouldn't believe."

"Says one hardhead to another," Toni clarified.

"No one is perfect," Nicole offered. "I know it's because of his childhood and everything. It's just going to take some time, but he'll come around."

"When did the kinder, gentler Nicole come out to play?"

Toni hoped that her best friend and her new husband could work out these serious issues soon. She didn't like hearing the strain in Nicole's voice over the subject. It simply reiterated the fact that she should be in Glen Knolls to fuss over her friends.

"I've got to run, Toni. Got to get up early in the morning. Let me know when you want us to run up there to help you pack and move," Shirley offered.

Everyone followed suit, ending the weekly call.

Toni slid under the covers and settled into bed. She shut her eyes tightly, hoping sleep would come quickly. Instead she thought about her friends and how much she missed them. They loved her unconditionally.

She wasn't sleepy, so she grabbed the book that she had

half-heartedly started to read. The celebrity biography was interesting, but bore no resemblance to her world. Staying out late, drinking and hanging out with the jet set wasn't in her world, not that she wouldn't like the chance to live life as a millionaire. She could learn to drink champagne, eat caviar and be a young sexy starlet for a hot second.

She heard her parents' muffled voices seep through the shared wall. A couple of words became clearer as their tone rose. Toni tried to ignore the conversation. She burrowed her head deeper into the pillows and focused on the words on the page.

"Shh, lower your voice, Wesley."

"I will not. It makes no sense."

"She's leaving at the end of the month."

"You baby her. That's why she's been in this house moping around for months."

"Don't be cruel. It's difficult for a woman to deal with what she's gone through."

Toni placed her finger to mark the page where she'd stopped. Kneeling, she placed her ear against the wall. So far, what she overheard didn't make her feel warm and fuzzy. But she wanted to hear everything.

"Do you want me to talk to her?" her father asked.

"Good gracious, no. You and she go at it too much. You're on her case about everything. She gets defensive even if you ask a simple question."

"I'm her father. I'm supposed to tell her like it is. I'm supposed to tell her when she's screwing up when she makes bonehead decisions. Doesn't mean that I don't love her. She's my daughter for heaven's sake."

"When has a kind word come out of your mouth? No, don't shoot back one of your crazy reasons."

"She's a tough girl. She doesn't need me to coddle her. That's your job. I raised a survivor."

"I agree that she's a strong person. Right now, she's beyond my help. It'll take time. And we can't measure how long. Home is where she can get her head together."

"All mumbo jumbo, if you ask me. She needs to pick up where she left off and continue with her life. While she's wallowing in self-pity, life and opportunities are passing her by."

"Wesley, I think—"

"Hush, now. I don't want to spend all night talking about our daughter. I don't know how we got on that subject. This is supposed to be our date night."

Toni heard the bed frame squeak and groan.

Oh dear, she thought.

She had hoped that she would fall asleep quickly. The squeaking repeated, growing increasingly louder. Toni pulled the pillow over her head. This had to be some kind of punishment. Goodness gracious, she couldn't possibly stay and listen to her parents' romantic moments. She'd learned about date night and always managed to be out or in the basement. She'd missed the cue this time. Maybe that's why her mother had seemed disappointed that she wasn't going out.

Toni threw back the covers, slipped on her bedroom slippers and hightailed out the room. She really wasn't going to listen to her parents' lovemaking. Already her face was flush with embarrassment. A squeaking bed was one thing. Overhearing rapturous moans did her in. Robe thrown over her arm, she tiptoed into the hallway and eased down the stairs, careful to avoid detection.

Her parents, despite their prim and proper demeanor, were like randy teenagers who couldn't keep their hands off each other. She was happy for them that things were going well in that department. Sitting in the kitchen drinking a glass of milk, she thought, who was the lame one? At thirty-five years old, she could do without this life experience.

She phoned Nicole.

"Toni? What's the matter?"

"Sorry to wake you. Guess you went straight to bed after we talked."

"It's okay." Nicole yawned. "Is something wrong?"

"No, no." Now that Toni had Nicole on the phone, she felt a bit foolish. "I needed to talk." She exhaled noisily. "You're waiting on my answer, right?"

"Yes, but not at this very minute. You're sounding a bit strange. Sure everything is okay?"

"You wouldn't believe me if I told you." Toni giggled.

"Try me."

"I heard my parents…doing it."

"Doing it? What…oh my gosh, do you mean *doing it?* That kind of *it?*" Nicole chuckled.

"Nicole, this isn't funny. Every Friday I can set my clock by their weekly ritual."

"They are married. Remember that's how you got here."

"I know, but you'd think they would show some restraint."

"Sounds to me like you may be jealous."

"I'm in the house, Nicole." She didn't think of herself as a prude, but when it came to her parents, she'd rather not imagine the scenario. "Nicole, who are you talking to?" She listened to Nicole explain about her parents' late night activities. "Are you telling Brad?"

"Yep. He thinks that it's funny as all get out." Nicole then dissolved into another fit of laughter.

"I'll take the trip."

That at least shut Nicole's mouth.

"Really?"

"Yes. I don't think I can take any more of this before I move into my own place."

"At least I know what motivates you. Maybe you'll get lucky and get yourself some lovin' under the tropical sun."

"Yeah, right. Forgot what some lovin' did?"

"Excuse my bluntness, but there wasn't any love in that equation. You have to learn from your experiences. You can't learn if everything is perfect and goes your way."

"Why don't you go on the lecture circuit?" Toni snapped.

"Whatever. You're only going to be there for a short time. You can let down your hair. We'll never know," Nicole teased.

"Not everything revolves around relationships."

"You may play Miss Pollyanna all you want. I remember the college years, the twenties and—"

"Shut up." Toni blushed at the memories best left tucked away with the fashion mistakes.

"Remember don't get hot and heavy over any dude. And my last bit of advice—use protection."

This time Toni not only blushed, but wished the floor would open and swallow her.

Nicole *and* Brad were laughing heartily over the phone.

Chapter 2

Derek Calverton sat at the beachside bar clipping his fingernails. His schedule was pretty light with only two excursions planned. A busy day usually had him giving up to eight tours. If the weather held out, he'd have another two or three in the afternoon.

A light itinerary didn't concern him. He had to meet with his other business associates later that evening. Balancing the two worlds of charter tours and software programming promised to be difficult. His heart couldn't choose between the two. One had proven to be successful, while the other meant starting over in a new field with different rules and risks. Right now, he enjoyed the freedom to chat with the bartender Cecil until he had to go to work.

Nassau, the most famous city in the Bahama Islands, featured major hotels with family entertainment, casinos and celebrity stars in Broadway-type productions. Although he wasn't born in the Bahamas, it was his home. The warm temperature drew sun worshippers who pursued outdoor activities. No matter how many times he conducted a tour, he admired the natural beauty of the Bahamas' many islands.

Despite the tourist traffic, he still managed to find quiet areas of the island where he could enjoy a secluded piece of beach. He'd sit on the sea wall sketching the landscape while admiring the azure water softly washing against the beach. The sound of the ocean eased the day's stress. Living away from the beach seemed unimaginable.

He glanced at his watch, calculating how much time he had to play with before dealing with the weather. "Hey, Cecil, could you hurry with the registration list."

"Yeah, mon. Gimme a second." Cecil served a few more customers. It was only eleven o'clock in the morning, but that didn't stop the flow of piña coladas and rum-laced fruit punches.

Derek had an exclusive arrangement with a few of the key hotels to provide excursions for their guests. Cecil's bar was strategically situated near the water and the hotels. The bartender, and longtime owner, helped him with some of the administrative details, including letting his bar serve as the meeting point.

"Here ya go." Cecil pulled out a list from under the bar.

Derek took the list and nodded. Two and a half pages of names for two excursions. Not bad at all. "Thanks. Let me go get the stuff ready. Tell anyone who arrives to wait here. I'll be right back." Derek could proudly boast that many of his patrons would return for tours to other parts of the islands once they took one of his excursions.

Derek had to consider that the weather could play a factor during the trip. More than likely, there would be a sudden tropical storm that would quickly depart after a torrential downpour. As the owner and captain of the boat, he had to make sure the boat returned to shore before the storm hit with damaging winds.

He directed his assistants to fill the ice chests and load them onto the boat. The snacks and refreshments were provided to the customers as part of their payment. Whenever American passengers were on board, they demanded lots of ice with their drinks. He shook his head. Too much ice diluted any drink. But he'd learned to accommodate their wishes.

Tourists had already formed a line when he arrived back at the bar. A survey of the group showed a lively bunch. Couples stood hand in hand or touching each other lovingly. About four couples wore matching outfits, which tickled him. Only a man in blind love would wear clothes that matched his mate's. A state of being that held no attraction for him.

A few men stood in one clump, while the women stayed in their groups. He didn't know whether the women were married or not, but in his experience that small technicality wasn't a factor. The "come hither" looks didn't sway him. If he chose to play, he wanted to be the one in the driver's seat. Call him old-fashioned.

"Excuse me, sir?"

Derek looked toward the woman standing off to his right. She held onto her wide-brimmed hat with one hand while shielding her eyes with the other. His eyes flicked over her body. Nice. "Yes."

"I heard that I needed to sign up for the boat ride here."

"Usually folks sign up at their hotel. But there is room for the occasional walk-ons." He smiled.

"Well, where do I pay?" Impatience laced her question.

"Pay the bartender over there." He tossed his head in Cecil's direction before turning his back on her.

"Do you know anything about the trip or even about the boat?"

She followed him to where he sat at the bar. He had to review his list, which he did for every trip. Sitting there also gave him a few additional minutes of quiet before having to turn on the charm for his customers. People expected all the natives to be smiling and happy for their business. There was no off day in the tourism industry.

"I've read this, but there isn't much information about the crew's experience or how old the boat is." She unfolded a heavily creased brochure from her purse. He didn't look at the information since he wrote and designed the marketing piece.

"You sound nervous."

She nodded.

Her admission surprised him. She didn't appear to be the timid type. There was a direct manner as she looked at him and held his gaze. "Don't worry, it's safe."

"Don't care for boats ever since I saw *Jaws*." She offered a shaky smile.

At least she had a sense of humor. Derek laughed.

Oh, oh, big mistake. He quickly squashed his lighthearted approach when he noticed that she had stopped smiling. She had pulled her hat low onto her head. Together with the dark glasses most of her face was hidden. But her lips were exposed and had tightened into a straight angry line.

"Sorry. I thought you were kidding. You couldn't be more than a child when that movie came out." Charm and flattery always worked. Plus he didn't think that he was far off with his observation. Her body was toned, curvy in all the right places. Her face revealed natural beauty, unaffected by any makeup.

"Doesn't matter. I've made up my mind." She walked over to where there was a clear view of the pier and shook her head. "I'm not getting a good vibe from this boat. Doesn't look very sturdy to me."

A strong gust of wind whipped off her hat. She reached out to grab it, but it tugged and dipped in the air and finally rolled toward Derek's feet. He reached down and picked it up. He'd thought that the glasses hid her face, but they only shielded her eyes. With the hat off, he could see her entire face. She had a heart-shaped face that revealed sharp cheekbones tapering down to a narrow chin.

Full lips covered with glossy lip color drew his attention. It took him a few moments to stop focusing on her lips to realize that she was talking to him.

"I've changed my mind. I'll give it a try. Is there another tour in the area?"

"Another tour company?" Derek didn't take kindly to being dismissed. But he especially didn't care for anyone turning up her snobbish nose at his boat. This stranger, dressed in her bright yellow shorts and crisp white sneakers, may have the body of a fitness instructor, but being scared was one thing, insulting him was another.

"It may not be an iron maiden like your cruise ships. The boat is only part of the equation. Her captain is the other factor. I can guarantee that you'll have the smoothest ride. You won't realize that your feet aren't on firm ground."

"What makes you so sure?" she said.

The implication was clear. She didn't think him worthy of giving her advice, but good enough to answer her questions like what other tours were in the area. Now he dearly hoped that Miss Snooty Pants would join him on the next excursion.

"I know the guy who operates the trip." He deliberately softened his tone. He wanted her to take his tour. "Have a free ride. Only if you enjoy yourself, you'll pay for your next ride. And I know that you'll want another trip. I think that's fair, don't you?"

"Maybe." A smile tugged at the edge of her lips. She took off her glasses and peered up at the sky. "Heard about the rain showers that pop up suddenly and then disappear. What if that happens while I'm out there?" She pointed toward the ocean.

As much as he would have loved to see her drenched, he did his part to continue reassuring her. "Rain showers don't last long. Think of it as a brief cleansing. Anyway, the boat wouldn't be that far from shore. The crew is aware of the dangers."

She had a bag that matched the hat, both were hand woven by a native merchant. He recognized the generic style that was quickly made and sold cheaply in the marketplace. She dove into the bag and retrieved a black umbrella. With a triumphant grin, she raised the umbrella.

He shook his head. There went his dream of a sopping wet Miss Snooty Pants.

"Since you can't help, I'll go check out the other services. Thanks for your time." She stuck out her hand.

So that was it. He hadn't passed muster. He shook her

hand, appreciating the touch of her skin. Close up, he savored the soft fragrance surrounding her. The smell of a bouquet made him look at her neck where he figured she had sprayed the scent. His gaze traveled upward to her face with its sharp contours and smooth skin that reminded him of brown sugar. Her soft brown hair framed her face in soft waves that moved gently under the breeze. He didn't want to let go of her hand.

"It's a small island. I'm sure we'll meet again." And that was a promise.

She squinted at him, her mouth curled dismissively.

He'd displeased her again. Who knew she was so sensitive?

He checked his watch. Too bad. He couldn't play any longer. "Gotta run. Boat's leaving in ten minutes." He gathered up his paperwork and walked past her. Since she'd dismissed him, he wanted to be the one to leave her standing there. She'd bruised his ego, but only slightly.

Derek marched down the walkway toward his boat—his pride and joy. He heard the passengers ask each other if he was their captain. Didn't he look like the man in charge?

His attire hadn't changed much since he started his business four years ago. One of the local fashion designers had created some shirts and Bermuda-styled shorts that he wore and marketed for his friend. While he stressed rubber-soled shoes and many passengers wore tennis shoes, he sported hand-woven leather sandals.

If these people and Miss Snooty Pants wanted a captain in a sailor suit, they were looking for the wrong man. No other water excursion service took the time to make their customers comfortable, at least not at the prices that he charged. Plus with his connections, he was able to take them past celebrity homes, as long as they didn't take any pictures or videos. Once he had to jump overboard to retrieve an over-eager fan who tried to swim to a celebrity's house.

He started the engine, and let it idle. The usual two-man crew knew that was their signal to start boarding. Sometimes he hired more crew for larger groups. As captain, he took his place at the gangway to welcome the patrons. There were no familiar faces—the lady in yellow to be exact—among the passengers.

As soon as he was done welcoming the passengers, he returned to the captain's helm on the upper deck. He scanned the group once more to make sure no one had been overlooked. Still, no vivid yellow outfit stood out among the floral and Hawaiian prints.

To admit that he was disappointed meant that he'd hoped to see her. She was one customer who wasn't blown away by his sex appeal. Though rare, it wasn't an impossibility. But it didn't generally happen with women who piqued his interest. All he usually had to do was turn on the charm.

He motioned to his assistant to untie the boat.

"Wait! Wait!"

Derek wasn't sure if he'd heard a call. The engine carried a powerful drumming and the revelry was underway.

"Mr. Calverton, wait." His assistant waved his arms at him from the bow. The teenager pointed over the side toward the pier.

"What's all the fuss?"

"We've got one more," his assistant shouted up to him.

Derek leaned over in the direction that the boy pointed. The boat was still secured. So what was the problem? He shifted his gaze to a familiar figure running toward the boat.

"Help the lady." A silly grin spread over his face. For some odd reason, he wanted to gloat. He was taking credit for her new decision. Because he knew it would irritate her, he stood with his arms folded until she was onboard standing in front of him.

"Hi again. I should have figured you worked on the boat, since you gave it such high marks. Could you tell your boss that I'd like to take the ride?" She patted her forehead with tissue.

"I could tell him, but I don't know your name."

"Toni Kimball."

"Toni." He said her name a few more times. "Suits you."

"That's nice." She looked around him, looking at the other passengers and then the boat. "Where's the captain?" She moved away from him, craning her neck.

"Oh, I think I see him. Come with me." He grabbed her wrist and pulled her along at a brisk pace. "Here he is."

"Are you mad?" She stared at the empty space and then glared at him. She pulled her hand away from him. "Keep it up and I'm going to file a complaint against you."

"When you see him, let me know so that I can lodge my complaint, too."

"What do you have to complain about?"

"Discrimination and bias."

"What nonsense!" She had a hand on her hip. "Based on what?"

Derek raised a finger for her to hold that thought. He pulled down the intercom and flicked on the public announcement system. Then he offered a wide grin to her bemusement.

"Welcome aboard the Caribbean Queen, ladies and gentlemen. I am Derek Calverton and I'll be your host. At this time, let me introduce you to my two assistants—Jarred and Bruce." As he progressed into his welcome greeting and emergency procedures, he teased Toni with a mischievous wink and toothy grin.

The surprise on her face filled him with adolescent glee. At least she did look embarrassed, even averting her eyes from his scrutiny. He would set her at ease before the end of the trip, but he wanted to make his point that she'd underestimated him. It was all a game. In a few days she'd be gone from the island, fading from his memory.

At the end of his speech, he flicked off the intercom, returning the microphone to its base. Her lips made a straight line in disapproval. He'd found the facial expression quite sexy.

"Did you think that you were being funny?"

"Actually, no. That wasn't my intent."

"Could have fooled me with that silly grin."

"Rubbing your face in it is not my style." He winked. "What do people say about the word assume?" He grinned.

"Fine!"

"I'll drop my complaint if you drop yours." He returned his attention to steering the boat.

When she didn't answer, he looked over his shoulder at her. She openly stared at him. It was more than staring, her eyes scanned his entire body as if she was making mental notes about him. He much preferred the verbal sparring because he knew the direction of her thinking. Instead, she scrutinized him. But he couldn't tell what her observations meant. Did she like what she saw? Or did the sight of him make her want to hurl her breakfast over the side?

She was in the driver's seat doing what *he* normally did. Frankly, it made him uneasy. If she kept it up, he'd have to put her in the loony category and keep his distance. He cleared his throat. Anything, to break her focus.

"Can I get a drink?" She licked her lips.

"Certainly. Bahama Mama?"

She shook her head. "Fruit punch is fine. Non-alcoholic," she stressed.

"If you insist. Be right back." He bowed.

Looks like she wasn't going to hurl her breakfast over the side, after all.

Toni waited until Derek had gone before slumping down into a vacant seat. She pulled out the brochure to re-read the information about the charter company. Nowhere did it mention Derek Calverton.

Only two days on the island and her mission was complete. She'd figured that it would take several days to find out if Derek Calverton lived on the island. She hadn't been prepared to bump into him, chat, and now spend the next two hours on his boat.

There was still the chance that there were other Derek Calvertons on the island. She couldn't exactly ask him if he had a father who lived in Baltimore. And, oh by the way, you have a brother named Brad.

She took a couple deep breaths to get herself together. First, there was no rush. She still had her vacation ahead of her, and had to confirm if this was Brad's brother before calling Nicole.

The passengers cleared a path to the little kitchenette. She watched him prepare her drink. He used tongs to place the ice cubes into her cup. He ladled the fruit punch from a large white container. Other passengers who saw him preparing the drink also made their requests. She watched him smile and joke with them with ease. They responded, clearly enjoying his humor and hospitality.

This man was in absolute control. He moved with a self-assuredness that wasn't egotistical. No brashness or in-your-face attitude. He was the captain and his demeanor said as much.

She noticed that he was darker than Brad, more than likely due to his being outdoors all the time. Where Brad had a smooth, cultured image honed by his career as a travel writer, this man, if he was Brad's brother, exuded a natural strength. She didn't picture him in a gym guzzling energy drinks. He belonged in a job where he had freedom and control. People were attracted to him. And he enjoyed the attention, bestowing on his admirers that bright smile.

As if he sensed that she was watching him, he looked up. It was too late to avert her eyes. They locked gazes until a female passenger stepped up, gushing over him. The woman threw her head back and laughed harder than was probably necessary. Toni didn't miss the way the woman's hand fell on his arm, then his shoulder, and then his chest where it rested.

She noticed that Derek stepped back allowing the woman's hand to fall from his chest. Without missing a beat, he kept the bright smile on his face, but handed the woman her drink and then ushered her out of the kitchenette.

Only then did Toni turn to look out at the sun glistening off the clear blue water. She closed her eyes and savored the breeze blowing over her face, barely noticing the soft bobbing motion of the boat.

"Your virgin fruit punch, as requested."

"Thanks." She moved over, so he could join her at the boat rail.

He didn't step up next to her, instead held out her drink. "How long will you be on the island?"

"About two weeks."

"So you're not on one of the cruise ships?"

She shook her head, not sure if that was a good thing. "This is a vacation, of sorts." To her ears, it sounded as if she sought his understanding.

He nodded. Then he took his place next to her at the rail.

"Where do you go for your vacations, considering you're already in paradise?"

"I head for the States. Got friends in Maryland, Texas and California."

"How about family?"

"My father probably has family in the States, but I don't know them. My mother's Bahamian."

This bit of news startled Toni. His mother? Bahamian? She frowned in an effort to sort through this bit of information. She tried to recall the details Nicole had shared, but she couldn't recall any mention of a family connection to the Bahamas.

"Will that be a problem?" he asked.

"Excuse me?"

"It sounded as if my mother's origin made you stumble."

"Sir, I don't know your mother. And that would be rude." She gasped, adding a touch of exaggeration to lighten the mood.

"Would you like to meet her?"

"I guess…I don't know." She gulped. How could she be so gullible? Of course, he was only joking.

"Good. I think that she'd like to meet you. Where are you staying?"

Maybe he was slightly crazy. She was on the island all alone being picked up by a sexy, handsome man looking like he was ready to play on the beach. She drained her fruit punch, glad that she had decided to stick to the non-alcoholic stuff.

"That was a bit too bold, even for me." He offered her an apologetic smile. "I'll leave you to your thoughts." He walked away and mingled with his other passengers.

Toni didn't think that she had been overly cautious. But she wanted a second chance with Derek, anything to keep the flirtatious conversation going. She did enjoy how he looked deeply into her eyes as if he was trying to read her soul. Not that she would let him, even if he had that power.

A part of her wasn't afraid of him and what he could do, but her own reaction to him surprised her. She wanted to steal little touches of him to stem the growing curiosity about him.

She saw Derek take the intercom mike and begin talking to the passengers. From her vantage point outside the main circle, she couldn't hear everything that was said, but the group seemed especially happy with what he had to say. They cheered, clapping their hands and jumping, until he made a signal in the air and music pumped out of the speakers, which were strategically positioned around the boat.

The tour had turned into a full-blown party. Once upon a time, Toni would have been the first person whooping it up and partying. Now she looked on with a detached air, feeling old and out of touch.

At eleven o'clock in the morning sitting out in the Atlantic Ocean, she tried to remain in the shade. Meanwhile her fellow passengers had ditched their virgin fruit punches for the more potent version. In a manner of minutes, they were dancing with no inhibitions, no limits.

T-shirts came off and skimpy bikini tops were the fashion of the hour. Toni didn't have to contemplate whether she would follow their lead. Her sunny yellow shorts were staying put. And next to these beach babes, she was not giving anyone, including Derek, a chance to think of her as the "before" in a before and after shot.

Calypso poured out of the speakers filling the air with the rich sound of steel drums. Toni remained tucked away in the shade. One man, who clearly didn't use sunscreen since his back was a light shade of strawberry, started a conga line. He grabbed the wrists of one of the shyer passengers and guided her to the back of the conga line. They promptly dropped their façade and yelled at the top of their lungs.

Toni decided to return her focus to the water. She kept her back to the increasingly loud party crowd. She avoided eye contact so that she wouldn't be sucked into the line by an overzealous participant.

Someone tapped her on the shoulder. She turned to find Derek standing with his hand outstretched, his head bobbing to the calypso beat.

"I'll pass."

"There's no such thing." He wrapped his arm around her waist, propelling her toward the line worming its way from one end of the boat to the other.

Toni resisted, but her feet didn't respond and she skipped

and hopped to keep up with Derek. A space opened up for his reentry and in the blink of an eye she was swallowed into the snaking line.

Bodies crushed against bodies. Sweat mingled with perfume. Drinks laced with alcohol splashed along her legs. Tightly packed in, she couldn't look down at her tennis shoes to estimate the damage.

"Enjoying yourself?" Derek said in her ear, as his breath tickled her.

At that moment, the line stopped and people crashed into those in front of them in a domino effect. Split seconds later, Derek barreled into her.

His hand that was loosely on her shoulder slid down the front of her body landing on the slope of her breast. She tried to take small breaths to keep her breast from rising, but it only made matters worse. She exhaled in a whoosh. Her breast rose and his hand slid farther down touching her nipple.

Derek pulled his hand off, but the crush of the dancers hadn't lessened. "Sorry," he mumbled.

Toni turned her head to the side, knowing that his face was only inches from hers. "Not a problem." Not a problem because her entire body warmed to his intimate touch. Her breast puckered under the inadvertent touch. She wished that she could slip away and suffer her humiliating reaction privately.

"Don't try to run." Derek's lips brushed past her hair.

"Mr. Calverton, are you trying to flirt with me?"

"Personally, I thought you were trying to seduce *me*."

She turned to see if he was kidding. "Yeah, seducing men is right up there with eating raw oysters."

"Oh, good, something to look forward to. Did you know

that you have a little teddy bear tattooed on your neck?" He touched the small graphic.

She jumped. His touch tingled, tickled, and hit a nerve. This man had hot-wired her nervous system in a way that no man had before. Two choices were in front of her. One urged sanity and reproached any lust-filled thoughts. That side reminded her of her marriage. Cold water couldn't have done a better job of snapping her back to reality. But did she have to be 100 percent good?

The other didn't care about the rules. She saw a way to leave her inhibitions behind and have fun for the next two weeks. Fourteen days of living out the fantasy of a carefree woman with no past and no thoughts of the future.

As the conga line disintegrated and people broke off into couples to dance, Derek pulled her into his arms and waltzed. Toni didn't care that the music pulsated and invited the listeners to work themselves into a frenzy. All she saw were Derek's dark eyes staring back at her, seeking, penetrating deep into her mind.

She lowered her eyes to block the feeling of dropping into a bottomless well. He lowered his head to hers. She only had to turn her face up slightly to accept the kiss. Her body reacted with a warm rush. What would it be like to feel his firm lips, defined and full, against hers?

"Sir, it's time to begin the tour."

Toni pulled back, embarrassed that she had almost lost her head.

"Round one, Toni." A mischievous grin played on his face. "Nine more to go."

Chapter 3

Derek wished he had told Bruce, his assistant, to conduct the tour. Now he had better things to do with his time and attention. Instead, he was wrenched from the pleasure of drowning in Toni's sexy charm. He had his own rules about being some lonely woman's fantasy, but he was drawn to Toni and her quiet intensity. Her mind seemed to constantly take in her surroundings.

Where did that leave him? For the first time in ages he thought about maintaining contact with one of his passengers after the tour ended and they went their separate ways. Would she be offended by his pursuit? Maybe she would be flattered.

He began the presentation, leading the audience through a history of celebrities' fascination with the island. He pointed out the vacation homes of Hollywood stars, European nobility, and the residences of a number of heads of states. He could only see her profile as she stared out over the ocean. There was no way he could walk away. Maybe knowing that she would leave in two weeks relieved him of the risks of anything heavy.

Half an hour later, they headed back to shore. Derek moved around the boat giving his passengers face time. It was really his way of getting all the pleasantries out of the way. As soon as the boat was secured and passengers disembarked, he wanted to have Toni to himself.

She didn't go along with his plan, however. He caught glimpses of her yellow outfit in the middle of a group of tipsy, giggling women. They headed toward the taxi area.

He was disappointed that she hadn't lingered to say goodbye. They'd chatted, danced, flirted. Well, he'd flirted. But she didn't appear to disapprove. He wanted to call out to her. He hesitated. Some women didn't like being chased. They did the chasing.

Her brown legs kept her moving away from him. She had almost reached the bar area, where the taxis waited. It was quite clear that she wasn't chasing him.

"Crap."

"Something wrong, sir?"

"Clean up. I'll be back." Derek turned an irritated glance at Bruce. "We have another trip scheduled in an hour."

He wasn't sure what he would do. But he ran toward the bar. She was talking to a taxi driver who stood next to the open car door, waiting for her to enter.

He considered yelling her name. But he didn't want to give her any warning, in case she hastened her retreat before he had his say. Instead he ran to the car, grabbing the handle as she slid into the car.

"Could I share a ride?"

She looked up. Surprise registered in her face.

"Sorry, I'm in a hurry. Can't wait for another cab." He settled back. "Fancy seeing you here."

"Good to see you, Mr. Calverton. Where to?"

Derek shifted his gaze from Toni to the driver. "That depends." He smiled at her. "Where are you going?"

She looked straight ahead. Her mouth twitched. He could imagine the wheels grinding away.

The taxi driver turned and looked at Toni.

"I'm going to my hotel—Nassau Imperial."

"Beautiful architecture." Derek was impressed. She'd selected a five-star hotel. But he should have expected nothing less.

"Yes. Although I haven't gotten to see much of it since I arrived late in the evening two nights ago."

"Nassau Imperial, it is," Derek told the driver, knowing the man wanted his destination, not hers. The driver shrugged and put the car in gear.

"I hope you have a memorable two weeks in my paradise."

"Oh, it's yours?"

"This is my home and this is where the rest of the world comes for fun and sun."

"Are you calling us intruders?"

"No, not at all." Toni Kimball was a very attractive woman. Sitting so close to her, he admired her smooth skin. Her medium brown tone made him think of the creamy cocoa flavor of milk chocolate, and he wasn't even a chocolate fan.

Unfortunately the ride was over in a matter of minutes.

Derek hopped out of the taxi, and went to open her door for her to exit. "Hope to see you again."

"I don't think I'll be doing any dancing-boat tours any time soon."

Her hair whipped up in the breeze and fell over her face. Without thinking, he smoothed the wayward strands back into place. He caught the slight flinch of her body and dropped his hand.

"Dinner perhaps?"

She bit her lip and averted her gaze.

"I promise not to keep you out late." He understood her hesitation to go out with a stranger in a foreign place.

She nodded. "Where shall I meet you?"

"The Gardens."

She frowned.

"Tell the taxi driver. He'll know the place." He grinned. By simply accepting his invitation she had brightened up the remainder of his day. He refrained from planting a big kiss on her beautiful mouth. She was sturdy enough to answer his overture with a punch to the gut. "See you at six." All of that would come in time.

She smiled, but he could still see the nervousness. She waved and turned to head into the hotel.

Derek got into the taxi. "Bert, take me back to the boat."

The driver looked at him in the rearview mirror. A huge grin on his bearded face made his eyes crinkle. "No problem, Derek."

Toni picked up the phone in her hotel room, too frustrated for words. She'd tried to reach Nicole three times. Where on earth could she be? She had news. Good news. Big news.

She walked with the phone onto the balcony. Ten floors up from the ocean granted her a wonderful, unobstructed view of cruise ships, deeply tanned sunbathers, and tourists armed with mini-cams and digital cameras.

Nicole's line rang a fourth time. "Answer, please." She had to tell someone. If Nicole didn't answer, then she'd be tempted to call Donna or Shirley. But Nicole may not have told them everything, although highly unlikely.

"Hello," Nicole answered, noisily sucking in air.

"Found him," Toni said, not caring that she sounded so triumphant.

"Really? I didn't expect such quick results."

"I'm shocked too. I stumbled upon him because I figured that I'd start the search in a day or two. I mean, how hard should it be to find someone on this island? The hotel concierge pushed me to start my vacation with a boat tour. But not any boat tour, mind you. Anyway I go to the pier and voila! You'll never guess who runs it."

"Oh my gosh, get out! Just like that? So he's self-employed. Can you believe that both brothers are in the same industry?" Nicole paused. "Running a boat tour. Is that lucrative?"

"Guess so. He has a steady stream of customers. And even if you're not sure you'll have a good time before you get onto the boat, after two hours, you're having the time of your life."

"Sounds like you certainly did."

Toni laughed. She'd walked by the mirror earlier. Now she understood the expression that her face was alive. Sitting in the comfortable wicker chair with no pressing issues for almost two more weeks, she finally believed that she could have a good time. She hadn't laughed at herself, much less at anything remotely funny in a long time. Maybe Nicole was right, she needed this trip to get herself together.

"Did you get to talk to him?"

"Yep."

"What do you think?"

"Quite the charmer."

"Didn't expect that. Brad was such a bear when we first met. Well, being charming works."

"Works for what?"

"Our plan, silly. I didn't think about you actually meeting him. But you can help soften him up. So when I come to introduce myself…well, you know what I mean."

"Oh no, you don't. There was nothing in this deal where I play with the island Casanova." Toni didn't mention the dinner plans. No need to bring it up. It wasn't a date.

"Don't go all ice queen on me, please."

"Didn't know that you wanted me to play the lonely, sex-starved American woman looking for her hot-blooded Caribbean prince." The idea somehow stirred a distinct feeling deep within her.

"Stop getting prickly. I didn't say jump in bed with the man. But at least, flash a smile every now and again. This is for a good cause, Toni."

"Said the spider to the fly." She wasn't jumping into anybody's bed. Derek was cute, but not that cute. Yes, he was tall and ruggedly handsome with a tiny scar running along his jaw. His personality was like a bright beam in a sea of fireflies. But she was immune. "I'm sure that I'll have another opportunity to meet him. I'll see what comes of it. You'd better make sure that you bring your butt down here next week to meet him. I came with very little baggage and I'm not trying to get wrapped up in your family drama."

"Wow! He really made an impression. I've never heard you this nervy over a man. Tell me what else happened on this boat tour."

Toni bit her lip to keep from revealing any details. Definitely no need to disclose the conga line. How could she share the way his body had pressed against hers, leaving a torrid memory. In her thin lightweight clothing, there was very little between her back and his chest and stomach.

She blushed and had to retreat into the air-conditioned room. She'd be lying if she said that she hadn't noticed his pants waist rubbing against her lower back as she danced. The tightly packed bodies in the conga line hid her occasional slow steps that only exacerbated the intense, sensual sway of body against body as she danced. It was her guilty pleasure and secret, especially since her body responded with an aching desire to take things to another level.

"Hey, earth to Toni, does he look like Brad?"

Toni thought about it. Derek wasn't the pretty-boy type. Once upon a time only a model or wannabe model could get her attention. Based on her experience, she didn't need a man who elbowed his way in front of the mirror as part of his daily routine. Derek didn't seem to be that type. He probably didn't have time to tell himself how devastatingly sexy he was because a slew of women filled that role.

"Seeing him separately, no I wouldn't think that they look alike. But I can see similarities in the way they smile or the way they hold their heads."

"That tells me nothing. Is he as handsome as my darling husband?"

"A loaded question that I'm not answering. I'll tell you his physical characteristics and you can use your imagination."

"Send me a photo."

"Why are you so pressed to know what he looks like?"

"Curiosity. Plus I wanted to know what man managed to pique your interest."

"Bull. A man is the last thing that I want."

"Hmm. You're in the Bahamas. You're a young, beautiful woman. You met a hottie. What's wrong with this picture?"

"He may be married," Toni reminded Nicole.

Reality had a sobering way of intruding on fantasy. Good grief, she couldn't bear to repeat the same mistake she'd made with her ex. With that thought planted firmly in her head, she had made her decision. She wasn't going to any Gardens to have dinner. The glow that she momentarily enjoyed faded, turning black and curling like a dying rose. "Goodbye, Nicole. I'll call you if I learn anything else."

She couldn't promise that she would dig up more information about Derek. Whatever else she did find out would not include any further contact. She couldn't be sure that she could resist his charm. No complications on this vacation. And playing flirtatious games with a man who had a wife or close to one in the background, gave her an unpleasant sense of déjà vu.

A part of her still wanted to go to The Gardens to ask him. But it was much easier not to show up. She could be the average tourist and do the normal things like shopping, sitting on the beach or going to a show. Why muck up the water?

After a cool shower, she wrapped herself in a thick bathrobe courtesy of the hotel. Refreshed, she relaxed in bed, flipping through a magazine.

She came across information regarding several nightclubs, cabarets, and restaurants. Although she was pulling a no-show, it didn't mean that she didn't want to go out and enjoy the evening. The nightclubs didn't appeal to her, however. She'd had enough dancing for one day.

A cabaret show should be entertaining, she thought. The glitzy song and dance production was bound to entertain her for a few hours. In the dark, she could sink into a seat in the back and sip her drink while the show went on. She wouldn't stick out as a tourist traveling solo without girlfriends or a boyfriend for company. At least, she could tell her friends back home that she did see a Vegas-style revue.

For the remainder of the day, she sat on the balcony reading a novel with the music playing in the background, talking and laughter and the ocean waves rolling in with soothing ambience. From her vantage point, she enjoyed the panoramic view of the palm trees in the white sand, the shimmering blue water in the pool, and the people who moved around without knowing they were being observed.

The show started at eight o'clock. But she had been watching the clock when it approached six. She wondered if Derek was waiting at The Gardens. Maybe she should have gone at least to tell him that she had changed her mind. Then again, why would he think that a woman would want to go to a strange place with a strange man, no questions asked? "Because he's used to women saying yes." Her voice fell through the silence with a hollow ring.

She didn't have it in her to be like the other women. When the six had turned to seven o'clock, she dressed in a dark pants suit with a satiny red shell under the jacket. Even if her heart wasn't in it, she could at least look the part of a fun-seeking party girl. She sprayed a couple blasts of her favorite perfume and applied a little makeup, focusing on the lipstick. It was too humid to worry about foundation.

Grabbing her small sequined handbag, she headed out of the room. Why was she so nervous? Her stomach tightened into painful knots. She pushed the button for the elevator and waited. All she had to do was go back down the hall and back into her room. She could order room service and select a movie from the menu.

The elevator announced its arrival. She had to make a snap decision. There was no getting around the fact that she was spending the evening alone. She took a deep breath and stepped into the elevator cab. Might as well be alone and feed off other people's enjoyment.

Outside the night was balmy. Her girlfriends would probably complain about the humidity damaging their hair, but she liked the thick tropical air. The sound of the ocean rolling onto the beach added to the exotic setting. It was the perfect night to stroll along the beach with a perfect someone. She sighed, talk about fantasies that wouldn't come true.

She took a taxi to the hotel, steeling her nerves to stick it through. Why did taking herself out on a date cause so much angst?

The taxi pulled up to a grand hotel that must have had more stars ratings than were available. The soft pineapple color of the exterior was illuminated with unique lighting fixtures that created intricate shadows that snaked around the building. The front portion allowed for natural lighting to enter the oversized windows. Even the upper floors, where the rooms no doubt were, had large windows. No balconies jutted out, allowing for admirers to run their gazes to the very top.

Toni looked down at her outfit and wanted to go back to her hotel to change. She was woefully underdressed for this posh surrounding. Too late, the taxi pulled off.

She adjusted her jacket and put a reassuring hand on her stomach to calm the butterflies.

Another taxi pulled up behind her. She heard the occupants before she saw them. Toni turned to see the commotion. A well-dressed, light-complected lady with sparkling jewels around her neck, ears and wrist stood on shaky legs. The taxi driver put a steady hand on her arm, which she angrily shook off. He hovered with his hands still in protecting distance, but clearly away from her. Toni couldn't help staring at the drunken spectacle, considering that the woman dressed and acted like money was her second skin.

Even the bellhop hovered as the woman walked into the hotel still wobbling on heels that looked to be three inches. Toni turned her attention to the man bending over to pay the taxi driver. When he straightened and turned in her direction, her hand flew to her mouth in full disbelief.

"Good evening," he stated. He wasn't smiling.

"Hi. I didn't expect to see you…here." Toni's mind reeled. What was he doing here? What must he be thinking?

"Obviously. But don't let me hold you up." He stepped aside and opened the door for her.

Toni didn't want to move. "I didn't go to The Gardens."

"I suppose you had a better offer."

"Looks like you did too." She waited for him to deny it, but he stared at her. "Are you going to the show?" To have him in the same room while he's there with his…whatever she was to him, she couldn't deal with. She would go into the show and then when it started, she'd leave. No need to run into those two after the show. At the end of the night, she'd still be alone and he'd be with this woman going off to do what couples do in a tropical paradise late at night.

"No. I've seen it several times."

That meant the woman stayed at the hotel and he was escorting her. Icy shivers snaked their way through her veins. Was that the kind of relationship he expected from her? The thought sickened her.

"You and Mrs. Calverton?" she blurted.

He looked past her for a few seconds and then back at her. "I'm my own man."

Did that mean he was married, but they had their own arrangement? Or that he was thankfully unattached? She let the silence in, giving him time to clarify.

"Well, I'm needed elsewhere."

No, darn it. You're needed right here. Toni watched him walk toward the elevator, no rush, no hurried gait. He had one hand stuck in his pants pocket, but it didn't pull the suit out of shape. He looked like a man with expensive tastes and a sophistication that ran the opposite extreme to the ruggedly handsome, bare essentials kind of guy she'd met earlier.

The elevator door chimed, announcing its arrival. She waited, hoping that he would turn and wave. Maybe even change his mind and return to her. But that only happened in romantic movies. Derek with his midnight-blue suit, silk shirt and funky, fashionable tie entered the elevator cab without another glance in her direction.

"Nice seeing you," she said softly.

She exited the hotel. The cabaret show was no longer appealing. All she wanted was to go to her room, order a large helping of vanilla ice cream, and drown it in chocolate syrup.

Obviously Derek was attracted to all ages, since his date was of the mature variety. Men like that didn't care, as long as women put out.

Toni slid into the back of the cab and pulled the door shut. She couldn't understand why she felt so disappointed and empty. It couldn't possibly be because of Derek. He may have been the perfect partner on the dance floor, but they were clearly from two different mind-sets.

She'd come to the island to find Brad's brother and she did. Now it was time to find herself and what she really wanted to do with her life. There was no time for a youthful fling, even if the opportunity presented itself. She'd better stick to the plan and leave Derek Calverton to his player lifestyle.

Chapter 4

Toni spent the next two days sticking close to the hotel. Her routine began with an early morning visit to the gym. She only managed about twenty minutes on the stationary bike and the treadmill. Then she ate breakfast at the hotel's restaurant. Afterward, she sat outside to read and later walked along the beach.

Lunchtime, she ate at one of the beachside restaurants, which were usually noisy with children and a younger crowd, but she didn't mind. In the evening, she had dinner in her room, relaxing with a movie.

She practiced avoidance and it worked. She knew that she couldn't keep it up for the entire trip, but she didn't want to go anywhere near the downtown area in case she ran into Derek. Nor did she want to be tempted to wander to the bar where he was sure to be waiting for the next trip.

Dressed for breakfast, she headed to the restaurant. As

was her habit, she made sure to request a table that over-looked the beach.

None of the hotel's luxurious amenities spoke to her soul the way the ocean did. Regardless of how many different people and cultures inhabited this island, the ocean remained timeless. A simple experience like sipping coffee was height-ened by the ocean view.

The vast blue water rolled in and out with predictable ease. The ocean deposited its treasures with the incoming tide, while anything left on the beach floated off with the outgoing tide. Toni saw nature's work as life moving at a steady pace with or without her. Her personal loss had ripped away part of her will, leaving her a hollow shell where deep emotions remained hidden. Her modern-day marriage of convenience didn't matter in the scheme of things because she'd never loved her husband.

Sitting in the corner of the restaurant with her chair facing the ocean, Toni broke into a grin. She actually wanted to yell. She didn't love him. She'd never loved him.

How desperate was she to think that she'd ever loved such a selfish man. Away from her home, family and friends, she only had herself as company. In many cases she didn't like what she saw of herself.

She happily paid the bill before heading out to the path she had been admiring. Her revelation made her strangely giddy. She wanted to feel the sun warm her body, giving her energy.

The flowers that only seemed pink, red and blue were now vibrant fuchsia, crimson and deep violet. The air was clean and scented with natural fragrances. She'd found her paradise.

The path wound around the hotel meandering through

landscaped, eye-catching formations with tiny bridges over man-made streams, gazebos for quick rests and sturdy wooden benches.

By the time she had worked her way back to the front of the hotel, thick clouds had gathered overhead, hanging low and heavy. Seconds later she felt the warm drops of rain. If she didn't hurry indoors, she'd be soaked within minutes.

The rain continued for most of the morning. Toni enjoyed hearing the heavy beating on the patio floor. She didn't want to go outdoors, but she certainly didn't want to spend the time in her room watching TV. This rain shower proved to be more than the occasional summer soaker that arrived unannounced, and then evaporated within minutes.

Waves and waves of rain poured down. Many of the sun worshippers called it quits after the clouds kept a tight curtain shutting out the sun. Toni didn't mind the rain. She had nowhere to go, no pressing appointments, no one to visit.

No further prompting was needed to stir up memories of Derek. With this storm, his tours would be grounded. She wondered what he did when that happened. Did he stick around at the bar flirting with the latest arrivals?

There was no way that she was going to sit in her hotel room pining over a man. She remembered seeing a sign for a spa when she walked through the hotel lobby. The idea of someone massaging her body seemed fabulous. She could pretend for a brief moment that she was a lady used to such luxury. She looked at her plain hands, inspecting the effects of neglect. Maybe she'd even get a manicure like the old days.

Excited about her new adventure, she walked purposefully through the hallways, following the little signs that were fashioned after street signs to the spa.

The spa was cleverly tucked away from the thoroughfare in a separate enclosure. If the doors were any indication of the type of establishment it was, Toni knew she was about to spend a few significant dollars.

The entrance doors were frosted glass with a swirling tropical scene. Soft jazz with the trademark West Indian beats filtered through hidden speakers. If she wasn't mistaken, there was a fruity scent as if she had walked through a grove of oranges, mangoes, and peaches.

No one sat in its lobby. As a matter of fact, there were no chairs in the lobby. Maybe looks were deceiving and no one came here for its services. If so, she needed to know before she spent a fortune. From the looks and smell, it would definitely be a large sum.

Toni walked toward a large desk managed by a stunningly beautiful woman positioned in the center of the expansive foyer. She had to be a model. Her hair was styled in small locks that had been dyed a honey blonde, lifted off her face into a colorful headpiece, and allowed to spill out along the edges of her face. When she smiled, her entire face lit up. She had beautiful features that spoke of an Ethiopian heritage. This woman knew how to enhance all her feminine qualities.

What better way to get a woman to buy all the services and beauty products. Next to this woman, Toni felt washed out and drab. All her brightly color-coordinated outfits couldn't help how emotionally drained she was. She was sure that her skin didn't glow like this woman's, even if her skin was enhanced by shimmering foundation.

"Welcome to Spa Paradise. Is this your first time with us?"

Toni nodded, thinking the spa's name was quite appropriate.

"Slow today?" Toni surveyed the lobby.

"Oh no, we're quite busy. Our lobby is only to greet our clients. We never have anyone simply wait to be served. As soon as you pass through our doors, you are immediately given our individual attention. Your name, please?"

"Toni. Toni Kimball."

"Toni, I'm Portia." They shook hands. "What will be your pleasure today?" The hostess handed her a brochure.

"I would like to have The Pleasure Principle and a manicure." Toni placed her finger on the brochure, indicating the massage with special oils and new age techniques.

"Wonderful selection. Lydia will be your attendant. She will also take care of your manicure needs." On cue, Lydia stepped out from a door that, when closed, appeared to be a panel in the wall.

"Hello."

"Hi." Toni fought the impulse to mimic the bubbly personality approaching her.

Instead of the customary handshake, Lydia pulled her in an embrace, sort of, with air kisses and grand gestures. Toni wondered how this energetic redhead would actually perform a massage which would mean that she would have to touch her and get her own hands greasy.

Portia handed a pad to Lydia. "Antonia? Antoinette?"

Toni shook her head at each name. All her life people assumed Toni was a derivative of some other name. At least she could be grateful that they couldn't shorten her name to make some quick nickname. "It's Toni."

"Toni, let's get started."

Toni followed Lydia through the door from which she'd emerged. They walked down a wide hallway with several closed doors on either side. She heard no sound coming from the rooms.

"Each door leads to a private salon for our client. There is also another door that leads to the pool, if you should desire a swim."

Toni stole a look at the brochure for confirmation of the price. The décor, saleswomen, and features of this place oozed money. Something she lacked. Nicole's purchase of the vacation package didn't include expensive treats. She could only afford the one-hour package, barely.

"Well, here we are. Each room is named after an African Queen. You're in Salon Amina." Lydia opened the door and waited for Toni to enter. "The salon is decorated with pieces from the queen's homeland. Queen Amina was from Zazzua, a province in Nigeria now called Zaria. She was a warrior queen."

"Beautiful." Toni fingered the clay vase, enjoying the mastery that went into creating the fragile piece. The room was painted a burnt amber with clay pieces decorating the shelves. To break up the earth tones, indigo wall coverings draped the room. Small cushions of the same color accented the lounge area built along the wall. They had managed to make the room look like a royal harem from a scene out of *Ali Baba and the Forty Thieves*.

"Is this what she looked like?" Toni stood in front of a painted portrait of an African queen framed in dark wood.

"We hired several artists to complete the works based on their interpretation of what the queen may look like. Sinaai Watson painted this one. She is also from Nigeria and painted her based on the traditionally dressed females in her culture."

Toni remained silent, a bit ashamed that she didn't know enough African history to recognize queens and their history beyond the famous Makeda, Queen of Sheba. She studied the rendition, happy with the portrayal of a black woman with kinky hair, blunt nose and full lips standing majestically with a decorated shield and spear in the African heartland. There was pride in her erect bearing. Toni wondered if she would ever regain that strength. Could she stop feeling wounded?

Lavender incense softly scented the air. The music was light, airy, as if magical folk had made it to soothe the non-believers. She imagined a harpist over in the corner. A litany of maids to serve her. A cute manservant to peel grapes and pop them into her mouth. Yes, she could get used to being pampered. She inhaled deeply and closed her eyes, allowing a long satisfying sigh to release from her body.

"Here. You may undress behind the privacy screen and when you are ready you may lie on our table. Then drape this towel around you." Lydia waited until she took the towel. "Just press this buzzer when you're ready."

Toni did as instructed and climbed onto the table. She groaned when she looked down at her body. Her rounded hips and heavy thighs seemed to have expanded overnight. When she got back to Glen Knolls, she had to sign up at a gym. At least when she got her massage and revealed her cellulite, she'd never have to see the perky Lydia ever again. She could only imagine what the woman would think as she ran her hand over every dimple on her thighs and hips. This was no way to relax her mind.

The Pleasure Principle aptly earned its name. Lydia's fingers and heels of her hands worked their magic.

"You've a lot of tension in your shoulders. Don't hold your breath. In order to relax, you have to concentrate on your breathing. Let the air fill your lungs and exhale slowly."

Toni listened and tried to follow the instructions. She cleared her mind, pushing away any negative thoughts that would nestle in the dark recesses. As she regulated her breathing, she thought about a brand-new day. She thought about her new job, new home, she thought about her depression rolling back, rolling down and falling off to the side. She fashioned her thoughts in the same pattern that Lydia used to coax her muscles to relax.

Derek stretched, yawning loudly. He had only managed to do one tour this morning before the rain started. Since it already rained for over an hour and the weather report called for rain until the evening, he had to cancel the remaining tours.

He could meet with the banker to discuss financing for his software business. He could also meet with the management of the four- and five-star hotels to broker exclusive relationships for the boat tour.

His concentration wouldn't let him focus on work. All he wanted to do was play. And he only wanted to play with one person.

"Hey, Cecil, have you seen that lady I was talking to a couple of days ago?"

"You've been talking to lots of ladies."

"I was not talking to them. They talked to me."

"Technicality. Who are you trying to hunt down?"

"Never mind." Derek had never cared about maintaining a reputation. But it now bothered him that people compared him to a shark. He knew that was Toni's perception. He sensed the disapproval in her attitude toward him at the hotel a couple nights ago.

She hadn't given him the benefit of the doubt that he was helping an incapacitated guest back to her hotel. Mrs. Crawford was more than a guest. She'd celebrated her fiftieth wedding anniversary on his boat.

Every year, she and her husband returned. Derek looked forward to their vacations when she'd arrive from America with his favorite snack, large bags of kettle popcorn. The unexpected death of her husband hit her hard. Over the years, Derek noticed subtle changes from the outgoing, charming woman she was to a quieter shell of one, in which depression seemed to linger.

While he waited in The Gardens for Toni to appear, he saw Mrs. Crawford sitting alone in the restaurant consuming several drinks without eating. No surprise that, within the hour, she was completely inebriated.

"Is it true that the tours are cancelled?"

Derek looked up and nodded. "It's raining too hard." He thought that fact was evident. "Don't worry, everything will be back to normal tomorrow."

"What's a girl to do now? I'm bored." She puckered her mouth into a pout. She slid onto a bar stool and folded her arms under her ample chest, proffering her breasts like fruit on a tray.

Derek swallowed his usual easygoing smile. He squinted at the woman, taking in the exaggerated application of her makeup, styled hair, and skimpy clothing. She waved a hand to Cecil and ordered a drink, never taking her eyes off Derek.

Most times he knew what was coming and played along

until he got bored. She'd picked the wrong time and the wrong person for her latest diary entry. No one was going to get her groove on or anything else on his behalf.

Cecil placed the drink with a cherry and umbrella floating on top in front of her. He winked at Derek and backed discreetly out of sight, but probably not out of earshot.

The woman picked up the cherry and pulled off its stem. Then she made an elaborate gesture of licking and sucking off the drink from the stem. Derek wished he could show her how ridiculous she looked. He leaned against the bar, propping up his head. Her big accomplishment was to tie the cherry stem into a knot with her tongue—been there, done that. Next.

"Ever had three before?" She tilted her head toward a table with two other women. One had the same caramel skin tone, shorter hair, but dressed in a similar skimpy outfit. The other woman was a blonde who must have just arrived since she didn't have a dark tan. Her hair was in a tight bun and she wore heavy black-framed glasses. Her face didn't look as if she was on vacation, but the other part of her body had gone the popular route with a low-cut blouse.

"Have *you* ever had three before?" He threw the question back at her, providing a frightening leer for effect.

Uncertainty and fear flickered across her face.

"Where you ladies from?" He continued with his game.

"The States."

It didn't really matter whether it was America or some other place. Experience had taught him to be wary of heavy pursuits. Yet that was exactly what he was doing with Toni.

"What do you do in the States?" he asked, but really couldn't care less.

"Tax accountant. My friends work for the Library of Congress." She'd picked up on his tone and now straightened up, adjusting her blouse.

"First, welcome to the Bahamas. For the most part, people are nice and friendly. You seem like nice women, but let me give you some advice. Don't stand in the deep end with the sharks when all you want are the goldfish."

Her mouth opened and closed a few times before she could utter a response. "You are rude." She slid off the stool. "I don't know what you mean." She marched out with her friends, who ran after her to catch up.

"Hey, you didn't pay," Cecil yelled.

"It's on me." Derek threw down a twenty-dollar bill and walked away.

Derek drove up to the hotel—Toni's hotel. He parked and hopped out of the car, tossing his car keys for valet parking. He didn't know how long he'd be here, but he wasn't going anywhere without talking to her. He wasn't sure what his fascination was with her, it was more than her looks. But he wanted the chance to find out.

The hotel wasn't crowded. He'd arrived after checkout time, which left the front desk clear. He looked at the people behind the counter, hoping to see a familiar face who would do him a favor. He didn't recognize the employees.

"Hello, Mr. Calverton."

Derek turned toward the concierge. Crap, it was Paula, an ex-girlfriend from a year ago. It didn't take a detective to know that she still had feelings for him, despite his deliberate casualness. This could get sticky, but he was desperate.

Taking a fortifying breath, he flashed a brilliant smile. As usual Paula was the picture of neatness and annoying perfection. She had been crowned Miss West Indies in the nineties and still took her accomplishment seriously. All she needed with the stiff posture was the sash running diagonally across her body and she'd be ready for the catwalk.

He dared not underestimate Paula's demeanor, knowing the range of her volatile behavior—shooting from fiery anger to cotton candy sweetness. He only had to witness her hysteria once to know that keeping his distance was imperative.

"Paula, could you help me? I'm looking for someone. Trying to return an item that she left on my boat."

"Sure. Name?"

"Toni Kimball."

She looked on the monitor at her desk, occasionally glancing up at him. "She's in the system. You can leave a message and I'll make sure she gets it."

"Can you make an exception?"

"Like getting fired for giving out personal information?"

"Please, Paula. I won't tell."

"So, this is how desperate you are, when you're involved with a woman—fancy that."

Saying the wrong thing could further inflame the situation. He waited, trying to remain calm. Only his fingers drummed.

"Room 1022. Nice to see what you're capable of doing." A frosty edge seeped into Paula's gaze.

He had no rebuttal. All he was willing to do was thank her again. She certainly had gone out on a limb for him. Before her mood took any more of a nosedive, he headed for the elevator and punched in the key. One step closer to Toni. His nerves came alive, clenching his muscles, making his throat dry, causing the tips of his fingers to tingle. He stuck his hand in his pocket and played with the change, watching the lights blink as he passed each floor.

At the tenth floor, he stepped out and looked both ways before spying the sign that indicated he had to go to the right. Three doors later, he stood in front of Toni's door. He shook his hand, trying to release some of the stress. He took a deep breath, then knocked.

A bellhop was pushing a luggage trolley. Derek didn't look up as the wheels squeaked past him. He knocked again.

"Mr. C, is that you?"

Derek glanced over his shoulder, not caring for the interruption.

"It's me, Todd. Mabel St. John's son."

"Hey, Todd, you're working here now?"

"For the summer. Then I start university."

Derek looked over at the closed door.

"I don't think she's in there, Mr. C. I passed her going toward the spa about half an hour ago."

"Really? Thanks, Todd." Derek pulled out a ten and gave it to the young man. "Have to run. Tell Miss Mabel, hello." Derek hurried past Todd to get to the elevators.

As he rode the elevator back to the lobby, he didn't have a clue what he would do or say. But he didn't want to waste one minute figuring out what sounded the best. If she was in the spa, then he'd be heading there, also. This pursuit was about to get expensive, but he didn't care.

At the end of the hour, Toni left the salon covered with the scented oil. She took a quick shower and then opted to take a dip in the pool. She slipped into her one-piece, pleased with this particular purchase. The tag advertised its enhanced slimming waistline and breast cup-shaper. Nevertheless she tied the sarong on the side of her hip, in case the bathing suit's slimming effect didn't live up to its reputation.

Thankfully, the pool leading off from the spa was separate from the main pool, allowing for a more private swim. She slipped off the cover-up and slid into the pool, submerging her entire body until her lungs screamed for air. Like a rocket, she exploded out of the water sucking in air before gliding through the water.

It had been ages since she'd swum, but it had been her favorite sport since being on the high school team. The power of her legs pushed her through the water toward the edge. She rested at the edge, preparing to perform her backstroke to the other side.

"Fancy meeting you here."

Toni turned around as quickly as she could in the water, feeling as if she were moving in heavy syrup. That voice. Only one person.

"Derek." She wiped her face, smoothing back her hair. On land, he was a gorgeous specimen. In the water, bare-chested, water dripping from his muscular shoulders, expansive chest, he was to die for. The water beads rolled down his face, past his eyes, cheeks, and mouth. She wanted to take her finger and follow their track to their unknown destination. They went through the casual greeting of acquaintances. She couldn't help being transfixed by his mouth.

And why did his mouth attract her? It was just a mouth, with the standard lips. But it was the thinness of his top lip that formed a cupid's bow and the fullness of the bottom one that drew her attention. Most times they had a soft uplift at each corner as if he was cynically amused at the world.

When she raised her eyes to his, she read his acknowledgment of her open admiration. She couldn't hide her desire. Nor could he. His reaction was equally bold and direct. They stared at each other. Neither one took the first step. The space between them filled with sensual tension bouncing off, colliding, swirling into a heady mixture of naked passion.

Derek had to pay a huge bribe to get into the spa, but it was well worth it. From the day he met Toni, he couldn't shake her from his thoughts. None of the tourists held his interest for more than twenty-four hours. Looking into her dark brown eyes, he felt himself drawn into their mysteries.

"This is a wonderful surprise." He grinned. Grinning always worked to ease an awkward moment. "Sticking around in the pool for a bit?" He pushed aside the doubts playing havoc with his mind. Her rejection was a distinct possibility.

"Planning to enjoy a quiet swim," she answered, switching her hands under the water's surface.

Ouch. He'd caught her emphasis on *quiet*. "Me, too."

She reminded him of a mermaid. Not that he'd personally encountered one. But he'd have expected one to look like Toni with her wet hair, wavy and dark, falling on her shoulders. He wasn't sure what magical lighting caused her face to glow with stunning radiance.

"I thought this was a private facility. For the hotel guests."

"It is, but I have friends in high places." Thank goodness he stood in water that could cool the feelings she stirred in a simple glance.

"So do your tastes from what I've noticed." She floated away on her back. Her red toenails peeked above the water line. Even the minutest detail caught his attention, like her lashes that framed her deep brown eyes.

The water lapped over her body seductively playing peek-a-boo over her thighs. He liked a woman with a little meat on her bones. He admired the muscular thickness, running his gaze over the entire length to her hips which the swimsuit covered. He didn't even want to think about her hips, deliciously curved in all the right places. Farther up, he had no choice but to admire all of her, including her breasts that poked up from the water. What was it about this woman that made him have to fight to stay in control?

He envied the water lavishing her; touching, stroking, and bathing her with its attention. If only he could touch her with similar intent.

There was no way that he'd only imagined her response. If he could help it, he wasn't prepared to let her hide behind decorum. Bottom line was they wanted each other.

He swam out to where she still floated. She closed her eyes, but he sensed from the small frown that marked her forehead that she was aware of his approach.

"Do you trust my taste in women?"

"What?" Her eyes opened. Her body sank and she struggled briefly to get her body righted. "Silly question. I don't know you."

He bit back the smile. "Then will you allow me to give you the opportunity?"

Her eyes fastened on him. She righted herself. He noticed that she could stand with no problem in the middle of the five feet section of the pool. "Is this your attempt at another date?"

He hesitated. She had completely disarmed his playful tactics. But he didn't want to scare her off with the wrong answer. "I thought that I was being subtle. And that you would be swept off your feet."

"Now you can stand corrected."

"Call me slow to take the hint, but I want to take you out on a date, Toni. Until you say no thank you, I'll keep asking."

Shocked, she was momentarily speechless. She knew that he was interested. She'd have to be dead not to have noticed. But to hear the words said matter-of-factly ignited panic, embarrassment, and curiosity. "I'm leaving in another week."

"So you keep reminding me. And I wish that you had more time. But it should make things more interesting and intense."

Was he suggesting a one-night stand or in this case, two-night stand? "Why start what you can't finish?" She stared at him, waiting for a sign that he got her drift.

"Is that how you see things? A set beginning and a cold hard ending?"

"The mystery of life…and love, are for twentysomething-year-olds." She shrugged. "And alas, I'm not in that category."

"And all the better for it. My philosophy is to live each day, focus on each day. Don't waste time going over the past. Don't cross your fingers trying to guarantee the future."

"Everyone is entitled to their opinion. Time for me to get moving. It was nice meeting you, Derek. Maybe another time." She held out her hand and headed toward the steps. All she had to say was *no, thank you*—three words that seemed elusive.

"Who made you so scared?"

"How dare you?" She stopped and faced him.

"Who sucked out the woman in you? You're so afraid of feeling. Good or bad. You're afraid. Any other woman, I would turn my back and forget about her. But damn it, I can't get you out of my mind. I'm not looking for a one-night stand." His hands waved through the air as he spoke.

"Keep your voice down," she whispered. Her temper skyrocketed like a missile. Her defenses couldn't keep up with the prodding.

He leaned into her. "This isn't about sex."

"Yeah, right. Men always think about sex."

"I'll admit that I was, and still am, physically attracted to you. But I'm a grown man and I know what intrigues me." He closed the already small space between them. "All I'm asking from you is good conversation and dinner with a desirable young woman. Sue me because I can't help your preoccupation with having sex with me."

Toni exhaled slowly, not sure when she had held her breath. Her chest rose and fell as she sucked in air. She took a step back and he grabbed her wrist. The touch of his hand took another swing at her armor.

"Never thought of you as a chicken," he challenged.

She knew that he egged her on to make her accept his request. She knew it, and it pissed her off.

Good gosh, he smelled good. But that didn't matter, she had to stay angry. Don't focus on the dark chocolate eyes. Don't admire the nose with its wide flair. Don't crave those delicious lips that defined him as a black man.

"As a reminder, I didn't break off the date the last time."

"I know. I did." She played with water, flicking it with her hand. "Are you married?"

"No!"

"Engaged?"

He shook his head.

"Vaguely interested in someone?" She bit her lip.

"You." He noticed the relief wash over her. "I want to have dinner with you."

"Are all the other rich, older women too busy?"

She could have flicked the water into his face and let the pellets sting his eyes. It would have had the same effect as her words, but not as lingering. He didn't know who had hurt Toni, but the hardness in her eyes when she spoke let him know that the damage may have been irreparable. No amount of charm and sexy smiles were going to dissolve the ten-foot-thick wall.

He was never a quitter. But he was a good procrastinator. He'd have to regroup.

"My apologies, I'll leave you with that iron wall around your heart." He turned and swam back to the stairs.

"Wait." She was not far behind as he ascended the stairs.

He grabbed his towel and rubbed his chest, waiting to hear something from her that could give him hope.

"I should be the one apologizing. You're only being gracious."

He continued drying off, not sure what to say so that he didn't offend her.

"I don't think...I mean, it could be wrong. Well, not wrong ..."

There was a time and a place for everything. This was no

time for words. They got in the way. They made things worse.
Both people had to be listening, hearing, understanding.
Forget talking.

He took a step toward her.

Her mouth continued moving. He had already blocked out
her words. He didn't want to register the doubts that crept into
her voice. If he let her, she would have talked herself into
being scared again.

He placed his fingers against her lips.

She swallowed the stream of words.

He outlined her lips with his finger. Her breath, warm and
moist, tantalized him. She flicked her tongue against his
finger and his eyes almost crossed. He wanted to ravage her
mouth, but restrained himself.

Toni deserved to be savored.

He stroked away the hair that dripped along the sides of
her face. His hand slid to the back of her head, her hair was
soft and curled along his hand. Softly and slowly he lowered
his mouth to hers. He hovered just above her lips, knowing
that he was entering a place where there was no return. She
tiptoed and closed the gap, sealing their lips. Only then did
he close his eyes to succumb.

He cupped both sides of her face and planted little kisses
along her cheek, tasting the water, making it his job to remove
the droplets. She moaned and forced his mouth back to hers.
Her hands slid along his body, settling onto his hips. She had
her fingers running along the inside of his swim trunks' waistband. He moaned.

Her mouth opened under his full pressure. She surrendered against him. All he wanted to do was take his time

sampling and memorizing, archiving every nuance of her beautiful mouth.

He embraced her, locking into his mind the feel of her body despite the offending swimsuit that stretched like a second skin. His hands slid over her hips and cupped her butt cheeks. Effortlessly he raised her, plunging his tongue deeper into her mouth. Her breasts rubbed against his chest doing their part to drive him insane.

She gave. He took.

A myriad of thoughts entered his head, but he couldn't logically follow their stampede. The more he partook, the more chaotic he felt. Her soft moans wound him up like a top. When she gasped against his lips, he wanted to run into a wall over and over in delirious rapture like his childhood toys.

Her mouth slid from his. She kissed his cheek, his chin and then his throat. The sexy minx licked his throat, a light stroke to his Adam's apple, causing him to gulp repeatedly, thereby drawing more of her attention. She was going to make him choke. All he could utter was a growl to which she responded.

This time, he gave. She took.

A nearby splash interrupted, barely.

It wasn't until the cold contact of the water splash hit against their legs that they pulled apart. He thought he heard the pop as their lips parted as if a suction cup had been pulled from its target.

They stared at each other. Chests heaving. Mouths swollen.

Reality was forcing itself in, not waiting for them to get grounded again. Slowly the surrounding noises soaked through their consciousness. Another guest was swimming at the far length of the pool. An employee was straightening the lounge chairs. Another was watering the plants.

Derek wanted to talk now that his pulse had returned to normal. He was excited. He wanted to snatch her up and twirl her around. But he was afraid that any sound, movement, even thought would break the mood and make her skittish.

He could tell she was self-conscious again. She wouldn't meet his gaze. Instead she had her arms crossed over her chest and she was staring at her toes.

"Toni, look at me," he begged. "No regrets."

"Oh, my." Her hand came up to her mouth. She looked up at him, then covered her eyes. "Sorry."

He knew before he looked down that his body had not caught up with his mind and that the moment was over. He dropped the towel in front of his swim trunks in an effort to be discreet. "I'm not sorry." He grinned.

Toni slipped on the spa robe. She felt a warm flush and knew it wasn't embarrassment. Yes, it was a shocker to see Derek aroused, but she couldn't deny the hot streak of desire that coursed through her like an express train.

She wanted this man.

"I'm going to get dressed." She eased around him to get to the ladies' dressing area.

"Yeah, me too."

Toni headed to the dressing room, wishing she could say something clever. She wanted to say words that still left the door of possibility open. But the only thing that kept playing repeatedly in her mind was that she wanted this man.

"Toni."

She paused and turned.

"Dinner. Tonight at six." Derek walked into the dressing room without waiting for her answer.

Toni smiled. Guess the matter was taken out of her hands. She brought the towel to her face and grinned. "Yes, Mr. Calverton, I'll be ready for tonight." Her body blushed, letting her know that it was also ready for tonight.

Chapter 5

The remainder of the day dragged. Toni had a fruit salad for lunch. Her appetite had disappeared, but she knew it was important to eat something, even if it was the plate of melon, kiwi, grapes, and orange slices with creamy strawberry yogurt.

Sitting on her balcony, her new favorite spot, nibbling on the pieces of fruit, she wondered what the night would hold. She was a grown woman, but still suffered a case of nerves like a young girl on her first date. Questions like what to wear consumed her. Maybe a fairy godmother would suddenly appear and dress her in a designer ensemble.

Her phone rang. She stared at the sleek white telephone on the desk. What if Derek was canceling? After all, she had done just that a couple days ago. She'd be disappointed, if that was the case. She walked over, picked up the receiver and answered.

"How's it going, sweetheart?"

"Hi, Mom." Toni couldn't stop smiling. Relief coursed through her body. "Everything, okay?" Toni hadn't called her mother in a couple of days. However, she had made the obligatory call letting her mother know that her flight arrived on time and the hotel was wonderful.

"Yep. Your father and I have decided to get away this weekend. We're going to the Outer Banks. He's got all that time off and I've been on him to use it before he loses it."

"That's good, Mom. I'm having a great time. Very relaxing. Weather has been awesome."

"I'm so glad. I was worried that you'd be in your hotel room the entire two weeks."

Toni heard the concern in her mother's voice.

"I'm in the room now because I just came back from the spa. I've made some friends and I'm going out tonight."

"Oh, sweetheart, that's wonderful." Her mother's relief was palpable even through the phone. "Did you have any luck with Nicole's situation?"

"Yes. I've found Brad's brother. Nicole will be joining me next week." Toni didn't want to talk about Derek. There was no point in doing so. She was coming to terms with this experience being a summer fling and nothing more. There was no need to talk about him. There were no parents to meet and complicate matters. She'd be boarding a plane in another week and he'd remain here.

They were both adults and could handle that reality.

"I'm glad you got that over with at the beginning of the trip. Now you can concentrate on having a good time."

"That's exactly what I'm going to do." Toni promised her

mother to call before they headed for their mini-vacation in North Carolina, then hung up.

She retrieved the remainder of her fruit and headed to her closet. When she'd packed for her vacation, she hadn't planned on attending anything fancy. Her budget didn't allow for posh restaurants, big-name concerts or expensive tourists' packages.

However, if Derek did have a romantic evening planned for her, nothing in her closet would suffice. On the other hand, she could be blowing things out of proportion and end up at a local hangout. Her abysmally small selection consisted of two dresses, four shorts outfits, two dress slacks, and three blouses. Nothing leapt out at her as the perfect outfit.

Figuring that, if she were home, she'd want a new outfit, Toni opted to go shopping. The hotel's stores weren't an option, knowing that the mark-up could wipe out her bank account with one swipe of the credit card.

On the concierge's advice, she took a taxi to Bay Street, known for its trendy shops. Familiar U.S. chains lined the wide brick sidewalk. Small, exclusive boutiques were interspersed among the bigger stores featuring European designers.

Toni wandered into several stores. She could tell immediately if the apparel suited her tastes. If a store's merchandise caught her eye, then she headed to the sales rack. However, the price on some sales tags gave her sticker shock. The definition of sales or discount was a matter of perspective.

What would she do if Derek wanted to keep taking her out? She'd be broke. But at least for one night she could look darn good. She tried not to get depressed when she exited the last store empty-handed. As a last resort she could wear her black slacks and her long-sleeve black shirt with shimmering pearl buttons. It was simple, but elegant. Maybe she should focus on purchasing shoes, instead.

Toni crossed the street and began her search again. She walked into a tiny store that featured a Bahamian fashion designer. The lady behind the counter looked distinguished with salt-and-pepper hair. She stepped forward and greeted Toni at the door with a bright smile and an accent that Toni thought could possibly be French. It made sense that a classy woman ran a classy establishment.

"How may I help you?"

"I'm looking for a dress for this evening. Something nice, but I'm not trying to break the bank, either."

The lady laughed. "Come with me. I have my daughter's latest designs over here."

"These are all your daughter's designs?" Toni surveyed the store, truly impressed.

"Yes, she works with one of the major designers in France, but she also has a small line of clothing specifically for the people and tourists in the Bahamas. I'm Ginny, by the way."

Toni gave her her name. She tried to look at the costs without picking up the price tags. If she wasn't mistaken, there were three digits before the periods. Yikes!

She headed for the door.

"Don't give up so easily. What are you looking to buy?"

"Can't really say. Guess I'll know it when I see it."

Ginny placed a comforting hand on her arm. Gold bracelets jingled as she gestured. "We've a few dressy evening gowns over there. In the middle, we have everyday clothes.

Over to the right are all the one-of-a-kind pieces. See, there are no duplicates. No mass production, which makes the purchase all the more special."

Toni followed Ginny to the unique pieces, wondering how she could diplomatically tell her that she couldn't afford the mass reproductions, much less the unique pieces. But gosh, they were gorgeous. She trailed her fingers along the dresses, pants, blouses.

"How about this?" Ginny held up a blood-red dress with matching lounge pants.

Toni liked the style but thought the red was too harsh. She wanted to make a statement, not a sensation. Toni shook her head.

Ginny moved around the rack and pulled out a floor-length Indian-cotton skirt that had swirls of colors that reminded her of autumn. The pumpkin, olive green, golden hues would go perfectly against her skin—too ordinary. Toni wrinkled her nose.

Ginny stopped and tapped her finger against her cheek. Toni remained in the background watching the proud mother scrutinize her daughter's inventory. "I think I've found it."

Toni didn't immediately react. She didn't think that she would find that special outfit. With a deep sigh, she walked over to where Ginny stood.

Toni melted. She'd never considered white. Yet, the halter dress had an intricate bodice that would provide the necessary uplift and then a tight corset for the midsection with an abundance of material for the skirt that ended midcalf. A cute bolero provided a peek-a-boo cover for a cool night. As an added touch, shimmering accents were sewn along the hemline, waist and the top of the bodice. As Ginny held out the dress, the store's lighting picked up the soft glimmer with the merest hint of pink.

"I can see from your face that this is the winner."

"It's so beautiful." Toni felt the tears prickle. The dress was perfect.

"Here, try it on."

Toni took the dress and went into the fitting room. She slipped into the dress afraid that the zipper wouldn't pull the skirt around her hips. She also feared that the corset would be too tight, but it fit like a glove. And when she was done, she exhaled slowly.

Vanity was never her thing, but she had to admit that she looked darn good.

"What do you think?"

"Ginny, it's so gorgeous."

"Come on out so I can see."

Toni complied and walked out slowly. She had kicked off her shoes because they ruined the look. Barefoot she danced around the store. Ginny directed her to a raised dais with three full-length mirrors so that customers could see themselves from all sides.

More customers walked into the store, the little bell announcing their arrival. Three women, who were clearly tourists, came upon them. "That is so gorgeous," one woman said.

"Honey, you are wearing that color. Too bad I can't wear white," the redhead said wistfully.

"Makes a good wedding dress, too."

Toni stared at the woman to see if she was kidding. The trio wandered off to another part of the store. Toni turned back to look in the mirror.

Tears welled up. When she saw her reflection, the dress did

remind her of a wedding dress. Heaven knows, that wasn't happening anytime soon. The reality filled her with sadness. She stepped off the raised platform and ran into the fitting room. She had the dress off and back on the hanger within a minute.

"Here, Ginny. As much as I like it, I don't think it's for me."

"Honey, I know you're wrong. But here's what I'm going to do. Take my card. If you change your mind, the dress is here."

Toni took the card, not meeting Ginny's eyes. She walked out of the store knowing that there would be no more shopping today. She couldn't get the dress out of her mind and anything else that she saw would pale in comparison.

She hailed a taxi, deflated to be returning to the hotel empty-handed. Only a couple hours remained. Her hair needed to be washed and styled. Blow drying and hot curling would eat up those hours.

Derek had spent the afternoon calling in favors. He wanted everything to be perfect. He wanted to show Toni that she was special to him. Although he didn't plan for any of this to happen, he wasn't going to walk away from it.

He splashed on aftershave, smoothed his new haircut in the mirror, and ran his fingers along his eyebrows for good measure. His cell phone rang, on schedule. He answered, confirming the details before ending the call. His heart started pounding. He hoped that the night went according to his detailed plan. He picked up his keys and headed out.

Toni walked down to the lobby to wait for Derek five minutes before seven. She didn't want to sit, choosing to pace in the lobby where she could see his arrival.

She wore the black slacks with the big legs that caused the gauzy material to swish around her legs. Instead of the black shirt, she wore a gold silk top with spaghetti straps. In case she grew cold, she had a black lace shawl draped loosely around her shoulders. Her only accessories were a tiny black satin purse, big enough for her lipstick and hotel room card. She'd slipped her feet into black mules that had gold strips interwoven around the toe area.

The women's restroom was in front of her. Although she recently had come from her room, she needed the security of a quick check. She hurried to the bathroom, promising herself that she only needed to check her hair and makeup.

A few women were also doing their checkup. Toni offered them a smile. She leaned toward the mirror for a closer inspection of her eye makeup. Had she used enough concealer? Hopefully the foundation wouldn't make her shiny in another hour. The onyx eye shadow didn't need a touch-up, but she would have liked to add a bit more crushed pearl to the upper brow area. After all, what was the point of having the painful eyebrow wax if she wasn't going to highlight the brow arch.

She pressed her lips together to reduce the high gloss. Beauty experts insisted that lipstick should always be on hand, just in case it wore off with eating or kissing. She blushed and had to grab a tissue to dab her face because of the instant heat that broke out on her face and neck. No more crazy thoughts or she would look like someone who'd recently hiked through the desert.

Smoothing her outfit with her hands, she took a deep breath and left the ladies' room. There was no sign of Derek. She tamped down the fear that he had changed his mind. Was this how he felt when he waited for her that night? He wouldn't be so cruel as to give her a taste of her own medicine. Would he?

She walked through the revolving door. The humidity lay thick like a fortress. Knowing that the weather would play havoc on her hair, she had pulled it back in a ponytail with spiral curls spilling from the pearl-encrusted clip. She kept a few tendrils out in the back to soften the look.

"Ma'am, are you Toni Kimball?"

Toni nodded to the bellhop.

"Your limo is waiting." He stepped off the curb and opened the door to a white limo.

Toni looked at the young man and then at the limo. She tilted her head to see if Derek was inside waiting for her. Instead only a white leather backseat, without a passenger, awaited her. She stepped in and slid along the seat. The bellhop closed the door.

The driver turned and tipped his hat. "Good evening, ma'am. I am Laurence, your driver this evening. There is a minibar, television, and stereo for your convenience. Should you need anything further, you may press the intercom button."

"Where are you taking me?"

"To meet Mr. Calverton." He turned around and pulled out of the hotel's driveway. With barely a sound, the privacy window eased shut leaving her alone in the rear of the limo.

Toni didn't want to drink, look at TV, or listen to music. But that didn't stop her from opening the console and bar to admire the luxurious amenities. She sat back duly impressed at Derek's idea of a date so far. Her dressy selection may not have been a bad idea after all.

"Wait till the girls hear this one," she said softly. Her mind thought about her move back to Glen Knolls. She missed her friends. This retreat of sorts might help her put her past in the past. All she wanted to do was think of the present, enjoy it, wallow in it without planning for the future, at least, for the moment. While in the Bahamas, she wanted to take a breather.

The limo slowed and Toni looked out the window. She didn't have a clue where she was. She shook her fingers to chase away the nerves. The limo finally stopped and she waited for Laurence to open her door. She took his hand and stepped out. No sign of Derek anywhere.

"You're to go through that gate."

Toni stood in front of the gate that had roses interwoven in the arched trellis. She smelled them from where she stood on the curb. She turned to confirm the instructions, but Laurence had already stepped into the limo and was pulling off. There were people strolling nearby, but no one stopped at or entered the place where she stood.

She pushed open the gate and entered. It looked like someone's house, or rather, a villa. The open front door beckoned like an invitation into the living area. She didn't know much about Greek or Roman architecture, but the interior with its columns and open floor plan begged for an elegant gathering.

Music played, soft and romantic, filling the house with no speakers in sight. She followed the sound, which led her onto a patio. To her surprise, a harpist and two violinists played. The surprise of seeing the trio with no one else made her nervous.

No one acknowledged her. She moved around them looking at their music sheets, which had an Italian title. Whatever the name of the song, it touched her heart with its light whimsical tone and made her want to spin around until she was dizzy. A ballet routine from her childhood days came to mind: *Glacée, glacée, assemble, assemble, la piroute, la piroute*.

Now wasn't the time to indulge in youthful fantasy. Where on earth was Derek? The limo had been a nice touch, but if she didn't find Derek soon, then she was heading back to the hotel. The music moved her, but the otherwise empty house was too creepy.

She left the trio and continued her exploration, walking past the dining room. Still there was no sign of Derek. The house was one level and expansive, she'd noted. The back side opened out onto the beach. Toni opened the double doors and stepped out onto another patio. The music drifted through the house.

Bouquets of flowers of various colors and types surrounded her. She felt as if she had stepped into a garden paradise that was separate from the world. A glass of champagne sat on the table as if waiting for her. She picked it up and took a sip, enjoying the crisp taste against her tongue.

"You look absolutely beautiful."

"Derek," Toni exclaimed, spinning around to discover him standing in the shadows.

He stepped out of the shadows and kissed her softly on her cheek.

"You did all of this for me?" She couldn't help the tears. His thoughtfulness touched her.

"Yes." He took a flower and snapped off the stem. Then he stuck it in her hair. "Come with me."

She held onto his hand and followed him through the

house. He led her back to the dining room. In the short space of time, the room had been transformed. Toni put her hand over her mouth to hold in the exclamation, not believing her eyes.

The windows were opened allowing the thin white curtains to billow with the soft tropical breeze. Toni slipped the shawl from her shoulders and draped it on the back of a chair. The table was set with white votive candles. The plates looked like real china with silverware of the same quality. The glasses were Waterford.

She looked up at Derek who only smiled at her amazement.

"Have a seat."

On cue, a man entered in a white suit and pulled out her chair. Once she was seated, Derek took his. Toni looked down the table, shaking her head, she couldn't help but be thrilled by this attention to detail.

The waiter cleared his throat. "We need your assistance, ma'am."

"Yes?"

"Would you care for tilapia, roasted lamb or duck?"

"I'll try the tilapia." Toni loved the selection of fish in Nassau.

He bowed and Toni almost giggled. She noticed that he didn't ask Derek. But since he'd planned all this, the chef probably knew what he wanted.

"You live well." Toni raised her glass to Derek.

"I'll probably have to do a million boat tours after this." He laughed.

"If you need a testimonial, I'd be happy to oblige."

"For the boat tour?"

She nodded, sipping her champagne and licking her lips.

"You're lucky that you're sitting all the way down there."

"That can change." She sat back and crossed her legs.

The mood, the lights, the champagne and her desire to be flirtatious all surfaced. Tonight she might have difficulty restraining any sexual impulses. She flicked her shoulder and a strap slipped down her arm.

"Don't you dare tempt me. I paid for that meal and we're going to eat…before anything else."

"You know you don't have to always follow each step in your plan consecutively. Makes things a little boring." She opened her purse and pulled out the lipstick.

Sitting back in the chair, she slid the lipstick along her lips, with her mouth in an open O. Then she made a big production of winding down the tube of lipstick, before replacing the top. "Did I keep it in the line?"

Derek growled and threw his napkin down. His hands gripped the arms of the chair. He took a deep breath, closed his eyes and exhaled slowly. He snapped his finger.

"Yes, sir?"

"The shrimp, please."

Cocktail glasses with shrimp were served to each of them. The cocktail sauce was in a small ramekin for dipping.

Once she had eaten the shrimp, a small salad followed with a vinaigrette dressing. Toni was afraid that if any other dishes came out, she wouldn't be able to eat the main course.

But when the tilapia fish with a hint of curry was served on a bed of fluffy rice with steamed asparagus on the side, Toni had to admit that she was pretty hungry. She saw that

Derek had chosen the lamb, which looked equally appetizing with a side of garlic mashed potatoes.

"What are you thinking about?"

"Actually trying not to think," Toni answered in between bites of the fish, which melted in her mouth.

"I want you to think long enough to tell me about you."

"Not much to tell." Toni didn't mean to sound mysterious, but she'd put him on a need-to-know basis. And there was a lot about herself that he didn't need to know.

"Looks like I'm going to have to drag some information out of you." Derek cut into his lamb and popped a bite into his mouth. He rolled his eyes and made all kinds of hand motions to indicate how heavenly it tasted. "Where are you from? Siblings? Parents? Friends?"

"Parents are my anchor. They still find each other attractive. No siblings. I like being the only princess. My friends all live in Glen Knolls, Maryland where I also live. How about you?"

"Similar. My parents dote on each other. I'm also an only child. And we all live happily ever after on the island." He scooped up a forkful of mashed potato. "Your turn to ask a question."

"Why me? Why do I interest you?"

"Wasn't quite expecting that. I was hoping for what is my favorite color?" He exhaled and repeated her question. "Give me a second to answer that one."

Toni could wait. This answer was important. If Derek answered incorrectly—and she didn't know what would trigger the red flags—if he did, then the night was over. All the harpists and violinists wouldn't be enough to make her sit through the evening. She continued eating, munching on the asparagus spears, and waited.

"I'll admit that when I first saw you, I was attracted. For the most part, people notice each other because there is a physical pull. Then we talked on the boat tour and you had this look as if the world not only sat on your shoulders, but had broken you down. I don't know why, and this may sound corny, I wanted to be the one to show you that there was sunshine beyond the clouds. You have some deep fears and doubts, maybe even about me and my intentions. I can't make any promises because it's my belief that you've heard them all before. I'm not going to ask you to trust me. Your heart is all tapped out. All I can do is demonstrate what I'm capable of and let your inner voice do the rest."

Toni listened with a keen ear, weighing and examining the words and their meaning. She pushed aside the plate. Only a few mouthfuls were left, anyway. But Derek's admission had created a lump in her throat. His honesty had touched her. *How to respond?*

She heard him push back his chair and she looked at him through the tears that sprung like a faithful geyser to blur her vision. One tear spilled and she vaguely thought about the streak it would cause down her face.

Derek pulled back her chair and she rose. He opened his arms and she stepped in as he closed his arms around her. He held her until her tears dried and she had swallowed the sobs that erupted into tiny hiccups. He kissed her forehead and gently laid her head against his chest.

Slowly he swayed to the music. She followed his lead. Their bodies locked in each other's embrace moving as one.

Toni closed her eyes and let the music fill her soul. She allowed Derek's legs to move, lead, guide her through their waltz. When the music ended, she opened her eyes to look into his.

His eyes were dark pools, mysterious and inviting. His face held no judgment. His lips, well, they held such promise.

"Ready for dessert?" he asked.

"I'm not sure."

"It's on the beach."

"This beach?"

He took off his jacket and tossed it on the chair. Then he slipped off his shoes and socks. He opened his shirt midway and rolled up his pants legs inches above the ankle.

Toni didn't wear anything that could be converted into beach wear. She looked down at her dress slacks.

"Don't worry, you'll be fine." Derek led her out the back door onto the beach. The music had faded. She turned and the house seemed far away. She looked out into the inky blackness. Her steps slowed.

"It's okay," he reassured.

They walked onto a pier where a small rowboat was tied. He stepped in first and lifted her into the boat.

Toni wasn't terribly comfortable on water. But she was game as long as the boat was big enough for her to sit down in. Watching Derek row out into the ocean was not exactly calming or romantic. Plus no one knew where the heck she was. She looked back to shore debating whether to jump into the ocean.

"Would you calm down? I can practically hear the crazy thoughts running through your head."

She turned around to tell him a thing or two.

Suddenly lights blinked on, bright and piercing on their boat. Toni shielded her eyes, realizing that a large yacht was anchored in the water.

Derek rowed up to the boat where a ladder hung from its side. He offered Toni his hand and then helped her place her feet for the climb. "Don't worry, baby, I'm right behind you…enjoying the view."

"Wait until I get up here," she muttered. He could have warned her. The wide pants legs were not designed for climbing. She constantly stepped on the hem and the spaghetti straps were not comfortable.

Once on board, a three-man crew met them. Derek made the introductions. The captain and one man returned to manning the yacht. The other man served champagne and strawberries with chocolate. She was impressed considering the humid weather.

A few minutes later, Toni realized that she had left her shawl at the house. The night on the ocean had proved to be a bit cool. She ran her hands over her arms and headed inside.

The large room in the yacht looked like an intimate sitting room with sofa, gas fireplace, and bar.

"Who does this belong to?"

"A man that can afford another fifty of these and then some."

"And he just loaned it to you?"

"Don't sound so doubtful."

"Hey, I'm not complaining. Just make sure that we return in time for me to get my flight home."

"Hmm. So I haven't convinced you of my pure intentions."

"Heck, no, and not when you say it with that grin." Toni swallowed a mouthful of champagne.

Derek moved closer to her.

"I've got the yacht until sunrise."

Toni stared at him. Her mind and heart warred.

"Do you want me to head to shore?" Derek asked.

Toni sank into a nearby couch, resting her head against the back of it. What the heck was she doing? Home and all its baggage seemed far away tucked behind a velvet rope in her memory banks.

Derek sat next to her, waiting for her answer. Toni turned to him and pulled his head toward hers. She surrendered. Now, she did what she wanted to do. She kissed him, lingering over the feel of his lips against hers. She inhaled the expensive cologne mixed with his own scent to seal his signature fragrance for the days when he would no longer be around.

"I want to stay," she whispered.

He didn't move, simply stared down at her. "One sec."

He went down a hallway and came back with a damp washcloth. Then he dimmed the room.

"I love how you made yourself look like a supermodel on a photo shoot. But I like you with a more natural look. You are so beautiful without makeup." He wiped her face, slowly and gently as if revealing a work of art.

Toni saw the bronze foundation mixed with the black eyeliner with streaks of the copper lipcolor on the washcloth like a painter's palette. When Derek had finished, he reached behind Toni's head and unfastened the ponytail clip. He ran his fingers through her hair, fluffing it out to frame her face.

"You're so damned beautiful."

"I hear that all the time." Toni bit her lip.

"You know we're supposed to be eating crème brûlée."

"Let's do that later."

"At sunrise?"

Toni nodded before rising to kiss him. She didn't want to talk anymore. Derek hungrily responded. But Toni didn't want to rush, either. Derek had planned and controlled the evening. But she wanted to take the lead now. She wanted him to see her as an equal in all things. His art of seduction worked, but she wanted to close the deal. She wanted to take ownership of his body and ask him whether he had it in him to last to sunrise.

She pulled away from his lips and sat up. They were both panting, but it was merely the beginning. She spotted the tray of strawberries and the chocolate syrup in a silver bowl.

"Hold that thought." She maneuvered around him and retrieved the bowl.

In the meantime, he came back with pillows and bed linens and threw them on the floor. He pulled off his shirt and put his hands on his pants waist.

"No." She crawled onto the sheet and raised on her knees. "That's my job."

She unsnapped his pants and unzipped. She locked eyes with him, enjoying the restraint that he wrestled with while she slid the pants over his hips. He grabbed his champagne glass and drank deeply.

She saw the champagne trickle down the side of his mouth and drip to his chest. She licked the path of the wayward wine. He growled and she smiled, pleased at his response. After she had taken care of the champagne, she continued pulling his pants toward his ankles. He stepped out. She admired the muscular length of his legs, tracing the outline of his muscles with her fingertips. She followed the quadriceps starting from the knee and moved up the inner thigh where she felt him twitch. Her fingers did their magic playing and massaging the large thigh muscle, then switching attention to his hamstring that led up to his backside.

She ran her hand over his behind and then around to his hips. From the time that she had unzipped his pants, he was aroused. She knew better than to tease him there. Although it would be fun, she didn't want him to lose control. Not yet.

Taking the bowl of chocolate syrup, she dipped her finger and traced patterns on his chest. She even wrote her name across his stomach. Finally she drew a picture of a sunflower with its stem growing out from his briefs.

His hands went around her waist to pull her top over her head. She resisted, pushing him back. "I didn't give you permission," she teased.

"You're killing me." Derek's voice was tight.

"Then I'll get to resuscitate you."

She stood, not to kiss him as he tried to do. Instead she gave her tongue the job of erasing the path of chocolate.

Chapter 6

Toni took her time, giving her undivided attention to each chocolate pattern. Derek's body trembled as she swirled her tongue around his nipple. She delighted in her power, enjoying the rapturous moans vibrating through his body. His hand stroked her hair.

"Nope. No touching allowed."

"You are wicked."

She grinned and then spread some of the chocolate on her lips before deeply kissing him on his lips.

"That should keep you busy for a few more seconds. Now back to business." Toni admired her handiwork. She'd scrolled her name in large capital letters diagonally across his stomach. Each muscle rippled like a washboard. First the T disappeared, then she moved to the O.

"No more!" Derek dropped to his knees and held onto her

shoulders. He had to keep her still. Her mouth and that tongue were dangerous weapons. She brought him sweet agony that threatened to cut off his air supply, thereby leaving him in a state of blissful unconsciousness.

"I'm not finished."

"I haven't begun." He pulled her blouse over her head and unfastened the strapless bra that fastened in the front. His hand ran over each breast, softly massaging it until her nipples hardened.

He unbuttoned her pants and disrobed her the way she had just done with him. "Even your underwear turns me on." His finger played with the red lace bikini that was cut high over the thighs. "I want to be the artist now." He stuck his entire hand into the bowl of syrup. Then he placed handprints on her back, stomach, shoulder, rib cage.

Gently he pushed her onto her back. "If you want to save these, I'd suggest you pull them off."

Toni giggled and pulled off her underwear and tossed them onto the couch.

Derek took the bowl and poured the syrup onto her belly button. It spilled down the sides of her body and farther down into the nestle of hair.

"Now I'm going to write my name." He set down the bowl and slid his arm under her to raise her hips. With a soft swirl of his tongue he lavished, celebrating what she had to offer. Her soft moans, mixed with her muffled giggles, when he planted his kisses made his head spin.

Toni turned over onto her stomach and crawled to the sofa. "I need to breathe." She rested her head on the couch. Her breathing was heavy. "What are you doing to me?"

"Do you like it?" He slipped on the protective shield.

"More than you could ever know."

He kissed the back of her neck. His hands roamed over her breasts, cupping them. He framed her hips with his as his hands continued their sensual exploration. Before he exploded, he eased his way into her.

He clawed the bed linens as he matched the natural rhythm that they shared.

"Derek, I want to see your face. I want us to look into each other's eyes. Let us get there together, in sync." She turned and settled on her back. She took him between her hands and guided him to the one place that ached beyond anything imaginable.

He raised her legs, propping them on his shoulders and plunged deeper and deeper. Toni arched under him. Her nails raked his back, sending him into further rapture.

They were the only people in their world. Nothing mattered, as their bodies interlocked, with only a thin film of chocolate melting between them. They devoured each other.

The rise up the mountain was swift, fast-paced, full of energy as they savored each other's bodies like gifts. Derek reached his peak first, exploding with a passion that he thought could never be. He reached down to the depth of his soul and pulled Toni up in a final surge. Then it was her turn to contract and convulse with guttural shrieks ripping through her.

Once they had danced their choreographed routine that only nature could have written, they came back down hand in hand, easing back to the base where they had once begun.

Wrapped in the cocoon of the bed linens, they slept in each other's arms, exhausted, but with a smile on their lips.

There would be no dreams tonight, only memories of their special union until the early light of the new day came knocking.

Music blared. Men and women writhed to the bass beat. Strobe lights lit up the dance floor and flicked across the tables and chairs. Toni squinted as the bright light occasionally blinded her.

"Let's dance," Derek shouted.

Toni nodded. There was no way they could have an intimate conversation in a nightclub.

They danced to the latest songs.

Toni felt woefully out of touch, not only with the lyrics but with the dance steps. Her body didn't twist and contort the way these young people did.

She had to laugh at Derek. He wasn't going to pretend to know how to do these moves. Instead he grabbed her wrist and they hand danced in the middle of the gyrating couples.

Then a slow song played and he scooped her against his chest. She rested her head against his shoulder. She had so much pleasure standing in his embrace.

"Can we leave after this?"

"Sure. Are you tired?" He pulled away looking down at her face.

She shook her head. "I want you," she whispered into her ear.

"And I have to wait until this song ends?"

"Yep."

"But you know Barry White doesn't sing quick songs."

"Consider it foreplay."

"And then I can make love to you on the dance floor?"

"You're silly."

"Okay, try me."

Toni looked up at his face. "Oh no you don't."

Derek only laughed.

Five minutes later, the song ended. Toni backed away from Derek. She didn't trust him not to do something outrageous. She still hadn't gotten over their night on the yacht.

Derek led her through a door, down a hallway.

"Where are we going?"

"The VIP suite."

"I guess this is another one of your friends in high places?"

"Something like that."

They entered a room and Derek flicked on the lights. Toni surveyed the room openmouthed. There were several booths with leather couches. In the center of the room was a dance floor. But the thing that made her speechless was the dance pole in the middle of the floor.

"Are we having a show?" She examined the pole. "I know you don't expect me to do something."

"Not at all. I was just bringing you to a dance floor. I decided to take you up on your dare."

"Derek Calverton, you are too freaky." She walked over to a panel of buttons and levers. She flicked them on. Music, colored lights came on. All she could do was laugh.

"What are you going to do for me if I dance on the pole?"

"Free boat tour?"

"Did that already."

"You haven't had my personalized boat tour."

Toni only had to look into Derek's eyes to know that it

would certainly be a custom-designed outing. She didn't need any further encouragement.

She pressed the start button. A hip-hop song played, the rapper bragged with a bluntness that grated her sensibilities. This wasn't the music to get into the mood. It was more like a war song to get hyped up to go into battle.

This wasn't a battle, but a dance of seduction. She needed the lyrical poetry that soothed, stimulated, and energized.

She continued pressing the buttons until Luther's melodic voice filled the space. Toni turned it up. She brought Derek to the floor, dragging a chair behind him. Then she danced around him, not daring to deal with the pole. She knew her limitations.

Under the club lights, music pumping, she straddled Derek. She pulled a condom out of her bra. "Figured it might come in handy."

She slid the condom on him, nibbling on his lips in the process. She kissed his neck, letting her tongue flick where his pulse beat. With one hand she held him in place as she slid onto him.

"Keep your eyes open," she ordered.

Toni teased his exposed neck with small nibbles. He grabbed her hips and increased the friction. Toni had to hold onto the back of the chair for stability. She bore down, gritting her teeth.

Derek awoke in her an appetite that could only be temporarily satiated. She rocked against him, clenching him between her legs. A contorted mix of wailing, screaming and shrieks escaped from her. Waves of orgasmic pleasure tore through her like white-water rapids crashing their way along her inner walls, spilling out. She hoped the room was soundproof.

Derek rested his head against her breasts that rose and fell under the exertion. If she kept this up, there would be no turning back.

They readjusted their clothing.

"I don't want to know how you knew this place existed." Toni ran her fingers through her tousled hair.

"Good. Because I don't want to know the circumstances of your lap dance experiences."

The couple walked out of the room and club into the balmy evening, holding hands.

Derek hadn't planned for his every waking hour to be spent thinking of, or being with, Toni. Yet, in the morning, he couldn't plan his day without knowing what she would be doing. He knew that he ran himself ragged with his boat tours and then their nightly lovemaking marathon. But he wanted it all. Call him greedy.

He pulled up in front of the hotel, excited that Toni didn't keep him at a distance any longer. Another day presented itself in which he planned to whisk her into his imagination. He had a picnic basket with wine, cheese, fruit, French bread, butter, and cold fried chicken. Five days on the island and she had spent more time in his arms than touring his island home. He planned to rectify that with a lazy boat ride to the Blue Lagoon.

"Today, we're having a history lesson."

"Does this mean that you get to dress up as a British privateer and I dress up as a barmaid?"

He drove through the congested streets leading to the pier.

Her hair whipped around her face as she smiled sexily at him. He took her hand and planted a kiss in her palm.

The day was mild with temperatures in the high eighties. Toni wore jeans, a bikini top, a light shirt and tennis shoes. He wore shorts and a T-shirt. Armed with the picnic basket, they completed the picture of a couple giddy over each other. And that wasn't far from the truth.

He set the boat on course, while Toni prepared the ice for their drinks. He observed her, humming as she busied herself. For an instant he wondered if she would consider extending her trip. He waved to a passing fishing trawler.

Why would she stay? What did he have to offer? It was more likely that she'd grow tired of him and, in her second week of vacation, make excuses why she couldn't see him.

Toni walked up to him with a plastic cup filled with fruit punch.

"Here." She handed him the cup. "Now tell me about this beautiful island, m'lord."

"We're seven hundred islands strong. Nassau is our capital city on the island of New Providence."

"All this land explains why it was so attractive to others."

"We have our own melting pot—like New York City. We've had the British, Americans who fled after the Revolution, Africans, Haitians, even Chinese and Greeks."

"That's amazing." Toni recalled seeing portraits of Prince Charles and Queen Elizabeth around the island. "But it's still very British."

"Yes, we drive on the left side of the road and have the changing of the guard in front of Parliament. Yet there is a strong culture that is uniquely Bahamian that has developed through the years."

"You're pretty proud to call this place your home, right?" She placed her arm around his waist and rested her head against his chest. "Were you born here?"

"Nope. But I came here at a very young age because this is all I know."

"And your mom is from the U.S.?"

"No. She's a local. My father came here with a job and then never left." He squeezed her to him, wishing that he could keep her there.

"Think he misses home?"

He shrugged. "My father isn't the outgoing type. It's pretty hard to know what he's thinking or feeling unless he chooses to tell you. And, well, I'm not exactly the model son."

"What do you mean?" Toni pushed away from him.

"He thinks that I'm wasting my life being a tour guide. After all I did go to college and got a degree in software design."

"But this is what you love to do."

"It'll do. I needed some time to figure out what was important. I'm planning to open a software company that will handle contracts from the U.S."

"That's great." She hugged him. "I know that it will be successful."

"But I'll miss this."

"When do you think it will start?"

"I'm tying up loose ends with the banks. I'll open by the first of October."

Toni showered his face with kisses. She hugged him

tightly. Her joy and acceptance touched him. Having her show her approval meant a lot to him.

"Here we are on the Blue Lagoon." He steered the boat to a dock.

"It's gorgeous. And do I smell food?"

Derek helped her off the boat. "You're smelling BBQ ribs. They make food for the special excursions."

"But, do you know someone who will let us eat without a hassle."

"Ah…actually no. Not this time. I'm sneaking onto the island and probably in about fifteen minutes, we may be asked to leave."

"You'd better tell them that you're *the* Derek Calverton, software genius and tour guide extraordinaire."

He kissed her full on the mouth.

"What was that for?"

"I'm getting stuck on you."

He saw the shadow flick across Toni's face. He wished that he could retract the words. He'd wanted her to somehow change her life's plans and hang out with him.

She slipped out of his embrace and walked onto the beach. She took special care spreading out the red checkered table-cloth, weighting each corner with medium-sized shells. Carefully she took out the food and set it in the middle.

"Come and eat, Derek."

He sat on the cloth, following her busyness with the food, while stealing surreptitious glances at her face. Her expressions intrigued him. One time she appeared to be enjoying herself. Another time, she seemed reserved. He didn't want her to panic. Heck, he didn't want to panic. All he had to do was enjoy what days she had left. He couldn't help pushing for more, even laying down a tad of guilt.

"Who made the chicken?"

"I did. I minored in cooking."

"You're the Renaissance man. When will I get to experience some more of your culinary skills?"

He leaned over and kissed her in the valley of her breasts. "As soon as I get to sample more of your amorous skills."

"You have a one track mind."

He put his head in her lap and looked up into her face. His fingers played with her legs, doing a spider imitation up her pants leg with a tickle in the most sensitive spot. She squirmed and then tried to push him away.

"I'm beginning to think that you only want me for my body."

"No, I want you for your mind." He slid his hand under the cup of the bikini top. "I want you for your soul." He rose up and kissed her stomach.

"Don't care what you do or say, Derek. I'm not making love to you on the beach."

"Do you want to make love on the beach? Or do you just want the drink sex on the beach?"

"Neither. You're making it difficult for me to think. There is no need to make love as frequently as you want."

"That sounds like a pathetic confession. Guess the men you dated didn't know what an appetite you have. I feel kind of honored to make the discovery."

"Stop sounding so proud." She pushed his head off her lap, giggling as he rolled onto his face.

"Most explorers that conquer new territory have a day named after them. What can I expect?"

"I'll tell you when I'm inspired." She stood up and ran toward an outcropping of rock.

Derek followed close behind. He didn't want to catch her. Instead he was curious as to where she was and what she was about to do.

"There's an entrance over here." The entrance to the cave invited her. She hesitated.

Derek followed her eager directions only to be surprised.

The opening was wide enough for a car's width with room to spare.

Toni ran ahead, disappearing from view in the semidarkened interior.

"Toni?" He strained to hear any discerning sounds. "Stop playing." Small rocks were tossed at his feet.

Toni emerged from a hiding spot at his left. Before he could recover, she wrapped her legs tightly around his waist. She smothered his face with wet kisses, nibbling on his earlobes.

"Did I scare you?"

"Yeah, I thought that you were a big, ugly bat coming at me." That remark earned him a sharp nip on the bottom lip. "Ouch."

"Sorry, forgive me?"

"No. Because you're not sincere."

She started to unfasten her top. "Sure there's nothing I can do?"

"You fight dirty," Derek accused.

Toni opened her shirt allowing it to fall open over her breasts, suggestively featuring her generous cleavage.

"What am I going to do with you?"

"If you have to ask, then I'd better be on my way." She made a production of buttoning her shirt. "Oops." She retrieved the sealed condom packet that had fallen out of his pocket. "Guess I'll give this back to you." She held the thin plastic square between her fingers.

There were rare instances when Derek needed obvious clues to understand a given situation. He took the condom, turning it over in his hand.

"I'm trying to be a respectable gentleman." He groaned. "You're making it too difficult."

"That's because I can hear your thoughts."

He stepped into the shadows. He propelled her back against the cool cave wall. His hands led the exploration with his lips and tongue. He made love to her with an urgency that knew no limitations. In the cool recess of the cave where pirates hid their booty, scavengers laid in wait for injured ships, lovers whispered their innermost thoughts, he laid claim to the only woman to seep deeply into his soul.

"Toni." Her name ripped from his throat. He squeezed her behind as he released himself in powerful thrusts. If this moment was akin to blowing out a candle on a birthday cake, he wanted to make his wish that Toni would always be with him.

Toni leaned her head to the side on the headrest. She enjoyed the ride back to the hotel in a dreamy state of satisfaction. From a period where there was no one special in her life, and certainly no sex, to this special man at her side, she would never have dreamed of such a thing.

Happiness shouldn't be a burden. The happier she felt, the lighter her spirit, though wisps of guilt still infiltrated. Derek's wide shoulder supported her head. It provided a solid base more than he knew.

"Will you come up with me?"

"Don't know if I have anything left in me." He kissed her fingertips.

"Is that the only thing on your mind? There's a wide variety of television programs to see." They'd shared so much with each other, but she wanted the simple intimacy of sharing a bed, sleeping side by side.

"I need to change my clothes." He noted her disappointment. "I'll be back."

"Here's my hotel card. I'll wait for you."

She hopped out of the car. At home in Glen Knolls, this would be normal. On vacation on a Caribbean island, this was foolhardy. Her father would burst a blood vessel. Meanwhile her mother would shake her head and mutter under her breath. Her girlfriends, well she couldn't imagine what they'd say. They'd mothered her so much in the past months that she suspected they wouldn't say anything. But she'd get too many phone calls pestering her to reassure them that everything was okay. She waved as he pulled off.

The phone rang as she walked up to the door. She slid in the card and ran into the room. She dived across the bed to reach for the phone.

"Hey, Toni," Nicole greeted. "Where've you been? I've been trying to reach you."

"I was on a boat tour today."

"Another one?" Nicole laughed. "And what else have you been up to. You sound so happy."

"I'm getting my share of daily rest. The sun is agreeing with me. Guess I'm coming back a new woman."

"You can save that upbeat mumbo jumbo for your mother. I want the nasty juicy bits when I get there."

Toni sat up. She'd lost track of time. She looked at the calendar on the desk. Once Nicole arrived, everything would be different. She pulled the pillow into her lap, she wasn't ready.

"So have you learned anything else that would be helpful to me?"

"He doesn't know anything about his father's first wife. Thinks he's an only child."

"This is going to be a kicker. I'm going to need you to help me when the time comes. He trusts you, right?"

Toni closed her eyes. She didn't want that responsibility. Why did his world have to be turned upside down?

"Toni? Are you listening? I'm so appreciative of what you're doing. I love Brad and I need him to move beyond this episode in his life. I would crawl across a desert for this man."

"I know." Toni felt bad for being selfish. She hadn't come to Nassau to pick up a man. She came to help her best friend. "I'll be here when you come."

"Okay, Brad just walked in the door," Nicole's voice dropped. "See you in three days."

Toni stared at the phone. Three days. Seventy-two hours. She didn't want to sleep at all for the next three days. She didn't want to share Derek's time with work, his customers, anyone.

She sat on the edge of the bed and buried her face in the pillow. She cried for the wonderful time that she'd enjoyed. She cried for the way he made her spirit reenergize. She cried for what would never be. The soft cries turned into muffled sobs as her body shook with pent-up anxiety more than with grief.

Suddenly she looked up at the clock. Derek would be coming up at any time. He couldn't see her like this. He couldn't know how her heart and its feelings had reached a critical juncture.

She stepped into the shower stall. The warm water washed away the sea salt and sand. It washed away the tears. It washed away the fear and sadness. By the time she turned off the water, she'd regained her composure.

She slid back the shower curtain to find Derek sitting on the toilet lid. Her towel was laid across his legs. He had the bath rug positioned in front of his feet.

"Step out."

She obeyed, standing on the rectangular towel.

He dried her off. With his usual attention to detail he tended to her arms, rubbed the backs of knees, wiped under her breasts. His hands didn't tease or perform foreplay. He simply dried her off.

He led her to the bed and slipped her nightgown over her head. She slipped on her underwear. Then she placed the lotion in his hand and waited. He applied the lotion to her exposed skin.

A knock on the door surprised her. He pulled back the bedsheet and she slipped in. He covered her before answering the door.

A tray of dinner and dessert was brought in. Toni inhaled the wonderful aroma.

"What did you order?"

"Filet mignon."

"Yummy."

He brought the tray over to her side of the bed. Then he retrieved the tray for his side. He pointed the remote at the TV. "What do you want to see?"

"Nothing. I wanted to spend a quiet evening with no pomp and circumstance."

"Then I look forward to honoring your wishes. We will enjoy our meal in each other's company, side by side like an old married couple."

Toni's fork clattered to the plate. Surely he had to be joking. She turned to look at him. He was forcing a relatively large piece of steak into his mouth. The statement clearly didn't mean anything to him.

If she used her parents as a model, it would be the meal and then a healthy and noisy amount of flesh banging. She smiled at the hasty retreat she'd made out of their house.

"Toni, I've told you about my dream to own my software company. What's yours?"

"I don't indulge in dreams. It lessens the disappointment if they don't come true."

"You don't have goals? Not even an action plan?" He studied her. "You don't strike me as that type."

"See, that's how much you know. I was the kick-butt one out of the group. I approached everything as if going into battle." She paused. "It's not always the best method."

"Let me make it easier on you. When you get back home, what will you do?"

"Are you trying to find out if there is someone else that I'm going home to?"

"No." He finished off his steak. "Is there?"

Toni shook her head. That was one question that she could answer without hesitation. "I'm starting a new job at an insurance company. I'll be moving into a condominium. And I plan to take one day at a time."

"Sounds normal enough. What gets you excited?"

Toni couldn't answer any of these probing questions. Any true, honest answer would open up the box where she had shoved her heartbreak. Since losing her baby, nothing excited her. All she could manage was a job that didn't hurt her head and life that didn't have a roller coaster ride.

Toni moved the tray to the table. She came back with apple pie and picked at the crust. "Coming to the Bahamas gets me excited."

"Don't try to flatter me." Derek leaned over for a piece of her pie.

"I'm not. It's true." She ate her pie, alternating servings with him.

When she was finished, they lay in the bed. Her head was tucked under his chin. Her arm casually crossed his body. She listened to the strong, steady beat of his heart. She wished that she could hold him there for seventy-two hours.

Avoiding falling into the doldrums took a significant amount of effort. She walked into the bathroom and looked at the sink. Derek had his toothbrush lying next to hers. She looked at her reflection and smiled. A small thing like that lifted her spirits.

She brushed her teeth, noting that she had gotten several shades darker. Even her hair shone with reddish highlights from her hours in the sun. The phone rang. She hurried to wash the toothpaste out of her mouth.

When she emerged, Derek was on the phone.

She ran over and grabbed the phone from him. She mouthed, "Why did you answer it?"

He shrugged. "You were brushing your teeth."

"Shh." Toni held her hand over the mouthpiece. "Hello?"

"Who was that? Was that him?"

"Yes."

"I want to hear all about it."

"Oh my gosh, you have Donna on the line?"

"Me too."

"Shirley?"

"Nicole, why are you wasting money," Toni scolded.

"I wasn't the one dying to call you. It's your crazy cousin."

"We want to speak to him," Donna yelled. "Put him on the phone."

Toni debated with the soundness of this proposition.

"What's going on?" Derek asked.

"Pick up the phone." Toni watched him pick up the phone by the desk.

"Hello?" Derek prompted.

"Hey, big guy. What's up? Is this Derek?"

"Ladies, could you act like you have some sense or I'm going to hang up."

"Since when did you get so stuffy?" Donna asked. "Derek, is she acting like a stick in the mud with you?"

"Nope. I have no complaints in any department."

"What departments have you checked out?"

"Nicole, please. I expected you to be the adult."

"Remember how all of you pounced on Brad. Payback, baby!"

"Who's Brad?" Derek asked.

No one spoke.

Toni wound her finger around the cord, biting her bottom lip.

Derek shrugged. "Ladies, it was nice meeting you. I'll let you talk to Toni."

Toni made small talk, listening to the round of apologies. She couldn't acknowledge anything, sensing that Derek was listening to her words.

Later when the light was out. The balcony door was partly opened to let in the natural breeze. She was lying in the crook of Derek's arm.

"Who is Brad?"

"Nicole's husband." Toni struggled to keep her voice calm.

"Good."

Toni closed her eyes.

"I don't want to think about you with anyone else."

Chapter 7

Derek awoke in the morning to a knock on his door that didn't cease. He groaned and buried his face in the pillow. The thought of swinging his legs over the side of the bed made him hug his pillow tighter.

The early morning visitor wasn't going to leave. Derek stood and stretched, sleepily scratching his body. Guess he'd better grab a pair of shorts. Only a microscopic segment of the female population who managed to wake up next to him knew that he slept in the buff.

An obscenely tropical, patterned pair of shorts sat on top a pile of clothes in a laundry basket. He picked it up between two fingers and performed a sniff test. He found the scent acceptable. A dryer sheet fell from the shorts near his feet. He stumbled through his bedroom as he pulled them up.

"Coming," he roared at his front door. "Man, I need

coffee." He licked his lips anticipating the taste of the bitter, dark liquid.

"If you don't have coffee, go away." He flung open the door ready to throttle the irritating knocker.

"Boy, who do you think you're talking to?" His mother glowered at him before pushing him aside. She strode into the house, looking over the living room with a discerning eye.

Thank goodness Patsy, his cleaning person, had just completed her once-a-week clean-up. It didn't stop his mother from trailing her fingers over the side table where he placed his mail.

"At least your house is respectable for visitors, even if you're not." She rubbed her fingers together and turned to look at him.

"One second." Derek knew that look.

He followed the silent directive and returned to his bedroom. His mother wouldn't talk until she was good and ready. She also wouldn't talk if he wasn't dressed properly.

He dressed quickly into a sweat suit complete with socks and tennis shoes. Knowing that he still wouldn't pass inspection, he headed to the bathroom and performed his morning ritual topping it off with mouthwash. Now any remaining notions about going back to bed to complete his ten-hour sleep cycle vanished.

His nose picked up the scent his brain craved. His body followed the smell of freshly brewed coffee in the kitchen.

"Here." His mother handed him a large mug.

"Thanks, Mom." He kissed her cheek dutifully. He tried to pick up any other enticing scents, like her delicious raisin rock buns.

"Stop sniffing like you're some animal. I didn't have time to bake. But I did bring you saltfish and freshly baked rolls."

"Just what the doctor ordered." He made quick work of unwrapping his surprise and headed for the small table set in the corner of the kitchen. "Would you like to share with me?"

"I'll stick with tea." She raised a small dainty cup with cream-enhanced tea. "But I will sit with you."

"What's up?" He put a forkful of saltfish in his mouth. His mother's cooking didn't disappoint his tastebuds. She had the right amount of onions, shallots, and hot pepper to give it flavor and enough zing.

"It's about your father."

Derek tensed. "What's wrong?"

"Nothing. But you know that his birthday is coming up this weekend."

"Yeah, and I also know that he doesn't like to celebrate it."

"Yes, yes, and he hates surprises." His mother waved her hand through the air. "But I still want to do something special."

"How about I send you both on a fun-filled night on the town?"

"No. I think we should do something that involves the family." Her eyes held a plea.

Derek leaned back, already sensing what his mother was about to ask him. He crossed his arms—his only show of defiance. "Are you planning to invite your side?"

"Stop it. They are *your* aunts and uncles," she admonished.

"That doesn't stop them from being the village idiots."

"Show respect."

"Why? They're not here. And they will never come here. Remember when you got all mushy and wanted them here for Christmas." He paused, but didn't wait for a response. "On the day that they should have arrived, they called to say that Aunt Lorraine was having a Christmas party. She would be really upset if they didn't stay. And as I recall, they wanted you to come, too. Never mind your family. Never mind your husband or child. As usual, Dad and I weren't good enough."

"Stop it."

"No, mom, you've got to face facts. The only people that will be at Dad's birthday are you and me." He pushed back his chair from the table. "He was never good enough for the judge's daughter."

"You don't know everything. You only see one side of everything."

"No disrespect, but you're too willing to lie down and let them walk all over you."

"You don't give me any credit."

"You're too sweet, Mom." It wasn't exactly how he wanted to say that his mother was gullible. But her sweet nature could always pull on his heart. He kissed her cheek. "Let's not fight." He refilled his mug and turned to face her, giving her his full attention. "Okay, what do you want me to do for Dad's birthday?"

His mother stopped staring into her teacup and looked up at him. Tears brimmed on her eyes. He felt like such a lout, pushing his point. Because, ultimately, what did it matter? He wouldn't win the affections of his mother's side of the family.

"I think that we should send out the invitations." She played with the delicate painting around the cup's rim. "Maybe we'll get a few that will come."

He nodded. He didn't want to fight anymore.

"I'll make the cake and the food."

"And…"

"Your father really likes the small carving you gave him. I want you to give him something special, something uniquely from you. He loves your talent."

"Sure he does. Mom, I'm not going to go down that fantasy lane with you. Dad wanted me to be a lawyer and nothing else would do."

She held up her hands in surrender. "Regardless of what you say, I know that he loves you. He wants the best for you, and he wants to know that you will be okay."

"I think owning my own house and business should provide all the security he needs."

"Don't be sharp-tongued. It's not your style." She stood and walked away from the table to come near him. "Your father and I worry about you. We'd like to see you settle down."

"Those magic words that cause my blood to freeze." He looked at the ceiling, knowing where the conversation was heading.

"Is it so bad to bring a young lady to the house every once in a while? Thank goodness the gossip died down over that rich television bimbo."

"Over a year ago, Mom." He didn't mind playing the role of island lover. But when he had fancied himself involved with Tamia Richards, a U.S. soap opera star, he'd toned down the image for what he'd hoped would be a long-term relationship. Back then, he'd thought it was as close to being in love as he would ever get. Now, he could only chalk it up to temporary insanity.

"Trash, that's what she is. I refuse to watch her stupid show."

"It's all over." He wasn't the type to hold a grudge. He

didn't blame all females of such shallowness. But just in case, why give them the chance. Keeping things brief and memorable was the only way to go. The key reason for keeping Paula, beauty pageant addict, from ever meeting his parents.

"I'm still going back to my point, Derek. Life is passing you by."

"Thank you for telling me that I'm getting too old to get a babe. I'm surprised you're not fixing me up with one of your friend's daughters." He shuddered and grimaced, which earned him a punch in his arm.

"As I recall, I introduced you to two women. Do I have to recall the details?"

"You picked an excessive talker and another one that was afraid of her own shadow." The words were no sooner out of his mouth than he thought about a true blooded woman who could stand toe-to-toe with him. He didn't want to share that bit of news with his mother. She'd probably drive over to Toni's hotel and do the talking for him.

"You're looking for perfection. You'll be looking until the end of time." She grabbed her car keys and purse. "I've spent enough time with you. Are you coming over for dinner tomorrow?"

"Sure, Mom." Yep, he was a mama's boy. He escorted his mother to the door. "Tell Dad I said hi."

Derek looked out the window until his mother had reversed out his driveway and headed down the street. He wished that he could erase the worry that she held in great supply on his behalf. She worried about his father, about him, about whether they were happy or if things weren't going right. Yet, it didn't deter from her strength as the matriarch of the family. She took no nonsense and he had witnessed his father getting a dressing down or two.

So there would be a party for his father, regardless of his father's wishes. There was no talking his mother out of this unsavory idea. His father was extremely private. He didn't like his mother's side of the family and didn't hide his feelings. The last incident almost had his father and one of Derek's uncles trading jabs in the backyard. His uncle was pulled away by his own family and shoved in the direction of his car. Before he pulled off, he yelled out that his father was a coward.

His mother had stopped him from defending his father's honor. She'd stayed quiet through the yelling and cursing. The minute he took a step toward the melee, she stepped in, advising him to stay out of it. From her anger, he could only sympathize with his father. Family relations weren't right before that, but they darn sure weren't right after that public display.

If he could entice Toni, maybe she would accompany him to his father's birthday. He was sure that she would fit his mother's high standards. Maybe he could even get his father to stop worrying about him.

Who was he kidding?

He just wanted to be around her. Toni had beauty, but that was not on the checklist of his universal ideals. Toni had a quiet determination that he both enjoyed and envied. He was sure they were the same age, but she had such a confidence and depth to her personality that it left him feeling as if he was all surface, lacking any emotional depth.

Since Derek was busy, Toni took the opportunity to go off on her own. She'd take the taxi into town, but then wander on foot. Things were getting hot and heavy a little too fast. She was afraid that the physical attraction had eclipsed other parts of the relationship.

The downtown traffic roared past her. Toni had to take care to watch for cars, trucks and the motorcycles that wove among the traffic. She studied the map of landmarks. Since she had missed The Gardens that Derek wanted her to see, she decided to check out the Versailles Garden.

She entered the area and felt as if she had come into another world. She walked around viewing the bronze and marble statues, including a life-sized Hercules. The brochure had mentioned that it was a popular place for weddings. She had to admit it was lovely. The fountains, reflecting pools and waterfalls painted the area with a romantic touch. She walked up to a gazebo that had a grand view of the harbor.

She stood in the center and slowly turned around. Then she closed her eyes to visualize what lay secretly in her heart. The rows of friends and family dressed in bright colors with wide-brim hats being held down because of the ocean breeze. She would walk down the aisle with her father. In the special white dress that she had already claimed, she would approach the gazebo where her soul mate waited.

"Hi there." A neatly dressed woman with a tightly held clipboard smiled up at Toni. "Do you mind if we join you? My clients are trying to decide if this spot is where they will exchange vows." She smiled with a wide mouth that had a thick coating of red lipstick.

"No problem." Toni edged out of her way and sidled past the happy couple. She assumed the twosome was the couple because they kissed and nuzzled, ignoring the coordinator's comments.

Out of the way, she lingered to witness the beginning plans. An older woman stood off to her side, dabbing her eyes. Toni offered a small smile, wondering why she looked so sad.

"That's my little girl."

Toni nodded. Her mother would probably be front and center bawling her eyes out.

"They have only been engaged three months. Met in university. They remind me of my day so many years ago."

Toni studied the young couple again. They looked so innocent and trusting of the world. She hoped they never had to experience the bitter edge of life.

"Would you believe she doesn't want to wear a white dress? Called it old-fashioned. I remember wearing my white dress, feeling like a princess coming down that aisle. I even wore gloves and carried a bouquet of flowers that went all the way to the floor."

Toni watched the woman dab at her nose. If she carried on about her wedding day like this all the time, no wonder the girl was running in the opposite direction of traditions.

"They want to wear matching Hawaiian outfits and after the vows, they want to go to the beach and swim. They expect the guests to do the same."

Now that piece of news had Toni staring at the young couple. The only people she envisioned diving into salt water with their beachwear were probably her buddies. Actually the sight should prove amusing. She forced herself from throwing back her head and hooting.

"I will have a private affair for my friends. None of this loosey-goosey stuff that breaks tradition. My reception will take place at the Palisades Hotel on Cable Beach. The room literally hangs over the ocean. I will introduce the bridal party and the in-laws-to-be in a formal manner." The woman dabbed at her eyes and looked at her. "After all we must show them that we have class."

Toni didn't know whether she had been included in the "we," but because of the disdainful sniff, she guessed that she should be grateful that she was brought into the inner circle.

"And in my opinion, I don't know why they went with this grinning hyena of a woman for the coordinator. I have a short list of highly recommended coordinators, all with training from British or French companies. But it's not my wedding, is it?" This time she blew her nose with a loud honk.

Eloping sounded better and better. Toni looked at the gazebo and resisted the urge to warn them. But the girl had to know what her mother was like and the future son-in-law, well, looks like he'd have to learn the hard way. Toni giggled softly and parted company with the distraught mother.

As she reentered the busy world where people were shopping and going to and from work, she realized what a fairy tale women tried to live. The whole idea of romance was of meeting that one special man, marrying him and spending the rest of your life with him and your children. It was so far from the truth.

It was a tall order to fulfill. She may meet the man, but never marry the man. She might marry the man, but may not be together long enough to have children. Depressing. This is why she wasn't going to give all of this any further consideration. She'd leave it up to girls who barely had a foot planted in womanhood and mothers who needed to relive their dreams through their daughters' lives.

* * *

Toni hung on to Derek's arm, partly for support and partly to keep him near her. He had invited her to a reception by the Board of Tourism and Trade. As he explained it, she was in the company of business owners, entrepreneurs, and venture capitalists. Again, she had to purchase an outfit. Well, maybe another excuse to shop worked. She chose a navy blue pantsuit. By the time she returned home, she'd be eating tuna fish sandwiches until her savings account was replenished.

"Relax, baby."

"I'm trying."

"Do you want me to get you a glass of wine?" Derek kissed her softly on her ear.

"Not if it means that you have to leave me to go all the way over there." She looked at the end of the room where a drink station was set up.

"Okay, we'll go together." He unfastened her iron grip on his arm. "I need the circulation."

"Circulation is overrated."

Toni followed Derek to the bar, then they moved to the appetizer trays featuring shrimp, puffed pastries, and a vegetable and fruit platter. Her stomach was too nervous, so she opted for cheese and crackers. But after meeting one gentleman with cheese stuck between his teeth, she decided to put down the small plate.

"There's one of my financiers. I need to go talk to him."

"And that's a solo event, right?"

Toni saw the difficulty he had with the decision. "I'm sorry, I'm being a big baby. You go do your thing. I'll be fine. If I pull on my right ear that means I'm in trouble."

"What does the left ear mean?" He leaned close to her ear and flicked the lobe with his tongue.

"Whatever you want it to mean."

"Considering that I haven't been with you for one whole day, I think that we need to rectify the situation."

"Mmm. Honey, your financier is walking out the door." She had to laugh, watching Derek fast-walk across the room, while trying not to be unsociable to the other guests.

She surveyed the room. She truly was in a sea of strangers. A few guests made small conversation with her, but once they found out that she was only on the island for a vacation, they moved on.

Half an hour later there was no sign of Derek. She imagined that he was in deep conference with his investor. Besides, he was also planning a big opening bash with politicians and millionaires on the invitation list. She wished that she could be here to see his plans come to fruition.

Tired of standing in the room with no one to talk to, she headed for the balcony. The scene on the patio wasn't much better. There were groups of people talking and laughing with each other. But at least in the shadows, she didn't have to pretend to be engaged in conversation, instead of praying for Derek's return.

"Hi there."

Toni spun around to see a familiar face.

"Remember me. I'm Ginny from the boutique store."

"I remember." How could she forget? It was the store that had her picture-perfect white dress.

"Sometimes these things get to be a bit much. But it's necessary from a networking standpoint." Ginny walked over to a stone bench. "Do you mind if I sit. My feet are killing me."

"Only if I get to join you." Toni sat next to the older woman. "Is the business profitable?"

"It's a lot of work, but it's worth it. It helps that my daughter is commissioned by the Bahamian Pageant committee to outfit the girls, and then some of the finalists also hire her exclusively. Last year her collection was used in a movie that also was filmed here."

"That's really good. Your daughter is really lucky to have you."

"Yeah, well, I have my own selfish reasons for doing it too. I was once a fashion designer, but I never got that big break." Ginny clasped her hands. "Guess that makes me a little pathetic."

"Not at all. I'm realizing that a mother and daughter may have more in common than they give each other credit for. I was thinking about my mother who chose to be a housewife and stay-at-home mom for me. I used to think that she'd settled for the short-end of the deal by not going out there and working. I equated her worth with the lack of a salary." A small hitch caught in Toni's throat. She swallowed the tears that were ready.

"She knows that you love her." Ginny raised a knowing eyebrow.

"It's not about love. It's about respect. Your daughter learned from you and forged a path for herself. A few days ago, I met another woman who had also showed her love for her daughter's decision, in her own way, but it was there." Toni recalled the wedding to be held in the Versailles Garden.

"Don't be fooled, Toni. My daughter and I have some major disagreements, especially about the direction of the business. Sometimes there is a happy ending, most times there isn't. This is why she is on another continent." She laughed hard and long.

Toni understood the humor in the situation and shared a laugh with her.

"I think part of my problem may be a touch of homesickness. I miss my family and friends." Toni looked through the doorway as people milled around. It was thinning out. She looked at her watch. She pulled her right earlobe, although Derek wasn't in sight to rescue her.

"You called, m'lady."

"Derek!" Toni shot up from the bench and ran into his arms. "Derek, this is Ginny."

"Hi, Miss Ginny." He bent to kiss her on her cheek. "Ginny's a friend of the family," he explained.

"Small world, isn't it, Derek." Ginny patted Derek's cheek. "Toni and I were keeping each other company."

"Thank you. I took longer than expected with Mr. Singh." Derek placed an arm around her waist.

"I hope that it went well."

"He has the responsibility of getting the U.S. ambassador to our open house reception. It's going to be fantastic." He lifted Toni into the air and spun her around before planting a long deep kiss.

Toni melted any time he held her close. Kissing her made her dissolution even more complete. She shared in his joy and wished him as much luck as he needed.

They pulled apart and then looked toward the bench at Ginny who was grinning from ear to ear.

"Sorry," Derek said, straightening Toni's clothing.

"Don't be, my dear. It's always good to see young people in love. There's no substitute for that courtship phase."

"Oh, but we're not…" Toni blustered. What was she going to say, that they weren't a couple? That wasn't true. That they weren't in love? She didn't want it to be true.

Ginny stood up and gave them a peck. "Derek, let me know how things are going with your business. Toni, remember, don't wait to live your dreams."

Derek dropped Toni off at her hotel. He declined her invitation to come up. The weight that dropped to the pit of his stomach hadn't dissolved after the near revelation that she made.

He couldn't put much stock in what Ginny said. She was a matchmaker at heart. As soon as she saw any woman or man together, she had her fanciful thoughts directed to commitment and marriage. Plus she had only just seen them together, how could she possibly conclude that love was in the air?

He answered his ringing phone.

"So, I had to hear from Ginny, instead of my son, that he's got a woman?"

"Mom, stop being dramatic." Miss Ginny had a big mouth.

"When do I get to meet her?"

"Have I brought any of my other friends to the house?"

"No, but those were sexpots that were looking for a man to take care of them or be a father for their children."

"And I've witnessed your brutality with the ones that are casual friends."

"They have to pass my standards."

He thought about Toni. She would pass any picky mother's standards. Yet he hadn't brought her around his family. He knew by doing that he was taking a step toward that fleeting, amorphous emotion that some idealist coined love. He wasn't going there.

"Derek, are you listening to me? Is this woman the reason why I haven't been seeing you or why my calls aren't being returned? Why don't you bring her over tomorrow? We can kill two birds with one stone. I can meet her and I can talk to you about your father's birthday. We need to finalize the details."

"Mom," Derek interrupted his mother's steamrolling ideas. "There's no need to meet Toni. She's on vacation, a short-timer on the island. We hooked up. But she'll be leaving in a couple days."

"You know this island is small enough for me to track down this woman. From what Ginny said, you're like a puppy around her. And, it sounds like she's putty in your hands. Ginny warned me that wedding bells soon may be ringing. And I don't think it's fair that Ginny's in the know and I'm your mother, and you are holding out on me."

Derek knew that his mother wouldn't let up. And he also knew that, if she wanted to track down Toni, she would. The last thing he needed was his mother springing up on Toni and delivering her motherly advice.

"Tomorrow at three. Don't be late." She hung up before he confirmed or refused the order.

Derek dialed Toni's number. He'd better give her a heads-up. As the phone rang, he knew that he also wanted to hear her voice before he went to sleep.

"Were you sleeping?" he asked.

"No. I was reading a book until I fell asleep."

"Are you available tomorrow to meet my parents?"

There were several seconds of silence.

"I'm not sure that's a good idea."

He was supposed to be saying that, not her.

"Is it because of what Ginny said?"

"Maybe. I think that we have to be realistic."

"Screw realistic. Toni, I want you there with me tomorrow."

"That's exactly why I can't do it. You're expecting something from me that I can't fulfill. And what we have is special, but temporary. Let's leave each other on a positive note."

"You're acting as if you're leaving tomorrow. You aren't, are you?" Derek didn't like the tone in her voice. She was giving life to his fear. But he wasn't ready to say good-bye, have a nice life, it's been fun.

"Derek, what we have is purely physical."

"You're right. Which is why coming to my parents' shouldn't be any major thing for you." He was angry at her. "And maybe after we eat dinner, we could go have sex somewhere. For old time's sake." He heard the swift intake of her breath.

Then he heard the dial tone.

As he returned the phone to the cradle, his heart grew heavy. He couldn't force her to love him. And his love wasn't enough for both of them. Darn it, he was in love.

With sleep eluding him, Derek lay in the bed regretting his angry outburst. He spent the night tossing and turning, thinking of ways that he could apologize to Toni.

After an hour of the sheets wrapping around his legs and

pillows tossed aside, he made a decision. He dressed, grabbed his keys and her hotel room card. He didn't care if he had to keep his secret revelation. He wanted to be with Toni and that was all that mattered.

It seemed as if he caught every red light or driver out for a joy ride. His tires squealed as the car made a right, then a left. The road was slick with a recent rain shower. He toned down his reckless speed. He had been reckless without regard once already.

As soon as he tossed the keys to the valet, he ran into the hotel. He pulled out the card once he stood in front of her door. Should he knock? But what if she didn't let him in. He slid the card into the lock and watched for the green light to appear. He opened the door.

The interior was dark. Only the lights from outside the building shed a small amount of light in the room, enough for him to see the outline of her body under the covers.

He sat on the edge of the bed, debating whether to wake her up or simply lie down beside her. In the stillness of the room, he heard her muffled crying. He pulled back the sheet that covered her frame. "I'm so sorry, honey." He smoothed away the hair and wiped her tears with his hand. "I didn't mean to be cruel."

She raised and hugged him. "Come to bed."

She unbuttoned his shirt and slid it off his body. He did the rest before sliding under the sheet. She wore a silky night-gown that didn't belong on her at a time like this. He pulled it over her head and tossed it aside.

"You know you mean more to me than the cruel things I said to you. I don't know where we're headed. I don't want to know. The only thing that I'm certain of is that you will always have a special place in my heart. No distance can take away what we have because I think it is something unique and—"

Toni kissed him with the attention of an ardent lover. She didn't mouth sweet nothings to pacify him. As she made love to him, he knew that she had forgiven him. All he could do was return her attention with all the love overwhelming his soul.

Chapter 8

Derek kept his emotions in check since his outburst had almost cost him to feel Toni's ire. He was glad that Toni had let him off so easily. But he vowed not to let that happen again. He hadn't changed his mind that he wanted her to stay. But he knew that he had to change his tactics, otherwise she'd feel pressure. He counted Toni's change of mind about meeting his parents as a big step.

In the beginning, he'd wanted to keep his personal life private. He didn't want any drama to unfold on his turf. As such he kept the dating and dinner, even the lovemaking away from anything that could emotionally connect him to her.

But his strategy had backfired. Toni had broken through his defenses and found her way into his heart. Now he wanted to open his life like a book and have her stick around and enjoy it. She'd seen his place of work, but she hadn't seen his house, the building for his new company, the things that brought joy or frustration to his life. This evening she'd meet his parents which almost never happened on his own free will.

Derek finished dressing and hopped onto his motorcycle. He strapped on an extra helmet for his intended passenger. His motorbike was from his younger, wilder days. But every once in awhile he brought it out and cruised the island.

The powerful machine was something of a babe magnet, but he'd long gotten over that phase. Now, as he rode along the coast, he enjoyed the simple pleasure of it. Some people jogged to let off steam. Some went sailing. He cruised with his bike.

The midday traffic proved to be an obstacle course, as he weaved his way along the island. He didn't have patience for bottlenecks. All he had to do was convince Toni to hop on, lean her body against his, and let him show her the place he called home.

Toni couldn't believe that she was on a motorcycle with her arms locked firmly in place around this man's waist who raced through the traffic like a bullfighter in the ring. Riding a motorcycle was never a fantasy of hers, secret or otherwise. Her mother would have a cow if she knew that her child was sightseeing on a land borne missile.

She tried closing her eyes, but that made the fear more intense. No, she'd much rather keep a close watch on what was going on. Buildings, roads, people, cars, grew into one big noisy blur. If asked to describe the view, she'd take five different hues of paint and smear it into a kaleidoscope of colors.

Admittedly she enjoyed being so close to Derek. Sitting

behind him on his bike could only have happened by having complete trust in him. She leaned her head against his back, enjoying another hour, minute, second with him. They'd gone against their own rules and found each other. She liked the image of two rebels turning their backs on what they were supposed to do and how they were supposed to act.

They had exited the downtown traffic onto a quieter highway that ran parallel to the ocean. Derek had slowed down to a speed that afforded her a chance to take in the surroundings. There wasn't much to see other than a peaceful setting with a beautiful landscape. The only sound that seemed amplified was the sound of the motorcycle. Toni wished that he would stop soon. She could admire the place without the heavy vibration rippling through her body.

Toni sensed the bike slowing as Derek shifted down the gears. Only then did she try to peek over Derek's shoulder. They approached a gated community, equipped with two guard houses for entry and exit. A uniformed security guard had stepped out to meet them, as they cruised to a halt.

His grim expression could explain why he held this post. The man's face held no friendly welcome. She had nothing to hide, but that didn't lessen the tension in her body. She was prepared to jump if the guard so ordered.

When Derek stopped next to the guard, leaving only breathing space between them, Toni braced for the worst. Derek planted one foot on the road, before pushing up his visor. Toni squeezed Derek's waist to communicate her warning to keep cool. After all, the guard had a huge black gun holstered at his side.

The guard squinted with eyes like flint chips. He inspected

her before returning to his examination of Derek. Then he broke out in a wide grin.

"Hey, *mon,* you've only got thirty minutes before the shift changes. Go on through. But listen, if I get fired, you'd better hire me."

"No problem. You know I'll need people I can trust. Look, I'll zip in, zip out." Derek shook the guard's hand.

Not until she had her arm fastened around his waist did he pull away. They meandered down the main road. At the first intersection, he turned. Only three houses lined the street. Toni hoped Derek would stop for her to admire the luxury homes. She tapped his waist to catch his attention when they drove past the first home. The super-sized properties and equally expansive houses used the entire length of the road. He did stop, idling the engine.

"These houses are gorgeous."

"Thought you'd get a kick out of them." He turned off the engine and set the kick-stand. Derek put his arm through hers. "I loved sneaking up here as a kid. These are newer homes. The original ones were built like colonial mansions, but had the typical, bright colors that you'd expect to see in the Caribbean."

"Who lives in these? These houses are huge. They look like they go out as far as possible toward the ocean."

"I know this one in front of us belongs to a British movie star. He doesn't come here much. Uses it for parties." He pointed to another house that had been built to resemble steps in a mountain. Each level had an unobstructed view of the water and surrounding area. "This one was owned by an architect. But I think he sold it. Might still be empty. Want to see if we can get in?"

"No, Derek." Toni was horrified. That's all she needed, an arrest while vacationing. "I'm happy with the view from here."

"Coward." He laughed, which earned him a punch in the arm.

"What's the going price on one of these houses?"

"Don't know, but this is the millionaire's club. This means that you have to have at least a million net worth to buy. Considering that the houses are probably more than that, a mere million in the bank won't get you in."

"I guess no welcome card for you," she teased. Nothing like this sat in her future, either.

"Not my style, anyway. I like living with the common folk."

"That's what I like about you." She kissed him on his lips. "You don't have any airs and graces. You are a real man."

"Don't go flattering me." He walked back over to the bike. "I do have a connection in here. Let me show you."

Maybe it was his stiff manner. Or it could be the angry tightening of his lips. She didn't want to question him. Whatever it was, he felt it important enough to share with her.

He got them back to the main road, riding deeper into the community. There was no meandering this time. She couldn't enjoy the expansive two-story flamingo-pink villa. There was no time to stop, admire and smell the botanical display in front of one property that deliberately hid the house.

Then they banked a left down a one-lane road. A wooden sign stated Private Road, No Trespassing. As if to defy the sign's intent, he accelerated until they came to a large wrought-iron gate and fence.

Toni followed his lead and dismounted. She looked at Derek's face which stared at the house looming behind the gate. Toni swallowed her critical comments about the last ride. She'd had about enough of the motorcycle. But Derek hadn't moved, even when the guard came toward them. His countenance glowered heavily with suspicion.

Toni grew uneasy. This guard also was armed. Derek didn't say anything. She didn't say anything either because she didn't know why they were in front of this house. She took a step toward Derek.

"Derek, say something. I don't like the look in the guard's eyes."

Derek blinked at her.

"Mr. Calverton, are you coming in?"

Toni looked at the guard and then at Derek. This man was full of surprises.

"Not today. Just showing a friend how the other half lives."

Toni laughed because she felt the need since neither Derek nor the guard followed up with a laugh.

"Who lives here?" Toni wondered about the tenants and their insecurities. She surveyed the majestic property that seemed a tad daunting, a fenced estate within a fenced community.

"My mother's father."

"Oh, your grandfather?"

"A mere technicality. For my purposes, he is my mother's father."

"I guess visiting him is not an option at the moment?"

"No one is home, Mr. Calverton. But if you wanted to stick around, I'll let you in." The guard motioned toward the gate.

Derek didn't answer the guard. Toni had to turn to see what he was doing. His face was inscrutable as he stared at the house.

"The original style started as a colonial mansion. As the family expanded, they added wings to either side. Now the family palace resembles a jumbo jet."

"Unless this is a touchy subject, why does your grandfather—I mean your mother's father—upset you so much? Is that why we're standing on the outside, looking in?"

"He's a judge. My mother grew up here. She had the best childcare, best school, tutors. You name it, whatever she wanted, she got. Then she went to school in the U.S." He kicked at the dirt. "She met my father who is much older than she, but when love is involved, there's no logic. They got married and her father hit the roof."

"Maybe there's more to it than you know." Toni didn't like this kink-love, family secrets, rebellion. She could take her pick and any of these conditions meant human emotion. One conclusion became clear. Derek was hurting. Now knowing the family drama, she was due to add another layer with Nicole and Brad springing onto the scene.

"Is that your way of making me feel better? I know what I'm talking about. I lived it. My father wasn't good enough for their daughter and I wasn't good enough to be his grandson. As a child, I didn't understand. I wanted his approval so badly. But I'm no longer a child and I don't have to wait like a pet for his attention."

"Do you come to this house often?" Toni heard his anger, but knew it wasn't really directed at her. Despite his bravado, his words spoke of the pain that must have had an impact on his childhood. She saw him standing out here wanting to belong, hating himself for wanting to belong, but in his heart, refusing to lose his identity.

"I wanted to share this with you, that's all." He put on his helmet, mounted the bike, and waited for her.

Toni stared at the house, wishing she could offer some profound wisdom and comfort.

Instead of taking her back to the hotel, Toni noted that they were now on the other side of the island in a residential community, farther inland. The neighborhood resembled any U.S. suburb, with modest homes, cars parked in driveways, children playing jump rope.

She noted that he'd turned into a driveway of a little bungalow. There was a low concrete fence that seemed more for decoration than for providing a boundary. Toni slid off, grateful for firm land under her feet. Her thighs were throbbing. If they rode any longer, she would've suggested that he call a cab for her.

Derek didn't say anything. He led the way. She presumed that he expected her to follow. Too curious to scold him on his manners, Toni followed. He unlocked the door and waved her in.

"Welcome to my humble home."

"This is a day filled with surprises." She stepped in and kissed him. She wanted him to relax. They weren't at his grandfather's home anymore. There was no need for the deep scowl that he still wore.

Toni walked into the house, surveying the rooms that were open to view. The modest size wasn't ideal for a family of four. This wasn't one of the expansive models that went on farther than the eye could see. From where she stood in the living room, she saw the kitchen and straight through the kitchen window to the unruly backyard.

For Derek's purpose, he had the perfect bachelor pad. Toni wondered how many women's eyes lit up when they saw Derek's place. Did he bring women here to impress them? She tried to keep her hang-ups out of everything, but her insecurity wasn't a faucet to be turned off with a simple twist.

"Make yourself comfortable." Derek threw a careless hand over the interior. "I've got to wash up for later this evening."

"I need to do the same. Plus I'm not getting on that bike again any time soon."

"I'll drive you over to your hotel."

"But then we'll waste time. I can head over there now with a taxi and then you can pick me up." She didn't want to admit, at least to him, that standing in his house made her uncomfortable.

She hadn't wanted to think about why he had brought her to his home. The gesture touched her beyond superficial emotions to the deeper feelings that nudged at the heart. She may have wanted to test the waters, but she also eyed the front door for the quickest escape.

"I want you to stay. Will you?"

Toni didn't immediately answer. She couldn't put the brakes on her insecurities to grant his wish.

"What are you thinking?"

"A bit overwhelmed."

Derek approached her, but didn't touch her. She was grateful. She didn't want him embracing her, kissing her, scrambling her senses to the point where she gave in to whatever he wanted.

"I want you to know that all I knew this morning was that I wanted you to see who I am, where I live, my total environment. Guess I wanted to do that before you left. And because I felt like we were saying goodbye to each other prematurely. I want to be with you, until you have to board the plane."

Toni had held her breath while he spoke. She exhaled slowly through her mouth. Without a word, she walked into the kitchen, opened cupboards until she found a glass. Then she took out the glass and opened the refrigerator. "One question."

"Yeah?" Derek peeked around the kitchen's entrance.

"Are you one of those men who stands at the refrigerator and drinks directly from the bottle?"

"Not usually." He grinned.

At least she felt refreshed after taking a shower and dressing up slightly above beach casual. She'd also gotten a chance to relax while Derek got himself together. Either he was a man who loved to take long showers or the big meet and greet family dinner had him as nervous, or more than, she was. When she offered to iron his shirt, he refused saying that he knew how to make the crease on the sleeve sharp and pointed.

His confident demeanor had definitely flown south by the time they had gone back to her hotel. Before she had finished dressing, he had made suggestions on her attire, even offered to buy her new shoes. She'd pushed him bodily out the door, before being able to dress without his unsolicited opinions.

Which parent caused him to act like a total basket case?

Toni turned up the radio in Derek's car in an attempt to break the silence. She had tried small talk, but that didn't get Derek to open up. His sober attitude was putting a damper on her.

"Must you keep turning up the volume." Derek turned down the volume on the reggae song.

Toni bit back the hot retort. Battling over the radio volume was minor compared to what ran through her mind. The scenery that they drove past was familiar. She couldn't quite place why it was familiar, considering they had driven around the island.

"Oh my gosh!" Toni exclaimed. "I don't believe this."

As soon as the car stopped, she hopped out. She looked at the house, then back at Derek. In front of her was the beautiful villa where Derek had hired the musical group and chef to fix her the delicious dinner.

"Talk to me, Derek."

He walked past her and pushed open the gate. "This is my parents' home. Are you mad?"

Toni entered the yard. "No, can't say that I am. But you are a tricky somebody."

They walked up to the front door.

"How did you manage it without them here or popping up unexpectedly."

"My father had to visit one of the hotel chains in Grand Bahamas. My mother went with him."

"Did they have a clue?"

He shook his head, then knocked on the door.

"No key?" She smirked.

The door was opened by a woman in a flowered dress and apron. "Hello, Derek."

"Hi, Cicely." He waved Toni into the house, introducing her.

"Everyone is on the patio," Cicely announced over her shoulder.

Toni looked around, amazed at how much furniture and decorations Derek had had to move for his elaborate date. Now it had a sophisticated, homey feel. She was glad that he moved it since the furniture was an eggshell color. She could only imagine the drama if she had dropped cocktail sauce on the carpet or upholstery.

Cicely walked onto the patio in front of them. Then when they were about to enter, she stepped into the center. "Ladies and gentlemen, Derek Calverton and Toni Kimball." Then she smiled at them and left the room.

It was only then that Toni realized Cicely was the hired help. Toni tried to reconcile what she'd seen earlier, Derek's story and this house. He didn't seem to lack for anything, even if his mother's family didn't accept his father.

The person who would have a fit would be Brad. Thank goodness he wasn't the one coming over to the Bahamas. She looked around at the faces, trying to figure out which one was Derek's father. Would she be able to spot him?

"Come with me. Let me introduce you to my parents."

Toni placed her hand in Derek's. She felt that she was giving him as much support as he was giving to her. Like in a movie, the scene played out in slow motion.

A tall woman with regal bearing stood shoulder to shoulder with an older man who had distinguished gray hair. The woman wore a black dress with pearl accessories. The way she stood with her posture erect, seeming to look down her long nose at Toni, Toni knew the pearls were real. This woman had been born into high society and it carried through everything about her. No wonder Derek sought perfection with his clothing and with her.

She tried not to look at herself and see the areas that needed improvement. She didn't want to compete against this woman's standards.

The older gentleman looked harmless and friendly. But she remembered Derek's recollection of his childhood. His father was from the old school and had high expectations, which caused many disagreements in their household.

"Nice to meet you, Toni. I've heard so much about you. If Derek didn't have the courage to bring you to me, then I was coming to you."

Toni smiled and wished that Toni's mother would smile, too.

"You may call me Mrs. Calverton. And when we get to know each other, then we can get more familiar. Too bad that you're leaving in a few days." She kissed Derek on his cheek. "Glad you could make it, son."

Toni squeezed Derek's fingers. Why didn't he warn her? His mother apparently had sharpened her fangs for this visit.

What had provoked such animosity?

"Mr. Calverton, I presume." Toni tried to wrest control of the situation. "How nice to meet you."

"Likewise, my dear." He kissed her on both cheeks. His smile crinkled the corners of his eyes. Deep grooves marked the areas around his mouth. "Never mind, Sylvia. She likes to give Derek's girlfriends a hard time." His eyes grew round. "I don't mean that Derek has a lot of girlfriends or that they come around. But the ones that have come, a long, long, long, time ago…"

"Benjamin, you're embarrassing your son." Sylvia hooked her arm through Derek's and literally pulled him away from Toni to head to the other side of the patio.

"Maybe this is more of a family event than I thought."

"Please, let's go inside." He ushered her into the living room, decorated with a professional touch for an admirer's eye more than for comfort.

Toni sat across from Benjamin. Not in a million years would she have placed herself in such a position with meeting Brad's father. She didn't have any prejudiced opinion about this man who had walked away from his son. Maybe it was because he looked normal. He acted normal. His life didn't appear to be lacking from knowing his second born.

"Sylvia's nose is out of joint because she heard about you, instead of Derek telling her. You know how mother's are."

Toni shrugged. Did this mean that Derek wouldn't have brought her to his parents' home and attention, if he wasn't forced to do so?

"Tell me a little about yourself."

"Not much to tell. I'm an engineer. I live outside of Annapolis, Maryland. That's outside of Baltimore."

He nodded. "Family?"

"My parents live in Maryland. I'm an only child, like Derek." She stared at him, wishing that she could read his mind. On impulse, she wanted to give him a hint of what was to come. How would he react when Nicole delivered her news? Or maybe she ought to worry about Nicole's safety after Sylvia got through with her. Unlike Derek, she planned to warn Nicole of this strange cast of characters.

"Derek is my only son. He's really made me proud with his tour company and the upcoming software business. As a parent, you always worry about what your son or daughter will do when it's their turn to be the adult. I tried to do right by him."

Toni saw the pride in his face and heard it equally in his voice. She had lost her chance to worry about her child's future.

"You don't have an accent, Benjamin. Are you from the Bahamas?"

"No, I'm a transplant. And actually my first name is Elroy, but I hated that name. Now I use my middle name. I'm convinced that it made a difference in my career." He chuckled. "You know, being in the hotel business, you get moved around quite a lot. I took the least favorite job placements until I was in the position to decide where I wanted to be. Now I'm in the twilight of my career, I used my clout, as much as I think I had, to get this assignment. Sylvia would have probably left me if I didn't bring her home." He laughed.

Toni liked talking to him. He had a very humorous outlook on life. Without interviewing him in depth, she felt that he had a good heart.

"Derek has your smile."

"He looks more like his mother."

Toni looked up in the doorway. "Sylvia." She didn't know how long the woman had stood there. How much had she overheard?

"Miss Kimball, it is Miss and not Mrs., right?"

Toni felt the flush run through her.

"Mom, stop it." Derek stepped into the room and sat next to Toni. He tried to pull her against his body, but she was too stiff with anger to budge.

"I'm the bad guy because I'm getting to know your friend. If I waited for you to tell me, I'd be old and gray." She looked at Benjamin. "Sorry, honey."

"I know, you only married me for my money and social standing."

Sylvia threw back her head and laughed. The sound was a mixture of a hooting owl and a hyena.

Toni didn't expect that from the model of decorum. Obviously the men had the benefit of hearing this all their lives and didn't raise eyebrows. Toni tried not to look shocked or cringe from the unearthly sound.

When she was finished laughing, she wiped her eyes. She kissed Benjamin on the lips, patted his cheek before turning a fierce gaze on Toni. "Okay, I've debriefed my son. Now it's your turn."

Toni looked at Derek who mouthed, it's okay—easy for him to say. Next to her mother, this woman was certifiable. Nicole owed her big time. She followed the statuesque woman out to the patio.

"Isn't this the most gorgeous house you've seen?"

Toni nodded.

"Liar! I heard that you went to my father's house earlier today. Now, that had to be the most beautiful."

"I didn't go in. Derek didn't want to enter the property." Toni paused, contemplating spilling the family secrets. "Why is that?"

"I like your style. This is my family, Miss Kimball. Derek and Benjamin are who I care about and who I will protect. Benjamin has paid his dues where life is concerned. When I met him, he was a broken man. I gave him a reason to hope, plan for the future. Derek, I love with all my heart. I know he tries to please me, but he's stubborn too. I don't always get my way." She smiled. "But I like a challenge."

Toni assumed that meant her.

"Are you planning to tie up loose ends before you leave?" Sylvia crossed her legs. Her scrutiny directed to Toni's face. "My son is in love with you."

Toni sucked in her breath.

"You mean you didn't know?" She leaned forward. "And you love him. So now what?"

"Now nothing." Toni felt the rising alarm. "We both knew going into this that there was no happy ending. We also know that neither one of us will pressure the other." Toni returned the gaze, holding it steady sending the silent message.

"Okay, okay. I'm backing off. I'll be here to pick up the pieces, I suppose." She sighed and dramatically fell back into the chair. "Guess it's time to switch over from the lovebirds to planning Benjamin's birthday party."

"Oh, when is his birthday."

"It's at the end of the week. There's not much more to plan. I've done most of it. I want it to be a big affair. Benjamin received a promotion to Vice President of Operations for the entire Caribbean. Do you know how big that is? I want all his friends to celebrate it with him. And my family." Sylvia twisted her hands together.

Toni realized that Sylvia had spent most of her married life trying to prove to her family that Benjamin was worthy of their respect. She understood Derek's pain and anger that the man he looked up to wasn't good enough.

"May I attend?"

"Oh yes, that would be a great farewell."

Toni resisted asking if she could bring her friend— Nicole. She couldn't even begin to explain who Nicole was and why she would want or need to come.

And for a few seconds, she wondered if it was necessary to tell this family about Brad. Brad didn't want to know. Benjamin acted as if he didn't know. And Sylvia would come down on her like an avenging angel to protect her men. Talk about tying up loose ends.

Chapter 9

Toni wasn't sure what time Nicole would arrive. Her friend flew stand-by in order to get a cheaper deal. On one hand, she missed her dearly, and looked forward to chatting about all she'd seen and done, minus the adult-rated goings-on with Derek. On the flipside, Nicole's visit wasn't an island getaway. She, despite her intentions, was bound to cause a ripple that could have unseen effects. Toni wanted to support a friend, but she also wanted to pay the airline penalty and book a flight home. Her conscience called her coward. Fine. She could live with that.

Plain and simple, an early frost had settled over the relationship since visiting Derek's parents. Toni feared that the rosy glow of physical attraction and budding relationship had faded. They snapped at each other, exchanged apologies, and carried on in a subdued manner. Toni reflected and concluded that their disagreements were superficial. The underlying cause was, so far, undeterminable. When the final act to this drama played to the end, her deepest wish was that they separated as friends. Maybe in ten or twenty years, she'd recall fondly the memories of this summer.

She sighed. It didn't help that their relationship would face a tough test with the introduction of Nicole and her news. Yet, she hadn't stuck to the script. Nowhere did the rules state that she should fall in love with Brad's brother.

Even after the first day of meeting Derek, she hadn't intended for anything beyond possibly a chance meeting. There hadn't been any designs for his attention. Not even her half-hearted attempt to be logical slowed down the terrific rate at which she fell, more like tumbled, into this briar patch called love. And any attempt to pick her way clean had the potential to leave a stinging reminder of why any emotions of the heart needed to be avoided at any cost.

She answered the phone on its second ring.

"I'm here," Nicole shouted.

Toni gave her the room number, but couldn't wait. She stepped into the hallway waiting for the telltale ring of the elevator's arrival. Nicole and an efficient carry-on suitcase burst out of the elevator car.

They ran toward each other, screaming and laughing. A few heads popped out of their rooms. Toni didn't care. Her best friend was there with her. Their tight hugs and joyful exclamations said it all.

"I can't believe you're finally here." Toni opened the door, propping it for Nicole and her luggage to enter.

"Heck, I thought that I would never get here. Flying standby is no fun." Nicole walked over to the balcony and slid open the door. "This is so beautiful." She turned and beamed at Toni. "You must be hating life now that your vacation is coming to an end."

"You don't know the half of it." Toni joined her on the balcony. She'd often tried to capture the sun setting against the ocean, locking the scene into memory.

Only a week and a few days had passed since she had last seen her friend, but the absence felt like months.

Nicole wore a long sundress with a leopard pattern. The variations of brown suited her skin tone. She always had a natural beauty that ensnared men. Brad had fallen for her and couldn't let go. The key difference with him was that Nicole loved him and couldn't let go. Their love story was the ideal. Nothing like what she experienced with Derek.

They looked out at the courtyard, pool area, the nearby beach and farther out on the water. All the while, Nicole exclaimed over the smallest thing that caught her attention. She admired the tall palm trees. How they swayed and bowed without upending. She squealed over the little kids in the kiddie pool, splashing and giggling with each other. One or two single males walking toward the beach drew an appreciative comment on their good looks.

Toni could relate to her enthusiasm. She reacted similarly on the first few days. At the time, she didn't have anyone to share in her exuberance. She wished that she could package all these qualities that made Nassau a vacation paradise into a small sandwich bag and take it home. She knew that it would probably only take a few weeks being home, working the new job for her to need to reminisce.

"Do you want me to order sandwiches?"

"Nothing heavy. Fruit would be good." Nicole took a seat and put up her feet. "By the way, I got my own room. It should be available by three. Don't want to cramp your style."

"Now that was silly. Why pay for two rooms? I know you got it like that, but don't go overboard. You call down now and cancel that room. There's no cramping of anybody's style."

"I'll call down, but then you'd better spill it." Nicole went into the room.

Toni overheard her try to cancel the reservations over the phone. From the sound of it, that didn't work and a minute later Nicole left to confirm the transaction.

In the meantime, Toni ordered the fruit platter and a glass of lemonade, Nicole's favorite summer drink, and a sandwich for herself. By the time she was done, Nicole had returned.

"That was fast," Toni remarked.

"A bright smile and a flicker of lashes can get a girl far." They shared a laugh. "I'm ravenous. When is that food coming?"

"Soon. Didn't you eat on the plane?"

"Pretzels and soda can only go so far. Although…" Nicole grabbed her pocketbook and pulled out a chewy granola bar. "I forgot about this."

"Well, room service is pretty fast."

Toni flopped down near the head of the bed. Nicole did the same near the foot of the bed.

"Let me go first," Toni said. "I can see that you're practically bursting to give me the third degree. What's going on with Brad? Did you give him any hints?"

"Are you crazy? I wanted to tell him, but the more I push, the more stubborn he is about the whole situation. I can't get him to open up."

"Even if you get Derek to agree to come to Glen Knolls, why would you subject him to Brad's anger?" Toni heard the accusation in her own voice. "You may be making matters worse."

"This isn't only affecting Brad. This is affecting our unit as a family. Derek wasn't at fault. I want to meet his father, but I'm not pushing for him to reunite. I know that is more volatile." Nicole punched the pillow in frustration.

They were interrupted with the food's arrival. Nicole sat cross-legged on the bed and balanced the fruit plate on her lap. Every mouthful had her sighing and exclaiming how delicious it all was. Toni enjoyed watching her eat, while she ate a roast beef sandwich.

"Have you been dieting?" Nicole had a piece of pineapple poised in front of her lips. Toni shook her head. "Well, you are looking great. Got the whole tan thing going on looking like a mocha latte. You do look refreshed, though. Back to the land of the living."

"Don't try to turn this on me." Toni really didn't want the attention, in case Nicole caught a whiff of anything newsworthy. "I'm still waiting to hear about the girls."

Nicole spent the next half an hour updating her on her cousin's promotion and Shirley's new passion for creating quilts. She talked about how well the bed-and-breakfast was doing and the increased number of return guests, a sure sign of success.

In the city, they were building a museum highlighting the path of the Underground Railroad and her house would be listed as the site of a safe house. Nicole had a lot to make her proud. Her hard work paid off.

Nicole stretched, then yawned. Toni relieved her of the plate, allowing her to slide under the covers with a sigh. "Looks like you're ready for a nap." Nicole sleepily nodded.

"I'm going to run out for an hour. Then when I come back you're getting your lazy butt out of bed. Don't try to act as if you're suffering jet lag," Toni teased.

Nicole offered a small smile before she finished the sentence.

Toni pulled the drapes to darken the room, set the dishes in the hallway, and grabbed her pocketbook.

Although she had turned up her nose at the idea of visiting any of the museums, now that she had downtime, it would afford her the chance to browse, not spend any money and give Nicole a chance to recover from the fatigue of traveling.

Derek wished that he hadn't taken Toni to his parents'. By the time dinner had been served, Toni had grown quiet. It didn't make him feel any better to see his mother in deep conversation with her. Occasionally Toni would look up at him as if she was studying him, weighing whatever his mother said quietly to her.

He'd tried calling her room this morning, but there was no answer. He had a couple items to take care of in his new office before he could do anything.

Every time he pulled up in front of his office, pride surged through him. One of his biggest accomplishments was to have a building created from the ground up. He'd brought in the island's best architect to design a structure that pleased the eye and generated pride with his employees. He had a re-cruiting firm hiring the staff, but he wanted to be in charge of hiring the managers. The company's leadership team had to be strong, innovative, and flexible with some risk.

His steps on the wood floor echoed in the empty building. The furniture was scheduled to be delivered by next week. Then the equipment would come. By month's end, his company would open its doors for business.

He envisioned a vibrant work environment. When clients walked through the doors, a receptionist would greet them. Programmers would work busily in their over-sized cubicles arranged in quads for a team aspect. Managers, who would zealously vie for his attention, would have to be equally respectful of his personal assistant.

This dream burst into his imagination and took shape. Over time his business enterprise transformed from an amorphous configuration to a living entity that greedily demanded his time and commitment with slavish devotion. So far, many of the decisions had been made instinctively.

From the onset, he didn't share any part of this with his father. He needed to be sure that it would be a reality. Too many dreams, like his, failed in their first year of operations. Plus he didn't want to be tempted or rely on his father's connections for his success.

Today he expected the landscapers and the men who were going to paint the lines in the attached parking lot to begin working. His outdoor plan didn't stop there. The features that had earned praise in the local business journal and local news were the fountains and small gazebos for employees to enjoy the outdoors. He wanted it to be a fun place to work. Happy employees meant good production. He didn't want to settle for good, he wanted excellent. When he approached his contractors for work, his reputation had preceded him.

* * *

The manicured lawn with precisely placed flowers brightened up the location. A Caribbean newspaper contacted him for an interview and photo shoot. He had one day to prepare.

Finished for the day, Derek's emotions were flying high. He wanted to tell Toni about all of it. Actually he wanted her at his side. She deserved credit for listening to his goals and giving him concrete advice. A copy of the article would serve as a good souvenir, a small part of their special friendship.

This break, even though it was only a couple days, wore on him. He drove to the hotel, not bothering to go to his house to change. He couldn't wait to tell her the news and watch that wide grin erupt into girlish giggles. Just thinking about her revved his system.

It had been days since they made love. He wanted to enjoy her scent, her soft body curved next to his, the moans of sensual pleasure.

He took her hotel card out of his pocket and slid it into the door. The faucet was on. He tiptoed in and took a seat at the table. He'd surprise her.

The stream of water stopped. He listened to the shower curtain being drawn back. Something dropped, followed by a sharp, colorful curse. He smiled. He'd never heard Toni curse. Guess she saved it for her ears only.

The bathroom door opened.

Derek's smile dropped. He sat up. "Who are you?"

A strange woman stared at him, equally startled. Then she ran toward the door.

"No you don't." Not only had this woman broken into

Toni's room. She had the *cajones* to stop and take a shower. Clearly this stranger hadn't thought through her plan. Escaping through the door, while he was standing in the room wasn't going to happen. He pinned her against the wall, the side of her face against the wall. "Who the hell are you?"

"Who the hell are *you?*"

Oh, but she had nerve. He pulled her away from the wall and sat her on the bed. He pinned her with his knee while he grabbed the phone.

"Get off me. I swear if you touch me…"

"Operator, send up security. I'd like to report a break-in." He told the room number, feeling proud of himself.

"I didn't break in." The woman struggled. "Could you please get off my back? I can't breathe."

Derek heard her labored breath. He wasn't trying to kill her, simply slow down her escape. "Sure. Sit up." He noted an open suitcase near the closet. Her shoes were strewn nearby. "How did you get in here?"

There was a knock on the door. "Security."

Derek opened the door and invited in the two uniformed men. "This woman broke in."

"I did not break in. I don't even know this man. I'm registered to this room."

"Liar! Toni Kimball is registered."

One of the security personnel pulled a folded paper from his jacket. He opened it and read. "Says here that Toni Kimball and Nicole Montgomery are registered to this room."

"What? I've been coming to this room and only one person is in this room." Derek looked at Nicole smiling smugly back at him.

"What's going on?" Toni stepped in from the hallway.

"There's some mix up." Derek stepped over to her, feeling that she was the only sane one of the group. "I came to see you and this woman came out of your bathroom. I managed to subdue her and called security."

"Derek," Toni said softly, "this is my best friend Nicole. She's joined me for the last few days of my vacation." She stepped away from him and went to the other woman.

"Are you okay, Nicole?"

"Yes, although he was about to break a rib or two." She looked him up and down. "So this is Derek." She clapped her hands and laughed.

Toni took the security guards aside and explained the situation to them. Shortly thereafter, they left. Then it was the three of them looking at each other.

"Derek, lighten up," Toni laughed, feathering his face with kisses. "You are my mighty hero."

He didn't see the humor in the situation. Maybe it was the way Toni and this new woman, Nicole, laughed at him.

"When you're less busy, you know where to reach me." Derek opened the door and walked out.

Toni hit Nicole on her shoulder. "Stop laughing, you're making it worse." She ran after Derek. "Would you come back? I want to formally introduce you."

"Why didn't you tell me that you expected a friend?"

"If you recall, we haven't been doing too much talking." Her heart raced. She needed him to meet and like Nicole. How was the plan ever going to unfold if these two couldn't get along?

"Meet me in the restaurant downstairs." She kissed him

softly, knowing that she was manipulating him. But desperation won out. She turned and headed back to her room. "Fifteen minutes, okay?"

Toni didn't turn around, but didn't hear Derek's footsteps going down the hall. "Fifteen minutes, Derek." She entered her room.

Toni leaned against the hotel door. She had to take several deep breaths to steady her nerves.

"He doesn't really look like Brad."

"He takes after his mother."

"How do you know?"

"His father told me." Toni went to the closet for a change of clothes. "I told him that we'd be downstairs for dinner in fifteen minutes. Get dressed."

"Are you mad at me?"

Toni sighed as she pulled out a pair of slacks and a shirt. "No, I'm not. I wanted a smoother introduction, that's all."

"I think it's more than that."

"Oh really."

"I think that you probably wished that I hadn't shown up. Maybe even changed my mind." Nicole stood behind her, not going into the suitcase for her change of clothes.

"That's a cold thing to say."

"No it's not. Just the truth."

"Nicole, please get dressed. Let's go down to Derek. Drop whatever it is that your crazy brain is trying to conjure."

Nicole didn't respond, but instead got busy selecting her outfit.

Twenty minutes later, they walked into the restaurant. Toni hoped that Derek had followed her request and didn't leave altogether. She told the hostess that a man should be waiting for them.

The good news was that the hostess remembered a man waiting. The bad news was that she also remembered the man leaving. Toni hoped that he was only wandering around the lobby.

"Come with me, Nicole. Help me find him."

"Sure."

Toni hurriedly entered the main part of the lobby. It had the usual hub of activity with guests heading out for the evening entertainment or the incoming guests who had spent the day on the beach.

She continued her search behind the fountain in the middle of the lobby and the comfortable nooks framing the outer edges. Four hallways lead off the lobby. One advertised the spa. One led to the restaurant from which they'd just come. Another featured the high-priced gift shop and elevators to the rooms. The fourth option had a piano bar, which she had never visited. Would Derek be in that place, of all places?

An elderly woman came toward her. After a moment's hesitation, she touched her arm. "I came from the piano bar. The man playing is not only good, but extremely handsome too."

Toni was too astonished to respond to this elderly woman gushing.

"I don't know about you, but I'm curious." Nicole laughed.

"Only for a minute, Nicole. We have to find Derek."

"If you ask me, Derek is a stick in the mud. I'll probably have his knee print in my back."

Toni rolled her eyes. "Why didn't you explain?"

"I tried, but he was too busy defending your turf."

They rounded the corner and immediately heard the music. Nicole moved ahead, weaving between the small crowd that had gathered.

"Ah…Toni, would you come here, please?" She beckoned to Toni, but didn't take her eyes off whatever held her attention.

Toni followed her progress, getting closer. The woman's enthusiasm amused her. It wasn't until she passed one of the Greco-Roman columns that she could see the piano and small seating area for patrons' listening pleasure.

Not even the glossy black grand piano and its melodic sound snagged her attention. No, her attention was reserved for the pianist. Derek's fingers did their dance over the keys, stroking, pounding to the rhythm of the music.

In front of the piano, she felt like a voyeur. Derek's face shone with a joy that she could respect. Once upon a time, she had that look. It meant a passion for a dream. The way Derek played, he put his whole soul into it. Each note, each chord, the beat, the rhythm, all of it poured out of his body which reacted to the tempo.

The music could have been any of the composers she had learned in music class in high school. Her ignorance didn't take away from the power of the music. She closed her eyes, relaxed, and soaked up the sweetness of the notes. There was a sadness that threaded through it, haunting and meandering, touching her emotions.

Then the tempo picked up, lightning quick and sharp. She imagined a lover playfully chasing his young love, shy and virginal. Toni opened her eyes, wondering if anyone suspected what her imagination had worked up. Thankfully, no one paid her any attention.

As the song wound down, he added flourish by trailing his fingers over the bass keys until the song ended with a ripple. Only then did he look up. His face registered his surprise at the appreciative audience who clapped and shouted for more. He waved, indicating that he was done. He shook the hotel pianist's hand, who now regained his position. He bowed, with grand gestures like a vain maestro. Toni laughed at his silly antics, clapping with great appreciation for his talent.

As he walked down, Toni was able to catch his eye. He headed over looking relaxed and pleased. She had seen him in several different settings. All of which showed his tendency to be playful, even flirtatious, as he relied on his sex appeal.

"Don't you look like the proud girlfriend." Nicole nudged her. "You're beaming so hard with your pearly whites that you could probably light up the room."

"Shut up and go be a pest elsewhere."

"No way. You wanted me to make a good impression. And I can't wait."

Toni noted that several women had stopped Derek's progress. They lined up and a few had taken out paper and were looking for pens. The woman who talked to him now kept touching his arm and then had the nerve to squeeze it, marveling at his muscularity.

Nicole pushed her way forward. Then she walked up between Derek and the attractive woman. "Derek, Toni is waiting for you. You know how your woman gets when she's hungry."

Toni could hear Nicole's clear declaration and the aftermath with, not only the woman, but the others bidding a hasty retreat. She smiled, silently thanking her friend for watching her back.

The two returned to her.

"I don't know about you two, but I'm hungry."

"Now that Nicole has returned your heroic favor by saving you from those women, I think that you owe her a meal."

"It would be my pleasure."

They headed to the restaurant. Toni and Nicole flanked him with their arms interlocking with his. Toni felt satisfied that things had taken a turn for the better. She couldn't deal with the situation if these two couldn't get along.

After they were seated in a booth on the patio of the restaurant, and wine and salads were ordered, there was an easy silence among them.

Derek looked at Toni from across the table. Nicole sat between them.

"Hey, beautiful."

"Hi, gorgeous," Nicole answered, sipping on her water. She winked at both of them. "Kidding. Toni stop kicking me under the table."

"Hey, yourself," Toni answered. "Didn't know you had it in you."

"Today has been a day of surprises." Derek sipped his water.

"Anything else that we have to look forward to?" Nicole piped up.

"No," Toni and Derek said.

"Where'd you learn to play?" Nicole asked.

"My mother taught me."

"Your mother?" Nicole asked. Toni heard sharp interest in her friend's question. Nicole looked over at Toni.

"My mother and her sisters learned to play the piano when they were kids. Guess she passed on the tradition to me. I played seriously until college. Now I play for pleasure. You know, a form of relaxation. Once in a while, I played in my father's hotels."

"Your father owns hotels?" Nicole could barely remain still in the chair. Toni placed a calming hand on her thigh.

Their entrees arrived, pausing the conversation.

"He doesn't actually own them, but manages the hotels."

"Guess the world of tourism and hospitality runs in the blood."

Derek shrugged.

"Do you think that you could take us to see your father at one of his hotels?"

"I don't see why not?"

Toni nodded. She had to sip her water to wet her dry throat. "Can we eat, please?" Toni pleaded. She didn't want Nicole to pry and dig away.

She knew that the time for revelations would come, but she wanted to hold it at bay as long as possible.

Chapter 10

"I can't believe you went straight for the throat and asked him about his father. Could you slow down please?"

"How can I slow down when we're leaving in a few days? This is important to me, Toni. Do you remember why I was doing this in the first place? I can't get caught up in your little love story."

"You're becoming tunnel-visioned. These are people's lives that you are impacting. It's not only you, Nicole. Have you really thought about Brad? Once you open the lid, you can't get everything neatly packed back into the bottle. You can't rewrite history." Toni's voice rose. She didn't want to state her fears that Nicole's plans would ruin the stable ending she had envisioned when she left the island. She didn't buy into any illusions that it would be happy, but there would be no lingering regrets.

The two women sat under a large umbrella on the lounge

chairs facing the ocean. They had applied sunscreen liberally, especially after Toni shared her sunburn experience after her first day at the beach.

Nicole had bought both of them handwoven, wide-brim hats. Their additional accessories were their sunglasses. Toni enjoyed people-watching, it was a dip into her adolescence casting a critical eye at the shapes, sizes, and various colors using the beach as a runway. It didn't help that she was slowly moving out of the "hot young babe" category.

"Toni," Nicole prompted, "I'm glad that your heart is healing. But everything comes with a risk, anything that involves the heart. I promise that I will do everything in my power to make it right between you and Derek."

Toni looked over at her friend. Now she was going to talk about affairs of the heart. The only person in their girl group who could possibly talk about that was Shirley. Shirley had a habit of opening her heart to the good, bad, and ugly. And for some reason, the good always left her. The good thing was that Shirley hadn't married any of the lowlifes.

She, on the other hand, had a lot of belief in her ability to change her man. She had performed a dive roll into the relationship and eventual marriage with enough confidence for the two of them. But despite his glossy exterior, like a Red Delicious apple shiny with wax, she had bought into the image of a self-assured, committed man. Everyone warned her, especially after he left her the first time. But she had wanted to make their union right in her father's eyes.

Her ex-husband didn't go out of his way to show that he would make the effort. He constantly threw it in her face that she was the one who wanted this. Looking back at it, she'd agree. She was the only one buying into the image of husband, wife, and child. All she needed was a pet to complete the picture.

He'd left shortly before she miscarried. She hadn't told anyone, for weeks. The clothes that had remained in the closet for show were the clothes that she had bought him. He declared that he wanted nothing as a reminder. The one thing that she could be proud of was that she didn't beg him to stay. She didn't call him names. She didn't fight with him.

Instead she did spring-cleaning at the beginning of winter. She had cleaned out the cobwebs. She had the carpet professionally cleaned. The locks were changed. She stripped away as much of his presence as she could.

She had avoided family and didn't want to see her friends. She wanted to suffer her heartbreak as privately as possible. Her final punishment was when her stomach tightened unnaturally. She had placed her hand on the small mound of her belly and knew. She drove herself to the hospital, wanting to avoid any fuss. The doctor told her it was nature's way.

Nature's way of doing what? Nature's way to say that she had married the wrong man? Nature's way to say that he would have made a terrible father? Nature's way of saying that she was too stupid to be a mother? The self-doubts kept rolling in, sinking her into a deeper and darker depression. Six months she festered in that state. Some days she struggled to emerge, but it was too difficult. Her mind had gotten used to not caring.

Nicole never let up on her. She offered that rope to lift her out of the quagmire. Her love and caring guided her to think about the future. The very act of planning and setting expectations again gave her energy. Now that this power had been turned on, she didn't know how to stem its flow.

What she was most afraid of was placing Derek in a position to be the rebound man. He was the first man to whom she ran after her devastating experience. One part of her wanted to declare her love, or to have him declare his. Then, they'd get married. This idealistic and very unreal view would have worked a few months ago.

The other part of her wanted to return home. She wanted to start her job, live in her new condo, prove that she could live her life unfettered by a relationship or move toward commitment. And one day when she was in her seventies and her children and grandchildren treated her like an old feeble woman, she would tell them about her steamy summer romance that rivaled anything in the movies.

"Hey, earth to Toni. What are you thinking?"

"If you must know. I wondered what makes you the great magician all of a sudden? You want to play the role of Mrs. Fix-it." Toni turned up her face to the sun, wishing its heat could burn away the heartbreak.

"I've been married for over a year. Time will fly past regardless of life's ups and downs. The only thing that I will have left is my family and friends. Those are the people that will be there. You're important to me. Brad's important to me. Can you understand?"

"I understand." Toni sighed. "How could I not understand when family and friends were there for me in my darkest hours." She stretched out her hand to Nicole. "Let's get this over with."

Nicole responded by grabbing hold of Toni's hand. They would take this big step together.

* * *

Toni was dressed, sitting on the bed while Nicole applied her makeup. Derek would pick them up in fifteen minutes to head for lunch at his father's hotel.

She agreed with Nicole's argument, but she also knew that Nicole was impulsive enough to blurt out everything today. That wasn't the plan.

"Hey, Toni," Nicole called from the bathroom. The door was partially opened. "You listened and accepted what I said about friends and family. But what I didn't tell you is that I'm afraid if I don't do this, Brad won't want kids."

"How do you jump to that conclusion?" Brad was so in love with Nicole. How could he not want kids with this woman? "What aren't you telling me?"

Nicole stepped out of the bathroom. "When Brad found out about his brother, he was angry. Boy was he angry. Then it looked like he'd gotten over it. We would get into arguments when I suggested that we try to find his brother and father. Then I let it go. Recently I told him that I wanted to have a baby. None of us are getting any younger." Nicole stopped with the mascara brush poised in her hand. "The most natural thing in the world after a couple is married is to think about your family with children. I see Brad and me with several loud-mouthed kids, battling for attention. Brad would be the stern, caring father. I'd be the pushover mom, screaming at the top of her lungs.

"I've got the bed-and-breakfast. Brad has his freelance travel writing. We're busy, but there is still some semblance of family life. But I noticed that whenever I brought up the subject about having children, Brad would change the subject. At first

I was baffled. Then, you know me, I started thinking that he had a medical problem." She laughed, but the humor didn't infuse her face. "I made an appointment for him to see the doctor. Brad wasn't happy, let me tell you. Maybe I should have told him that it wasn't a regular exam." She finished applying her mascara. "I explained why I did what I did. I explained how worried he was making me. Then I came right out and said that I wanted to have children. Doesn't he? Without blinking an eye, he said that he doesn't and never will."

Toni sat still. Her friend's pain spilled over to her, she felt its sharp edge.

"We haven't really been the same since."

"Is that why you're trying to get to Derek? Create a family reunion of sorts. Show him that he has a family and how that can feel?"

Nicole nodded.

Toni didn't like the direction her mind was taking, it brought up all kinds of negative thoughts that she wished that she could bury. "Did he ever suggest that he wanted to meet his brother and probably his father?"

Nicole shook her head. "I can't just sit by and do nothing. Having a child or not having a child needs to be a mutual decision. Shoot me for not discussing it prior to us getting married. But it's done. I want a child."

Nicole thought about her loss. She had the image of a perfect family in mind. Not having that chance after that wish grew in her mind made it become an obsession.

"Although it might seem a tough thing to do, you might try just talking to him before opening this door to his past."

"But this isn't for Brad. This is for me, too. I want to know my brother-in-law. I do have mixed feelings about my father-in-law, but this man's heart may have changed over the years."

"Go on, get ready. We need to go downstairs now." She grabbed her pocketbook and did a once-over in the mirror. "I will give you some motherly advice because I know that you haven't told her any of this."

Nicole rolled her eyes.

"I want you to tread lightly when it comes to bringing them together. Think about what you've got now and what you could lose." Toni headed out the room.

"And you want me to think about what you'll lose, too."

Toni ignored her. They rode the elevator cab down to the lobby, neither one talking. She felt like she was entering a situation that would be hard to trudge through—like walking in molasses.

She planted a kiss on Derek's lips when she climbed into the car. Maybe she was trying to send him some reinforcement. He didn't have a clue as to what was about to hit him. That made her feel low. But how to warn him about something like this? She wouldn't stay quiet until Nicole made her declaration.

"You smell delicious," he whispered to Toni while Nicole climbed in the backseat. "I've missed you so much."

"Nicole, looks like you got some sun," Derek teased.

"Yep," Nicole answered.

Her tone must have sounded off because Derek turned to look at Nicole, then back at Toni. Toni shrugged emphatically and leaned over and kissed him.

"My dad is excited at seeing you again," he remarked to Toni. "You really made an impression on him."

"You sound relieved," Nicole remarked.

"Don't we always want to get our parents' approval?" Derek asked.

"Yeah, I guess you're right. I want my parents' approval. My husband, though, is an orphan."

"Nicole," Toni said through gritted teeth. "Let's keep it light."

"The princess has spoken." Nicole stared, her defiance expressed.

"Am I in the middle of a spat?" Derek looked in the rearview mirror.

"Not at all. Where's your father's hotel?" Toni wanted to get out of the car with a new desperation. She didn't know what had gotten into Nicole. Despite all that she had said, there was an undercurrent of something else.

"It's in Cable Beach. It's the other concentrated area of hotels outside of Paradise Island."

They drove the additional ten minutes in silence. Only a jazz tune played over the radio. Toni enjoyed the soft stroking of Derek's thumb against her hand.

"Hello, Toni. Hi son. And you must be Nicole. I'm Benjamin, Derek's father."

Toni held her breath.

Nicole nodded. She returned Benjamin's handshake. Only then did Toni relax, a little.

"What brings you here? You really don't want to see me at work. It's boring."

"I own a bed-and-breakfast, along with my husband. I wanted to compare some notes and pick your brain about the hospitality industry." Nicole stepped forward and took a seat.

"Oh, wow, a woman after my own heart. Since my son has

no desire to follow in my footsteps, I'm sure that he would rather be elsewhere." Benjamin waved him out.

"I'm taking the hint. Toni, let's go before he launches into the history of the first hotel built in the Bahamas."

Toni stood, feeling torn. She desperately wanted to spend her time with Derek. But she saw how relaxed Nicole was sitting in the chair. She reminded her of a spider spinning a web for her latest victim.

Derek decided the matter by placing his hand on the small of her back and ushering her out of the office.

"You worry too much," he whispered into her hair. "My father will be the perfect gentleman."

"And why do you think that I'm worried about him?"

He laughed. "You're right. Maybe we do need to check on them."

"Or maybe we can get away." She unbuttoned a button of her shirt and trailed her finger.

"Where will we go?"

"How about the suite for the VIPs or high rollers?"

"I see you like to make your challenges tough."

"I'm sure you can do it, Big Boy." She unbuttoned a second button. She pulled the lapel of her shirt open to show the black lace bra.

Derek growled and kissed her neck, nibbling on her earlobe. "What you're about to see is only for you."

They walked into the lobby. Derek dropped her hand. His posture changed subtly. He stood more erect, stuck out his chest, and kept one hand in his pocket. Then he changed his demeanor with a highly flirtatious smile that wasn't for her, but dazzled the concierge in front of him.

"Hey, doll, how is it going?"

"Hello, Mr. Calverton."

"Oh, you know who I am? I'm flattered, babe." He took her hand and kissed it.

Toni stayed in the background, but if he kept up this schmoozing, she was going to deck him.

"Of course, all of us know who you are." The concierge indicated the other smiling women at the front desk.

Derek made a bow, his smile got brighter and cockier.

"I want to show a client the VIP suite."

The concierge looked over at Toni. Her eyes full of venom. She cast a scathing once-over before shifting her focus back to Derek, with a highly flirtatious smile.

"I'd be happy to show you."

"Maybe another time." He waited for her to get the key. He looked at Toni. Toni wasn't amused. She had her arms crossed, mouth pursed.

Once they were making their way up with the special key, she turned to him. "If I find out that you are with that woman when I'm gone, I'm going to make a special trip."

"Promise?"

Toni waited until the elevator door opened. She stepped out directly into the room. She had planned to jump on Derek and start their foreplay until they made it into the bedroom.

But for a few minutes, she couldn't stop her exclamations over the decorations, the expansive area, the furniture. She couldn't stop her imagination from unfolding a wonderful scene with Derek and her sharing the space.

"The rich live well, don't you think?" Derek came up

behind her and wrapped his arms around her. She leaned back against his chest still admiring the layout.

"My condo can probably fit in the living room and dining area," she joked.

"Let's explore and then I want that black bra off."

They giggled and headed off through the room. If they were amazed at the living room and dining area, they hadn't seen anything like the master bedroom.

"This isn't a bedroom, it's a small apartment." Toni ran her hands over the heavy wood furniture.

The floor was uncarpeted with light area rugs. The soft caramel and almond colors added to the expensive look with touches of ivory. The bedroom had a private deck that overlooked the ocean.

"What a view." Derek whistled.

"When you make the big bucks with your company, let's get this room."

"Okay."

"I wanted to make love to you up here, but now that I'm here, I can't. I wouldn't want someone doing the nasty in my hotel room before I checked in."

"I would say that I'd pay for it, but I don't even want to know how much a night is."

"Plus there is Nicole and your father." She looked at her watch. "Let's go check on them."

Toni followed Derek into his father's office. He and Nicole were eating and drinking. They waved soiled fingers at them.

"We wondered where you'd gotten to," Benjamin said.

"We were doing a bit of touring."

"You went up to the diplomat's suite. Yeah, I know you did. I know everyone that has the key to the VIP suites. When you used the key it activated the security system. I knew no one was using it until tomorrow. I checked with the concierge and she told me."

Toni turned knowing eyes to Derek. His father finding out about their private moment would be too much.

"I'm starved. What do you have there?" Derek thankfully switched subjects.

"Fried wontons. Hot wings, only I got them mild. Cheese fingers." Nicole licked her fingers.

"Derek, I think we'd better stop for medicine for Nicole's upset stomach."

"I don't have an upset stomach."

"You will in a couple hours. I couldn't eat that much."

"Benjamin, it's time that I get going before Toni insults me any further. Any moment now, she'll call me a human vacuum cleaner."

Toni giggled.

"See, I know how she thinks."

"Nicole, I've had a great time with you. Toni, make sure you bring her to my birthday event."

"Dad, you weren't supposed to know about that."

"I didn't. Thanks for confirming."

"You can't tell Mom."

"I'll second that for him," Toni added.

"I'll stand behind their plea because I've heard of the infamous Sylvia Calverton. Personally, I can't wait to meet her."

"I think you and she will get along very well." Benjamin smiled.

Each person hugged the other. Toni really enjoyed being with Benjamin. He was such a genuine soul, kind-hearted and full of fatherly advice. She could not correlate the image of a father abandoning his son to achieve his own dreams with this man.

Toni promised Derek that they could have their special date tomorrow. She was too curious about Nicole's report to spend the evening in Derek's company. And she wanted to spend it unhurried, relaxed, and without wondering if they were being watched.

Nicole lay across the bed, staring up at the ceiling. Toni flopped down next to her, lying on her stomach. The balcony door was open for the night breeze that ruffled the sheer curtains.

"I didn't expect to like Benjamin," Nicole started. "He is the model of a father, even grandfather. We talked about the business. We chatted about his family—Derek and Sylvia. He had a hard life, but he succeeded. I so wanted to tell him about Brad. I know in my heart that something prevented him from coming for Brad. I can't believe otherwise."

"That's what I was trying to tell you." Toni looked out and up to the sky.

The night was like a black canvas with brilliant stars twinkling against that backdrop. She couldn't wait for a star to fall to make her wish. Right here, right now, she would throw a wish up that all would go well.

"I'm glad that Benjamin extended an invitation to you. I wasn't sure how I was going to pull it off."

"I want to talk to Brad."

"I think that you should."

"No, I want to talk to him now."

"Do you need me to leave?"

"Of course not."

"Okay, that didn't sound convincing. What if I go take a soak in the tub? I'll turn up the music so I don't hear your mushy stuff."

Nicole rolled on to her side. She took Toni's hand and placed it on her stomach.

"This wasn't exactly the way that I was going to tell this news."

"You're pregnant!" Toni raised to hug her friend. "I can't believe it. This is great." She danced around the room. "Now it's making sense why this was so urgent for you. Say something."

"I'm trying, but you won't take a breath." Nicole laughed and danced around with her.

"How long have you known?" Toni recalled how her friend had slept most of the day and then her appetite later in the day bordered on ravenous.

"I knew before I left for the Bahamas." Nicole wasn't dancing anymore. "I couldn't tell Brad after we had the dis-agreement about having children."

"But you're willing to tell him now?"

"I'm a coward because I'm not in the same room. This is also one of the reasons that I'm pushing with Benjamin. I'm hoping that by the time I return, I would have planned the family reunion."

"I'm putting my stock in Brad. I think that hearing he's got a little baby on the way will soften his heart."

Toni prepared her bath. She filled the deep tub with water hot enough for her to stand. She sprinkled in the bath salts.

In over one week, her life was zigzagging down a path on which she didn't know what was coming next.

And now she would be an aunt. She was very happy for Nicole. She knew that she had definitely moved to another place, a more positive place because there was no sense of regret that she wasn't the one who was pregnant. That alone made her happy.

She turned off the faucet. Then she listened. Not that she wanted to listen to Nicole's conversation, but it was eerily quiet. She cracked the door and peeped out. Nicole was sitting on the bed with her shoulders hunched talking on the phone.

Toni reclosed the door. This didn't look good. She expected Nicole to be elated, maybe not dancing around the way they had, but several degrees above this quiet version. Announcing a pregnancy shouldn't be treated as a diplomatic mission by peacekeeping troops.

She debated whether to get involved.

This was her girlfriend. She marched out of the bathroom. "Let me talk to him. If he's going to make you upset, then he's going to have to deal with me." She took the phone from Nicole motioning to her to stay put.

"Brad? What is your problem?"

"I don't know. What is Brad's problem?" Toni recognized Nicole's mother.

"Oh. Nothing." She handed the phone back to Nicole. "Why didn't you tell me that it wasn't him," she scolded. "Why are you looking so sad?"

"My dog is very ill."

"Yikes. I'm sorry. So you haven't talked to Brad?"

Nicole shook her head.

"Whew." Toni laughed.

"There's nothing funny about any of this, Toni."

"I know. I know. I was worried about your telling Brad."

Nicole simply glared at her.

Now was not the time to explain what she'd thought. They could laugh about it in a couple weeks.

She opted to take her bath. Now that her fears were unfounded, she could sink under the suds. Nevertheless she did keep an ear out for any conversation. She closed her eyes with a smile on her lips when she heard Nicole giggling and talking rapidly.

All would be well.

Chapter 11

Derek walked into his father's hotel. He had gratefully accepted Toni's suggestion that they take a taxi to come to the birthday party. His mother had tied him up with tasks until the party started.

The coordinator and his mother were in a heated battle. He edged past them to head into the main room where the tables were set.

"Derek!" his mother's voice rang.

Derek hunched his shoulders, debating whether to ignore her. He plowed ahead into the room. The transformation of the main conference room had changed the interior into a fifties Hollywood movie set with black movie actors from the silver screen. His father was a movie buff and would appreciate this.

The sharpest pain shot through his ear. He'd pull away, but he was afraid that his ear would be ripped from his head.

"Didn't you hear me call you? I know you heard me. I saw your shoulders flinch."

"Could you let go of my ear, Mom?"

"No. I'm going to pull it off because you told your father about the party."

"I did not."

She tugged on his ear, eliciting a scream from him. "Okay, I did tell him. But he tricked me."

"He thinks that it will be the usual birthday party at the house. And he's planning to rebel by not getting dressed. I have Laurence dropping by with the limo to bring him here. Now he won't get dressed."

"And you want me to go talk to him?" He eased his ear away from her fingers.

"Good. Your brain is working again."

Derek didn't have much time to waste. The party was due to begin in two hours. His mother wanted his father to show up when most of the guests had arrived, but not significantly late.

"Mom, keep an eye out for Toni and Nicole. They are arriving by taxi."

"Who is Nicole?"

"Toni's friend. Dad invited Nicole."

"When did this occur? How did your father invite someone to a party that he didn't know about?" She took a step toward him.

Derek placed his hands over his ears. "I'm leaving now."

He rang the doorbell of his childhood home. The maid answered, letting him know that his father had just returned from the beach and now sat on the patio. Derek went to the patio, hoping that it would be an easy discussion.

"Dad." Derek tried to use his serious voice. He felt as if they had switched roles. "I need to talk to you."

His father sipped his soda, munching on the ice cubes loudly.

Derek sank into the chair opposite him. It didn't look good for his power of negotiation having to start with his father in swim trunks and a towel around his shoulders.

"The party isn't happening here," Derek stated.

"Really. Where is it?"

"At your hotel." Derek sighed.

"Figured that you and your mother would make this into a spectacle. And if I recall, I asked her not to do this. I wanted to spend the day with her. I wanted to take a trip."

"She worked pretty hard. And so did your employees. You'll be amazed when you see it."

"If I see it. Why is it that you aren't listening to me, either? I know why she did this. It's for her family."

"Look, Dad. I'm not going to get into that. That's between you and Mom. All I know is that there are over two hundred people waiting to celebrate an important event in your life. You are a great man. You've accomplished a lot. People respect you. Heck, I've tried to live up to your abilities and have come nowhere close."

His father hugged him. Then he pushed him away. "I'll hate every minute of it."

"That's your prerogative." Derek watched him go inside and waited until he heard the shower before pumping his arm in the air.

* * *

Toni walked arm in arm with Nicole, following the big band sound. Evidence of a large party poured out of the room. Music blared. People milled around in their best outfits. The aroma of enticing hors d'oeuvres wafted in the air, stirring her appetite.

"This is fabulous." Toni edged around the room. She craned her neck for a better view of the entire room. Derek was nowhere in sight.

"Are you going to the front?" Nicole asked, her focus was on a passing tray of caviar on toast.

"I don't want to sit too close, but not so far away that we won't be able to see the goings-on." Toni did a sideways shuffle to select a seat closer to the middle aisle. She found two perfect seats and made her way to them.

"Toni, I see you made it. Is this the famous Nicole?"

"Yes, it is. And you are Sylvia. I'm glad we finally meet." Nicole shook Sylvia's hand.

"Come with me, you must sit closer. With me."

Toni followed the slim figure of this matriarch. She squeezed Nicole's hand as they made their way to a reserved table. She still couldn't locate Derek.

"Derek had to get his father. The stubborn man was going to make it difficult for us." She pulled out two chairs for them. "Have a seat. I'm going to check on them."

"She's a glass of ice water," Nicole remarked after Sylvia's retreating figure.

"No kidding." Toni sat, glad for the new seat which gave her a direct line of vision to the doorway.

Since they had arrived, more people had poured in. Tables

quickly filled and the din of conversation rose. The waiters served three appetizers for each table. Toni nibbled on a fried wonton dipped in plum sauce. Nicole ate her third caviar on toast.

"I think the baby likes this one." Nicole patted her stomach.

"I guess when you mow through the food in massive quantities, we know who you'll blame."

"Have a caviar and hush."

"Don't do that." Derek appeared from behind Toni.

"Don't do what?"

"No caviar. I don't like caviar."

"I wasn't giving it to you," Nicole said, making a face at him.

"Yes you were. I don't like caviar, and if you gave her caviar, I couldn't do this." He leaned toward Toni and kissed her firmly on the mouth. In an instant, she responded. He slipped in his tongue and played tag until he felt someone smack him on his shoulder.

"I get your point." Nicole hid a smile behind her hand.

"Behave, Derek," Sylvia said the words with the most fake smile pasted on her face. "And you, too, young lady."

"Yes, ma'am." Embarrassment brought a warm flush to Toni's face. It didn't help that Nicole giggled. Nor did it help that Derek didn't look the least remorseful.

"Where is your father?" Sylvia used a tissue to rub her son's lips.

"He said that he wasn't making a grand entrance. He was going to use one of the side entrances. Said something about the kitchen."

"Oh no he doesn't." Sylvia picked up her evening gown

and marched off toward the kitchen. Even the servers made a path for her.

"Is he really going to do that and risk her wrath for the entire evening?"

"No. He's over there shaking hands. He just wanted to walk in without any grand announcements."

"You do have lots of tricks up your sleeve." Toni played with his neck.

"Not only my sleeve, baby."

"Look, don't you two get all hot and heavy. Wait until later," Nicole said through another mouthful.

"No problem. Will you stay with me tonight?"

"I thought you'd never ask. I did pack a few of her things." Nicole held up a small bag that looked perfect for the beach and not an evening party.

"I wondered what that bag was. I thought it was for you." Toni snatched the bag from Nicole.

"I couldn't find your father," Sylvia reported to Derek, the accusation loud and clear.

"I think he double-crossed us. He's over there."

Sylvia slapped Derek's arm in frustration. She flopped into the chair with the dramatic flair of a fifties movie star. "I give up. I try to bring a little class to the affair and this is what I get."

"A very classy affair, if you ask me." Nicole raised her water glass at Sylvia.

Sylvia turned shrewd eyes on Nicole. Then she looked at Toni. "Derek, I need to talk to you."

Derek left with his mother.

Toni kept an eye on them. She didn't like the way Sylvia was pointing in their direction. At least Derek didn't look as if he was buying into his mother's speech. Once he looked over at her, but she didn't look away. Finally he put his hands on his mother's shoulders and said his piece before she walked off.

"Everything okay?"

"Yep," he answered.

"I think it was about me," Toni pressed.

"Nothing to worry about. The night's events are about to begin."

Toni took the hint and let the matter drop. She looked at Nicole and even Nicole wasn't looking so confident. Now she understood that Sylvia was a force to be reckoned with.

Toni had never experienced a party that extreme. The budget could have probably paid someone's salary. When she saw the cabaret act, she knew that it cost a pretty penny. Sylvia must have dipped in the trust fund for this one.

But she had to give the woman her props. All her hard work had paid off because her parents and siblings showed up with some of the other family members. Even Derek was tongue-tied when his grandfather shook his hand.

She felt the tension, but at least it was a first step. Sylvia was a fighter, that was clear. She wanted her family together no matter what. That was the similarity that Toni recognized in Nicole. No matter what, she was going to have her way.

"Hey, why are you out here all alone?" Derek placed his arm around her shoulders.

"Needed some air and a little quieter spot." She kissed his hand. "You don't have to watch over me. I'm fine. Your family is probably looking for you."

"I'll go in a moment. You would think that after four hours, people would start heading out, but it looks like the party's revving into high gear." He nuzzled her neck. "Oh, Nicole said that she had an announcement to make to the family members."

Toni sat up. "To the family members?"

"Strange, isn't it? What could she possibly have to say?"

Toni kissed him on the lips, before hugging him tightly.

"You know, don't you?" he accused.

She didn't answer.

"I can see it on your face."

Toni looked down at his feet. She knew that he now stood, probably looking down at her head. "I need to go talk to Nicole."

"You're making me uneasy, Toni."

Toni looked at him and tried to smile, but her lips trembled. He didn't know the half of it. She walked away to find Nicole.

She easily spotted Nicole who was in deep conversation with Benjamin. Toni tried to read the situation, wondering if she was breaking the news to him. She'd never agreed that this was the setting for it and she wished that she'd worked harder to make Nicole understand.

"Nicole," Toni called as if speaking to a child. "May I talk to you, please?"

"No, no, I finally got a chance to talk to Nicole. She has such a sense of humor. And too many people keep interrupting us." Benjamin waved Toni away.

"Nicole!" Toni held her ground.

"Benjamin, my friend is going to nag us to death if I don't see what the problem is."

"I'll be waiting."

Toni pulled Nicole by the elbow and steered her down the hallway. There were other rooms for meetings and conferences that lined the hallway on the left and right. Toni tried one door and then the next. They were locked. Nevertheless she kept trying until one door did open. She pushed Nicole into the room. She had to take a minute to catch her breath and to calm her anger.

Derek heard the warnings that his mother had tried to drum into his head earlier that evening. At first he thought that she had major issues with Toni, but it became clear that it was Nicole that had set off the bad vibes. She didn't like Nicole's vivid interest in Benjamin or the way she stared at her as if studying her. He'd called it an overactive imagination.

But Toni's reaction and what he just saw when Toni practically pushed Nicole into the room, set his senses on alert. He walked toward the door, knowing that, if it swung open, he'd be caught like a little boy with his hand in the cookie jar. Like his mother, he was getting bad vibes. While his mother focused on Nicole. He focused on Toni. If she did anything to harm his family or was in some conspiracy with Nicole, she would wish that she had never stepped foot on this island. He had already figured out that Nicole was probably some young thing about to accuse his father of being the father of her baby.

He didn't have to push open the door to hear them. Their voices were raised, but he wanted to see them. He wanted to see the woman who had captured his heart.

"You can't tell that sort of news here." Toni gripped Nicole's arm.

"Why not? Don't you think his family would want to know."

"You want to humiliate him."

"Why should this humiliate him? He should be proud."

"Proud isn't the first thing that comes to mind. I can't talk you out of disclosing it, but not now. He's the happiest man out there."

"It's not all about him, is it?"

"We would all like to enjoy this. Sylvia wanted to invite her family and get their respect and love."

"Isn't that a little one-sided?" Nicole pulled away her arm.

"You sound cold, selfish. And for a mother-to-be, maybe you should be a little more empathetic. You are casting judgment and meting out the punishment."

"And what are you doing? Huh! What are you doing? You're using Derek to repair your broken heart, then you'll use him as your doormat, wipe your feet and head home. Don't you think that you're being selfish. And if your ex comes back in your life again? Are you going to drop everything and everyone like you did before. You are a hypocrite."

Derek couldn't remember entering the room. He didn't know how he got across the room where they stood. His voice sounded as if it came from outside of his body. Then as if time and space caught up, he heard Toni sobbing.

"What is going on in here?" Sylvia ran forward and placed a hand on Derek's arm.

"You were right, Mom. These two are more than bad news. Nicole fancies herself pregnant by Dad. Toni was the scout to make sure we were in place for the big news."

"Have you lost your mind? I am not pregnant by your

father. I like your father and all that, but eeww." Nicole shook her head.

"Derek, Sylvia, it's not what you think," Toni interrupted.

"Say another word and I will strike you down right here." Sylvia raised her hand.

"Enough. You all are drawing a crowd outside." Benjamin walked into the room, adjusted his tuxedo, and surveyed the scene. "Since I didn't hear everything, why don't you, Nicole, tell me what you think I need to know."

"I don't think that this is the time."

"Oh, now you have second thoughts. This is sweet." Toni wiped the tears away with her hand.

"Speak." Benjamin's attention focused solely on Nicole.

"My name is Nicole Calverton. My husband is Brad Calverton. He grew up with…"

"His grandmother," Benjamin finished.

"In Baltimore. When she died, they couldn't locate his father—Elroy Benjamin Calverton. The other relatives didn't want him. He was placed in social services. He graduated and went to college. He became a travel writer reviewing hotels and resorts, including bed-and-breakfast inns. He also writes travel guides." Nicole's voice broke.

"You're a liar." Derek looked at Nicole and he didn't like what he saw. He didn't want to see the sincerity. He looked at Toni and she had her arm around her friend. Then he looked at his father. He stared over their heads with tears glistening on his cheeks.

"I wanted you to know because Brad found out the truth that he had a father and brother. It's killing him to know that you didn't care enough to come for him. It's eating him up inside and because of it, he doesn't want children. Well, he didn't, but then I found out I was pregnant on the day I left to come here. Now, I think with your first grandchild about to come into this world, that you should know."

Sylvia was the first to break formation. She walked over to Benjamin who had a decided droop in his shoulder. She guided him out. Derek could hear her explain that Benjamin was fatigued, but they could all stay.

Then he looked at Toni and Nicole. The revelation had skipped along the surface of his consciousness. But it didn't make sense. He couldn't wrap his mind around the fact that his father had another child, his brother.

Now wasn't the time to sort out the feelings about Toni. He didn't want to. She had played a part in the pain he felt. He backed away from her. Then he turned and walked away, biting down against the urge to answer her calling his name.

Toni watched Derek leave. She took in a shuddering breath. Maybe she would retell this story at the dinner table in her seventies. Maybe by then there would be some way she could erase unpleasant memories. And this one had earned its way to the top.

"Let's go." She walked next to Nicole.

"The only thing that I'm sorry about is the timing."

"You think?"

Toni entered the hallway which was like a different world. The music continued to blare with hits played in the big band style. People still danced or chatted. No one seemed to know the drama that had recently unfolded. She was grateful for that.

Toni rode back to the hotel with Nicole. There was no conversation. But then again, what kind of conversation could they have? They had both unloaded on each other with the effect of a double-barreled shotgun. Not too many pieces left to be picked up.

When the taxi pulled up, Nicole hopped out first. Toni stayed behind. "I'll catch up with you later." She closed the door and gave directions to the driver.

She didn't bother to look out the window for Nicole's reaction. She was a big girl. Plus she thought it best for them to be apart tonight. By tomorrow they could salvage their relationship for their trip home.

The taxi pulled up at Derek's home. There were no lights on. Toni wondered where he'd gone. Her fears surfaced that maybe he had gone to a lady friend, one that he could trust.

"Could you stick around, please? Let me make sure that someone is home." Toni stepped out of the taxi and looked around. She didn't see his car, either. She walked down the path leading to the front door. She knocked, but already knew that he hadn't returned home.

"Where to, miss?"

Toni sat back in the taxi. She gave him the only other address she knew. It might not be a smart move to go into the lion's den after what they had all gone through, but she was prepared to be as humble as it took.

This time the house that had been the site of her first official date, and that doubled for Derek's home at one time, had on all the lights. She paid the driver. She worried that if they saw the taxi driver outside, then they knew she had the option to leave and would tell her to do so.

She rang the doorbell. Sylvia answered still dressed in her

evening gown. Her hairstyle was slightly askew. Her eye makeup was smeared, making her look even more ferocious.

"What do you want?"

"I'm looking for Derek."

"Do you have another revelation? Not quite finished?"

Toni saw the glass half filled with amber liquid sloshing in it. She didn't know how to deal with Sylvia when she was sober. Having an unhappy inebriated woman could get ugly, since Sylvia looked like she would be happy to belt her across the face.

"May I come in?" Toni looked over her shoulder as if the neighbors might hear. She had to appeal to Sylvia's desire to appear respectable.

Sylvia's response was to turn away and walk into the living room, leaving the front door open. Toni jumped at the invitation.

There was no sign of Derek or Benjamin. The house was quiet, but seemed alive with tension. Sylvia's shoes were strewn in the living room. She had a half-empty bottle of Scotch in her hand. Toni watched her toss back a good mouthful before she lost her balance and fell over backward in the chair.

She hurried over and tried to wipe up the spill. Sylvia pushed away her hand. And to make her point, she poured the remainder of the drink directly on the chair.

"You're going to be so mad at yourself tomorrow." Toni wrested the glass from her, figuring that Sylvia's next action would be to toss the glass against a wall or maybe even at her.

"I haven't seen Derek."

"Is Benjamin upstairs?"

"No. He sent me home and went to his office. Said that he wanted to be alone."

"Do you want me to stay with you?"

"Why the heck would I want that!" She laughed, which then turned into a sob. "Do you think that I'll get my family back together again?"

Toni moved around the chair. She held out her hand. Thankfully Sylvia responded. Toni took her down the long hall to the door of her bedroom. She knocked to make sure that Benjamin wasn't in there before opening the door.

The decorative style hadn't changed much from the other parts of the house. There were more African carvings and pencil etchings of landscapes. She wondered if those were places that they had visited.

She helped Sylvia to her bed. She didn't know whether to undress her and put something a little more comfortable on her. Although the evening dress looked stunning on her, she had felt the stiff corsetlike fabric when she helped her into bed. It made her think of someone sitting on her chest, squeezing the breath out of her.

Sylvia took the matter into her own hands. She unzipped her dress and let it fall to the floor. Then she slid under the sheets with her control-top panty hose on. Toni accepted the compromise and turned off the lights before leaving.

"Try his office."

"Benjamin?"

"Derek's new office. Like his father, it may become his new hiding place."

Toni made a mental note of the address that Sylvia gave in a heavily slurred, sleepy voice.

Chapter 12

Derek heard a car pull up and then a door slam. He pushed himself off his couch and walked over to the window. The woman who had invaded his thoughts, now stood down there in the street looking up. He hadn't brought her here, wanting this to be the last surprise before she left.

He opened the mini-blinds to get a better look at the street. No car waited to take her back to her hotel. It would have given him a reason not to open the door and wait for her to realize defeat and head back.

Instead, he opened the door.

"How did you know to come here?"

"Your mother."

"Haven't you had enough. Why are you still harassing my family?"

He was glad that his furniture had arrived earlier than

scheduled. It meant that he could take the farthest chair in the reception area. But it would help if she didn't approach him.

"I can't leave you like this." She touched his cheek. He jerked away.

"Unbroken?"

"Don't be cruel." She raised her hand toward his chest.

He grabbed her hand, released it immediately. No contact. Touching her would destroy his defenses.

"You have more secrets for me? Is that why you're here? I think your friend Nicole was pretty clear about your motives."

"I'm not a flirt, Derek. I don't play games. No one knows what is in my heart since I've met you. What I've experienced is only between you and me."

"You started this mission with the advantage of knowing what was expected of you and of me. I was seen as the pawn to be manipulated." He held up his hand to stop her. "I can see it now." He walked away, re-establishing the space between them. "You and Nicole probably concocted this plan while watching a sitcom. You, being the single one, took on the job of finding me and my family. Then on the side, you figured out that you could get more out of the deal for yourself. A sort of summer fantasy that could be fulfilled, without any lingering complications." Derek saw her mouth twitch, but he wasn't going to fall for tears. "Sounds like I helped you with some therapeutic stuff, so do I get paid now or later?"

"You're deliberately being nasty. You don't want to face what we have. But I'm not going to let you ruin this."

"Again, it's all about you." He flicked on the lights in the reception area.

The dim lighting was adding to the confusion between

his mind and body. Toni in her pants suit was looking too sexy for words.

"Unlike you, I'm telling you the truth. So I'm not being nasty."

She flicked off the light.

He flicked on the hall light, illuminating the stairs leading up and the signs on the restroom doors on the main floor. He ascended the stairs.

"I have faced what we have. It's like looking into a trash can—full or empty, take your pick."

She flicked off the light.

He walked into his office. The desk lamp was on. He walked over to the desk and sat in his chair, waiting for her to enter.

He leaned forward because she didn't enter as he expected she would. Whatever, he wasn't going to look for her. If she wanted to snoop around the office, then fine. He reached for the button on the base of the lamp. Toni appeared. His finger paused and then withdrew.

The lamp blinded him, but he knew, deep in his soul, that Toni stood naked in his doorway. Now she walked toward him. She emerged from the shadow and the light revealed her full breasts, nipples erect. Then, the light spilled across her stomach plunging what lay below her belly button in darkness. She leaned over on the desk. He looked up at her face, witnessing the naked desire. Or from the way he felt, the desire was a reflection of his need.

He watched her press the button. The room was pitched in darkness and he was momentarily blind. He didn't know where she was until she took his hand and laid it on her breast. He tried to pull back, but she didn't allow him to pull away. Sitting on his desk facing him, he wanted to wave the white flag of surrender. She would not leave him in peace.

"This doesn't change anything," his voice sounded strained.

"You talk too much. You think too much." She guided his hand down between her legs.

She was driving him out of his mind. At the end of their crazy meeting, they must have decided to make him insane. As he sucked her breast, teasing, cajoling the sensitive puckered tip, his fingers played their own tune against the hidden inner folds.

"I'm a simple man, Toni. I work hard for a living. I don't know what you want from me."

She leaned back on his desk, arching for his attention. Somehow he didn't think she was listening. And he was finding it increasingly difficult to focus.

"I am yours, Derek." She sat up. With one swift motion, she ripped open his shirt and then opened his pants, stroking his arousal. "Let me stay with you tonight. Let's watch the sunrise in each other's arms."

He kissed her, tasting the saltiness of her tears. Was this how addicts felt doing drugs and then falling down the never-ending abyss, which was strangely titillating?

They kissed each other, their bodies sliding across each other in a frenzy of emotion. He kissed her neck, running his tongue along the edge of her jaw until it found its home in the sweetness of her mouth.

She used too many tricks on him. She wrapped her legs around his waist and erotically rubbed herself against him. He took a deep breath and pushed himself up while she lay on his brand new leather blotter.

"You're demanding something that I'm not prepared to give," he panted. "If I lie down with you and have sex, because heaven knows this is not love, I would be no better than you." He felt her legs slacken and eventually come down from his waist. He bit down for strength because his inclination was to kiss her on her right breast and then her left until she clenched him in a vise grip. "Sex is what you offered me when you decided to play Jamie Bond. And again, sex is what you offer me as a thank-you schmuck gift." He zipped his pants and retrieved the rest of his clothes. "You shared the best of what you have to give. I'm going to hold onto the best I have to give. I want a relationship, a commitment." He paused to wait for her answer while he made a production of putting on his tuxedo jacket. Instead she walked out the door and he could hear her getting dressed. "Say something," he whispered.

She came back into the room and picked up his phone. She dialed a number and he heard her order a taxi.

Then she walked downstairs. He stood at the top. She wasn't crying. She was very calm, but hadn't spoken to him or looked in his direction.

Fifteen minutes later, the taxi honked. Toni walked out the door. He remained at his desk consoling himself that he had made the right decision. There was no way that he could or should fall in love with a woman like her. It didn't matter that he missed her already and the craving had already begun.

He used Nicole's latest news about his father to stir the embers, make him angry. If he focused on what he'd heard tonight that he had a brother, then he didn't have the room to think about Toni Kimball.

* * *

Toni headed back to the hotel, wishing that she had another place to retreat in private. The pain had built enough pressure to make her erupt like a volcano, bawling like a baby. She and Nicole had unfinished business. But it would have to wait because her emotions would remain in check while she sat in the back of the taxi cab.

As added punishment, she rode up the elevator with a couple who couldn't wait to get to the bedroom. Their kissing and groaning were like spikes being driven through her heart. They obviously didn't care about her witnessing that side of their relationship.

She tumbled out when the elevator stopped at her floor. She gasped for air, but only a shuddering sob popped out. She clamped her hand over her mouth to subdue the noise, while fumbling with the room card. Her hand shook. It was like the ignition for her entire body so that she trembled as if a cold blast of air had washed over her.

She opened the door and entered the dark room. Her body decided that it was now safe enough for the tears to fall. She knew that, if the light was on, she'd be blinded by the volume of water pouring from her eyes. She felt her way to the bathroom and took a seat on the closed lid.

The toilet paper acted as her tissues and helped to muffle the sobs that were escaping with a sickening frequency.

"Toni?"

Toni couldn't answer. She tried, but another sob escaped in a massive heave.

"Toni, I'm coming in."

Toni hadn't locked the door, figuring that Nicole was

asleep. She didn't feel like getting up to lock the door. Actually she didn't care about anything. So what if she looked the pathetic mess sitting on the commode.

Nicole looked down at her and turned away. "Ah...here's water." She picked up the bottled water that was left on the desk. "Damn. Four dollars for this little thing." She unscrewed the cap. "Oh well, this is an emergency." She poured the water in a glass and brought it to Toni.

Toni shook her head. She didn't think that she could possibly drink and cry at the same time. Right now, she only wanted to cry. Crying had to mean that she was getting it out of her system. Getting Derek out of her system.

"You've got to drink this water," Nicole pleaded. "Make me feel useful, please. Then I want you to talk to me. And not in here. My butt can't fit on the edge of the tub. And I'm not sharing the toilet seat with you." She giggled and let it die when she didn't get a reaction.

Toni drank the water, hoping that would silence Nicole. She had enough warnings, advice, anger rolling around in her head that she didn't need another one with rollers in her hair to play the couch doctor.

"Toni, please talk to me. I'm supposed to be packed in an hour."

"Packed? Where are you going?"

"I was able to get a stand-by flight this morning. It'll cost me, but I can't stay. Call me a coward. But right now, I want my husband."

"Can you see if you can get a seat for me? I'll pay you back."

Nicole opened her mouth, then closed it. "Sure, honey." She picked up the phone and placed the call.

Toni left the bathroom when she heard Nicole thank the lady for helping her. She couldn't think about staying on this small island where so many things would remind her of Derek for another two days.

Since they were leaving soon, she slipped off her shoes and lay on her side of the bed.

"Let me start this conversation. Did you see Derek?"

Toni didn't respond.

"It's over?"

Toni thought about the scenarios that really could make the situation a pleasant reality. But they were from different worlds.

"I didn't end anything because there was no beginning. Why the heck would I get involved with anyone for a week or two? That's no time to develop anything. You need months, a year or two." Toni punched the pillow. "I can hear my father's lecture now."

"Forget your father." Nicole held up her hand in surrender. "I mean that in a nice way. Stop waiting for someone to tell you what's right and wrong. You had a misstep or two, but that's life teaching you how to detect the fakers and the players. Listen to your heart."

Toni didn't want to hear the clichéd advice about her heart. Her heart wasn't reliable for more than pumping blood through her body. She opted to start packing, something unemotional. She simply had to open the drawer, take her clothes and place them in the suitcase. Nothing that required feelings.

"I know you're mad at me. And when Brad finds out, oh boy."

"You didn't tell him? I thought you were big on not keeping secrets."

"Yeah, well I changed my mind."

Toni stuffed the last pair of pants in the suitcase and zipped it.

"Are you ready?"

"You're scaring me." Nicole readied her suitcase, keeping a close eye on Toni.

"Why, because I'm not acting like the blithering idiot that came through the door earlier?"

"Yes. Don't try to play the game of closing off your emotions. He hurt you. That's obvious. I'm here when you're ready to talk about it."

"Again with the clichés. Let's get out of here."

Toni walked out of the hotel that she had called home. She was becoming an expert at walking out of rooms, relationships, feelings. She wouldn't die from her heartbreak. She wouldn't lose her mind because she loved a man who now hated her.

Nicole and Brad were the lucky ones—in love, married, and about to have a baby. Timing had played a crucial part in their relationship.

On the other hand, timing had played a cruel joke in her life. She couldn't turn back time. She couldn't redo what she had done. She couldn't make her heart fall out of love with a man. This is what she would have to live with.

Derek didn't go to his parents' house for two days. The growth of hair around his jaw showed that he hadn't cared much about his overall appearance. He had turned over responsibility of his tours to his eager assistants.

He parked his car and stepped out. Only his mother's matter-of-fact summons got him over to the house. He hoped that there was no family dinner involved. It was no use pretending that they were a normal family. There was nothing normal about what he'd heard.

"You look a mess. How can you show up with wrinkled clothing?" his mother scolded.

"What do you want, Mom?"

"Watch your mouth. Your anger at me is exactly that, with me. Show some respect."

"Sorry, Mom. Is that it? I'm busy." He didn't make eye contact with either of them.

His mother knew him too well and he didn't risk having her scrutinize him. Once she had deduced why he looked a mess, there was no way that she would sit idly by as he suffered. He didn't want her help.

"We want to talk to you, son."

Derek tried to push his anger aside. He didn't want his father to be the bad man, the coldhearted villain. Derek ran his hands through his hair. He couldn't sit here any longer.

"If this is about what Nicole said, I don't think there is anything further. It is what it is."

"Life is never black and white. You can't judge things in that manner, not when it involves the human spirit." His mother took hold of his chin and then stared deeply. "Sit down, Derek. Don't be so quick to judge. Don't turn away until you hear everything."

Derek walked over to the bar. He needed a little help. "Anyone else for a drink?" He poured himself a splash of rum and filled the rest of the glass with cola.

"No," his father answered.

"I don't even want to smell it," his mother responded.

Derek took the chair closest to the front door. He suspected that after his parents continued their confession that he would have to separate himself from them for several days again.

"I was married to my high school sweetheart. We'd decided that we were old enough and madly in love with each other and we could overcome the odds.

"Soon after, she got pregnant. By then we were having problems. I wasn't the best husband, still learning how to be a man. We would argue. Several times she left and went to her mother. Let me tell you that her mother didn't like me even when we were dating in high school. She had big plans for her daughter and I had screwed them up. Looking back on it, I did.

"Then you were born and when we finally broke up, she took you. I couldn't go to your grandmother's to see you. But I would get little gifts to you through mutual friends. Your mother and I tried to patch up our marriage behind your grandmother's back. Your mother still lived under her roof.

"Then your mother got pregnant again. Later she got sick. Your grandmother didn't have a choice and allowed me to take you, while she tended to her daughter. Later she told me that the baby didn't make it. Shortly thereafter, your mother died. Once I'd heard all this news, there was no reason for me to stay behind, so I left and didn't look back."

Sylvia got up from her seat and walked over to Benjamin. She perched on the arm of the chair and put a loving arm around Benjamin. She dabbed at her eyes.

"It's my fault that he left. We worked together. I didn't want him to remain in Baltimore. Once I graduated, I talked him into applying for positions out of state. You are my son. We are a family. Maybe if we had stayed put a little longer he would have learned about Brad."

Benjamin kissed his wife's hand.

Derek hadn't taken a sip of his drink. He held it tightly in his hand looking into the potent liquid. Even though he didn't ask any questions, he had heard every word. He heard the pain in his father's voice that reflected his fatigue. He listened to his mother's love for her man in a difficult situation.

And yet he couldn't move.

"I have two sons."

"Successful sons, my love."

Derek set down his glass.

"I'll leave you men to talk. Then I want to talk to you, Derek." His mother left the room. He heard her go to her bedroom.

Derek looked at his father, envisioning another young man standing next to him. Maybe Nicole had a photo of her husband, his brother, but they hadn't gotten to that place in the conversation.

Would his brother look like him? Or his father? Or his mother? He had no recollection of this woman. Sylvia was his mother.

He looked at his father with his gray hair, and heavily lined face. His father aged well, looking distinguished, rather than a kind old soul. The anger toward his father had faded into nothingness. He could not hold a grudge against his father. He loved him too much to abandon him at this point.

"Dad, I can only imagine how hard it was to live through that, but then to hear it at your birthday party. Let me just say that this was not part of the planned activities."

They shared a laugh.

"I love you, Dad." Derek hugged his father. "I'll support any decision you make about this."

"I've been thinking about it. I couldn't live with myself if I didn't try to make contact with Brad. You have a big heart and can love me, but what must he be thinking about me and my actions? I can't make up for the years that I haven't been in his life. As a family we can open our hearts to him. I already like Nicole and know that I would like my son."

Derek squeezed his father's arm, glad to know that he was being positive about it. Unfortunately he wasn't so blindly optimistic. The fact that Nicole came to the Bahamas and was the one to break the news meant that Brad wasn't on board.

No matter what the new family relationship was, Derek wasn't about to have his father suffer rejection. He was going to protect his father as much as he could. He wasn't sure how or what he would do, but his father wasn't going to walk into a situation on blind faith.

After he was done talking with his father, he headed to his mother's room. Walking down the hallway was like walking down the hall of shame. He knew even before going in to her bedroom suite that she was going to pick him clean.

Once she allowed him entry, she directed him to take a seat near the window. She was already dressed for bed and looking at a nighttime television show.

"How's Toni?"

"Fine."

"When was the last time you saw her?"

"Don't remember."

"I didn't think that I would like her, but she has a good head on her shoulders."

His mother reminded him of a shark swimming around its prey. Sooner or later, she would dart in and take a bite. Maybe he could hurry the slap on his wrist. "I have an early day tomorrow. I've got to get some sleep."

"Never thought of you as a wimp. You only ran away from a fight once and that was because that boy was three years older than you."

"And that was in elementary school." He didn't like being called a wimp.

"Was this your first time?"

He frowned, not understanding.

"That you've fallen in love."

"I think that's an overused word."

His mother turned off the television and put down the remote. "Why does it always take a woman to recognize the feelings of another woman?" She rolled her eyes. "Toni is madly in love with you. It practically oozed from her, she walked around with a glow of love for you. It was worse when she was around you. Ginny told me. And I didn't believe her. Then I saw you when she came into your life and you lit up like a beacon. You were excited about everything, not just her. She inspired you."

"Maybe you didn't know everything. What Toni could do for me wouldn't have lasted for the long-term. And that is something that you or Ginny wouldn't know."

"I'm not going to argue with you or push you. You'll dig

your heels in and frankly, I'm too tired to fight your stubbornness. But what I do want you to do is be with your father when he goes to Maryland."

"What?"

"Your father and I discussed it and we think that he should go. He can't wait for Brad. Nicole has done her part. We don't think that Brad will want to see me at this point. He wants to go. I want you to go."

"Is this part of your manipulation to make me see Toni."

"Get over yourself, Derek. I don't care what you and Toni do or don't do. I'm interested in that man out there. I don't want his heart broken while he is in a vulnerable state. See, that's what love is."

"Fine."

"Good. Now could you give this note to Toni."

"Mom!"

"I would have it delivered to her hotel."

"And…"

"I can't. She left two days ago." His mother clicked on the television. "Seems strange that she didn't say goodbye. She took care of me that night after the birthday party. I was walking around here like a drunken sailor, but she was kind to me. The last thing I told her before she left was where to find you."

Derek's memory of that night picked up from where his mother had stopped talking. Knowing the facts presented a picture that was ugly. More precisely, he had stepped knee-deep in a mess and he wasn't sure he knew how to extricate himself and make it all better.

"Are you sure she left?"

"On the 6:50 a.m. flight."

Right after she'd left him.

He dropped his head in his hands and squeezed his eyes shut.

Chapter 13

Toni managed to survive the week living with Donna. Her cousin didn't push or question her about the trip. Nicole, more than likely, had filled her in on the details. And all she wanted was to move into her new condo.

Life in Glen Knolls had a strange sense of déjà vu since she was familiar with the small city. She and her three friends had discovered this piece of suburbia and settled down. Settling down became more permanent when Nicole opened her bed-and-breakfast establishment. It provided a central location for the four friends to meet.

The farmers' market was open on Tuesday and Thursday featuring locally grown fruits, vegetables, and floral arrangements just outside the historic downtown area. Once a month, other artisans were included in the list of retailers. Toni always made a point to shop on one of those days. There was no denying that the fruits and vegetables from small farms tasted better.

The mega supermarkets and superstores had successfully managed to set up their creations on either end of the city district. Toni did some of her shopping there, but felt overwhelmed by the sheer size of the stores' interiors. Besides, she lived alone. Why did she need supplies packaged in huge sizes that she could stock for the apocalypse?

Instead, she preferred browsing down Main Street and the side streets that herringboned off the central hub. When she needed a new cookbook, she could wander into Merlin's Cubbyhole and get the latest on the soap operas by chatting with the owner. On the days that she had no willpower, she would follow the smell of freshly baked cakes at Sweet Dreams Desserts to buy a cupcake still warm from the oven. Then there was the hardware store, a couple of real estate offices, accounting and legal firms before reaching the best barbecue house on the coast—Buckey's Wings, Ribs and Fish.

Not much had changed in the protected historic area. But Toni noticed that on the outskirts, new construction was everywhere. People had discovered their little paradise that gave ready access to Annapolis, Baltimore, and Washington, D.C. Since she was gone for a year and a half, she would be considered one of the new arrivals.

Even her condominium was a new addition. She particularly liked the garden-styled two bedroom apartments. Her selection offered an additional den unit. The common areas around the building offered covered gazebos, picnic benches and tables, and playgrounds. Toni particularly enjoyed the second floor view from her unit that overlooked the rolling grassy hills of a nearby farm. She was under no illusion that this could change by year-end with tract housing. In the meantime, she would appreciate the view.

Her kitchen featured one window that overlooked the parking lot. The view provided ample warning of any visitors, such as the arrival of Donna, Shirley and Nicole. She left the remaining dishes in the sink, turned off the faucet and wiped her hands on an embroidered hand towel.

There went her peace and quiet. Everyone had walked on eggshells around her. She appreciated it and hoped that it would have lasted longer. More than likely Donna led the charge to invade her home. On a Friday night, there was no telling how long they would stay.

She got the courtesy of one doorbell ring before she heard the key in the lock. Good ol' Donna, always predictably pushy and a pain, breezed into the foyer. She held three boxes of pizza and had a duffel bag slung over her shoulder as her heels clicked across the kitchen tiles.

"Here you go, sweetie." She set down the boxes and kissed her on the cheek. Donna never called her sweetie. Toni kept a wary eye on her as she headed down the hall into her room. "I need to change out of this suit," she called over her shoulder.

Shirley bustled around the kitchen taking out bottles of wine, water, and diet sodas. Then a low-fat, low-sugar cake emerged. Great, Shirley was on another diet. And they must all suffer along with her. Toni decided that she would play along with her for a bite or two, then she was taking out her praline ice cream.

"How are you doing?" Shirley had her in a bear hug that

prevented any kind of response. Then she played with her hair, stroking it as if she were comforting a child. With a quick pat on her cheek, she walked into the living room to scope out which chair was the most comfortable.

"I had nothing to do with this." Nicole remained at the door.

They had not spoken since they went their separate ways at the Baltimore-Washington Airport. Brad had picked up Nicole. Of course, he offered her a ride. Thankfully, she had already scheduled a ride with one of the airport shuttles. Their separation avoided the awkwardness that Brad would have noticed in the car.

"Come in. As the saying goes, what happens in Nassau, stays in Nassau." Despite what her girlfriends had in mind, Toni had no intention of having a therapy session with them with her as the patient.

"I brought chocolate chip cookies."

"And…"

"Peanut butter cookies, also."

"Good." Toni and Nicole had started the tradition since college to offer cookies as the token of apology. Nicole liked the chocolate chip cookies. She preferred peanut butter cookies.

After they each got two slices of pizza, they moved to the living room. Donna sat on the floor where Nicole joined her. Shirley remained perched on the love seat. Toni took the single armchair to ensure that her private space wouldn't be invaded by this lot.

"How is the new job?" Shirley asked.

"I'm getting used to it. Before the insurance company underwrites a property, I go out to take a look. Make a recommendation as to whether the manufacturing plant is insurable as is or whether changes need to be implemented before extending a policy. Keeps me outdoors. And no two jobs are alike. It'll keep me motivated for a bit."

"Any cute men in your unit?" Donna nibbled on a slice of pepperoni.

"I don't know. I didn't examine my coworkers." Toni didn't mind staying on safe subjects. But to have a discussion about men, specific or general, set her nerves on edge.

"Why are you sounding like a cold fish? Nicole, you haven't said much other than you met Brad's father and brother. Both of you are acting weird." Donna wiped her greasy fingers on a napkin. "I've got time. Still don't have a man waiting for me at home."

"Me, neither, girl." Shirley leaned over and exchanged a high-five with Donna.

"I told you everything," Nicole answered.

"No you didn't because you didn't say what was going to happen now that Benjamin, Brad's dad, knows. When are they coming?"

"*They* aren't coming," Toni replied. When they turned curious looks in her direction, she wished that she could retract her statement.

"That doesn't seem natural that Benjamin wouldn't want to reconnect with his son. At the very least, the brother shouldn't have any issues with meeting his younger brother. Nicole, what happened? Wasn't that what you were trying to accomplish?"

"It didn't go too smoothly. Some time needs to pass before I'll deal with it." Nicole rubbed her still flat stomach. "I don't want to deal with anything stressful."

"That's right. You shouldn't have to deal with anything, but making that stomach warm and cozy for my niece or nephew." Shirley looked in her pocketbook and pulled out a pair of booties. "I got this baby-blue set, but I think it'll work for a boy or girl."

"Could you wait until I get past my first trimester?"

"Oh, yes." Shirley looked over to Toni. "I'm sorry. How inconsiderate of me." She pushed the booties back into the pocketbook.

Toni set down her dish on a side table. Then she shifted to the edge of her chair. "I'm only going to say this once. I don't need you to treat me with kid gloves while Nicole goes through her pregnancy. You're making me uncomfortable and making Nicole restrain unnaturally her enthusiasm. It's been over a year and a half, and it's a memory that will fade. But it is mine to keep. I was having a fairly good day today. You have managed to come in here and suck the energy out."

She took her empty plate to the kitchen. Standing in the entryway between the kitchen and dining room, she looked back at them. "Bye."

Nicole took another bite of her pizza and rolled her eyes. Shirley looked mortified and scooted off the couch and headed toward her. Toni knew what that meant. Shirley was about to scoop her up again. She side-stepped her and used a chair from the dining table to separate them.

Donna mirrored Nicole's response with eating her pizza and drinking soda, but she accentuated hers with a loud burp.

"I don't know who you think you're talking to? Shirley sit and stop playing around with that twit. Fine. We'll stop treating you like we love you. Now that's over with, I want to hear about Derek."

"What about Derek? Take my word for it, there's nothing to tell," Nicole offered.

Shirley hadn't resumed her seat. Toni knew that she wouldn't until she had the chance to hug her. She remained still, accepting the love.

"I can look into your eyes and know that you're in pain. I bet there's a connection to Derek," Shirley said.

"Why are you badgering me about Derek? If I wanted to talk about it, then I would have done so. We had a good time. Now it's back to reality." She wasn't about to tell them that she had fallen in love. They would be quick to remind her that she fell in love too easily. If they would leave her alone, she would overcome this heartbreak. She could be strong. It was a skill that she had to learn and hone.

"Nicole, would you please talk some sense into her? I'm afraid that she'll reach an emotional low and have a meltdown." Donna stood. "Where's your bathroom?"

Toni pointed to the door near the front door. She knew Donna wasn't finished. She had been a bully as the bigger cousin two years her senior. When they became teens, Toni grew solid with a highly toned physique as a sprinter. Then she had the physical advantage over Donna.

"Toni would have to be the one to share any information about Derek," Nicole said to Donna who poked her head out of the bathroom.

"Okay, I see that I'm going to have to fight dirty." Donna dried her hands and aimed for the kitchen to snag a few cookies. She took a big bite of a peanut butter cookie. "Let me see, we know that there's a brother named Derek Calverton. He owns a charter boat service. Unfortunately I don't

know the phone number, but I think I can reach his father."
She pulled a number out of her pocket. "Can I use your
phone? I'm good for it."

Toni didn't move. She wasn't going to let Donna manip-
ulate her like a puppet. From Nicole's face, she didn't know
where Donna was going with this angle. Even Shirley looked
curiously at Donna for more information.

Donna picked up the phone and dialed. The other women
formed a semicircle. Toni held her breath, her body stiffened
with a mixture of dread and a slither of excitement.

"Hello. How are you? I'm calling from America. I'm
trying to locate a Mr. Derek Calverton." Donna smiled a
toothy grin. "Ah…you are Mr. Calverton. I'm Donna, cousin
to—"

Toni had rushed forward, pushed Donna to the floor and
pressed the button to end the call. "You have no right. How could
you?" She wanted to sit on Donna's chest and slap her silly.

"Calm down, Toni," Nicole urged in hushed tones. "You're
acting immature."

"I'm acting immature because you all are being rude about
my personal life. Derek and I had a physical relationship. I
said it, so sue me. I met him, thought he was reasonably good
looking. We hooked up for a couple days. When my trip came
to an end, we parted, agreeing to go our separate ways."

"You know, Toni, it's okay to show your emotions,"
Shirley urged.

"I've been doing that, but you all can't seem to get it
through your heads." The anger boiled over. They had stirred
the pot, unearthing all those things that she had worked hard
to bury. They didn't need to know that she had written three

letters to Derek, addressed them and put stamps on, but never mailed them.

She would hide the fact that any commercials advertising Nassau as a vacation instantly brought tears to her eyes. She didn't like feeling out of control. She couldn't very well walk around crying one second, arguing the next, and pining for something that could never be.

Toni stood over Donna, her chest rising and falling with anger, humiliation and frustration colliding to knock the wind out of her.

"Donna, are you all right?" Shirley dropped to her knees to help her.

She nodded. "By the way, Toni, the weather tomorrow will be in the upper nineties with a chance of an afternoon thunderstorm." She stood with the help of Shirley. "Now, stop being a brat and talk." She brushed off her clothes. "May I have a wineglass? I feel the need to celebrate."

The three friends performed high-fives.

Derek arrived at his office by six. Only a month ago, his morning started at nine, maybe. He'd grab a coffee, stuff a slice of sweetbread in his mouth and race to the pier for the first tour. Now he was in the coffee room, filling up his mug for the second cup dressed in a white polo shirt and khaki pants, the company uniform.

His secretary had a list of appointments as he entered his office. Since he was an off-shore contractor, most of his meetings were telephone conferences or Internet meetings. There were also the meetings with local city officials as a new entrepreneur reaching out to the business establishment.

He liked his days to be packed with meetings and work. The heavy schedule demanded that he multitask, burrowing under the paperwork until the muscles between his shoulders sent searing pain that radiated out his upper back and neck. Being incredibly busy saved him from answering his mother's phone calls. By the time he left in the evenings, it was so late that he could barely make it home, take a shower and fall across the bed without dinner.

For weeks this was his daily routine. When he got too tired in the evenings to risk driving home, he slept in his office. By the time his employees arrived the next day, he'd showered and shaved, donned a set of fresh clothing ready to begin the new day.

As long as he drove his body to the point beyond fatigue, he could count on falling into a comalike sleep. His body didn't have the reserves to dream. That suited him.

On the nights that his mind and body weren't taxed to the limit, he drifted into his recurring dream. Without fail, Toni would enter through an unseen door to talk to him, blush over his compliments, dance and spin around him with childish abandon.

Dreaming about her at night and thinking about her during the day had the same effect as sprinting five times around a football field. He awoke with an adrenaline rush and shortness of breath ready to kiss her awake as she lay in his arms.

But that was the past.

Now, he had to live with regret. He'd thought the worst of her, unfairly heaping all the blame on her. He could only imagine the courage it took for her to approach him. But he didn't have the reputation for being a hothead for nothing.

Any chance he had to rectify the situation would have to include a trip to Maryland.

Not all of his appointments were about the software business. He had one in particular that sat heavily on his mind. It had caused a sleepless night or two.

As a professional, he was determined to take on the demeanor of a business owner who made practical and wise decisions. There was no room for making choices based on emotions.

As the day went on, the need to resolve the problem loomed like a thundercloud gathering strength. The idea seemed to play on his guilt, his dreams, his regrets—none of which he could control. The only choice that provided some comfort to his conscience was a fast and clean break.

"Mr. Calverton, your three o'clock appointment, Fred Dundalk, is here to see you."

"Thanks, Juliette, please make him comfortable in conference room A." Hopefully in an hour, he wouldn't feel as if he'd sold his most precious body part—his heart.

The meeting room was on the first floor. As he walked down the hall, the pride he felt having his own company still gave him daily motivation. The designer had done a good job decorating the office space with pleasing colors and decorative art. They had brought the ocean vista indoors where employees would be spending most of their working hours.

He passed two managers chatting about the latest project. He greeted them easily, happy to see that they had adjusted to their new jobs. He dreaded having any disgruntled employees.

Fred Dundalk was reading the company's mission statement, which was framed and hung beside a limited number of lithographs in the conference rooms. Derek greeted him as he entered the room.

"I'm hearing only good things about you, Derek. This company is a shot in the arm for a lot of different reasons. Maybe we, Bahamians, can be known for more than tourism, don't you think?"

"I agree, although I can't say the tourist industry has been bad to me. And after all, it's why we're chatting today."

"Everything you touch is a winner. It is the key reason for my interest in the charter business. I'll replace the boat of course. But your exclusive contracts are worth some major dough."

"The boat is in good condition." Derek barely grasped the words that followed the remark about his boat. His "baby" served him well and he had conducted hundreds of tours with only two major repairs in the tour boat's history.

"I have a fleet that I currently use on the other islands. Got to keep things going to maintain my brand and continue development. Well, you understand as one businessman to another." Dundalk grinned.

Derek didn't.

He had no reason to be annoyed with Dundalk. It wasn't as if he hadn't done his homework and known the strengths of Dundalk's ecotour business. Plus, Dundalk had wanted in on his action from the first day.

"What about the employees?" Derek asked, trying to pull himself together and continue.

"They're welcome to join my team. We'll want to make sure that they're a good fit. My senior team will interview—"

"Interview? These people can't afford to lose their jobs.

It's a small number, I only hired two new ones and that's because business was too much for the other five." Derek tried to recall previous conversations with Dundalk. They had covered this very topic. Now Dundalk was trying to change the rules.

"Look, Derek. We're friendly competitors. I know you. You know me. All these little details we can work out later." Dundalk leaned back in the chair and pointed to his briefcase. "I came ready to deal. Look, this is what I'm willing to hand over today." He scribbled numbers on a notepad and flipped it around to Derek.

Derek didn't look down at the paper. Again all of this was discussed. Dundalk knew what he had to pay and the conditions of the sale. There was no negotiation.

Money didn't drive his motivation to sell his business. He didn't want to split his focus between the past and the future. His financial consultant wasn't impressed with the profits from his boat tours. Therefore, she didn't equate the labor with the earnings. And he certainly wasn't going to admit that he needed to do something drastic to erase his and Toni's first meeting at the pier.

He simply no longer enjoyed going to the dock, looking over the passengers for her familiar face, telling his assistants to wait a few seconds in case she came running up like that first day. Each time he was disappointed and relieved. He acknowledged that he'd done her wrong. And if she appeared in front of him without warning, he wasn't sure that he knew what to say after the initial, "I'm sorry."

"Derek, I'm offering you more than you asked. I'm showing good faith." Dundalk turned the pad around. His pen poised over the number before he scratched it and replaced it with another number. He spun the pad back to Derek. "I've got the public relations team on hold. Let's make this deal happen. Let's make history."

An urgent knock on the door interrupted any further discussion. Derek looked up to see three employees from his boat tour march into the room with solemn faces.

"Mr. Calverton, we need to discuss a matter with you," Todd, his second in command, said.

"Is there an emergency?"

"Yes!" Their collective voices filled the room.

Derek didn't hide the fact from employees that he was about to sell his business. Nevertheless it was an awkward moment with their potential boss and his unhappy employees in the same room. The awkwardness didn't prevent him from making his employees' needs the top priority.

"Fred, give me a second." Derek didn't wait for a response. He ushered the men out to the hallway, walking a few yards away from the conference room. "What's up, guys?"

"We want to make a counteroffer," Todd said.

"What are you talking about?"

"We decided to pool our money together and we want to go up against that guy."

Derek admired their initiative and loyalty for wanting to counter Dundalk's bid. These men didn't have much, but did have a family bond with the business. He also knew that they couldn't outbid Dundalk.

"Come with me, let's find a conference room."

They went into the biggest conference room since it was available. It took them a few minutes to settle down as they effusively praised the vastness and technological sophistication of the room and the office.

"Okay. Talk to me."

The men looked at each other. Then Martin, the newest hire, stepped forward. "My father works for a brokerage firm and he can get us financing to buy the business. We'll have to put together a proposal, but my father says it sounds good."

"Outside of the money, why do you want this business? It's entirely different when you own the company, rather than when you work for the company."

"Mr. C., I enjoyed coming to work. You cared about the business and you cared about us. There were times when I didn't understand why you gave us so many chances. But over time, I do understand. We're lucky enough to work together and like each other as people. We hang out at each other's houses. We help each other when times get rough. I don't think Dundalk can do that. I don't think he wants to. I know that I couldn't work for him."

"But you don't know him. He could probably pay you more and give you the benefits that I couldn't give."

"Only on paper, Mr. C. I've heard from his folks that he is mean with a penny."

"My father also suggested that we form an employee-owned company. This way anyone with a certain tenure level or seniority gets to buy into the company."

Derek liked the way Martin's father thought. It was also evident that Martin was soaking up his father's knowledge and advice. He could visualize him one day being a major businessman with his financial savvy.

"This is what I'll do. Give me twenty-four hours to

consider your offer. I won't make a decision about Fred, either."

"Thank you, Mr. C. Thank you. If you need any information from us, let us know. We'll get it."

Derek escorted them to the front door, making sure that they left. He didn't need them to gloat within earshot of Fred Dundalk.

Little did the men know how much he really liked the employee-ownership idea. There was nothing to think about. In the meantime, he had to stall Fred. Though he knew Fred would be furious about the delay, he couldn't stop feeling euphoric. In this high mood, he walked into the conference room with his chest stuck up, head held high.

He didn't want to get rid of the boat, their boat. When he was with Toni, they had always referred to it as theirs. With the employees owning part of it—since he still wasn't convinced about their ability to get financing—he would rename it Toni's Palace. Of course, with the new arrangement the employees had to vote on such a substantive change. But he didn't see any problems since they were like putty whenever she was around. If she held a conversation with them, they acted for the rest of the day as if they could leap tall buildings or complete some miraculous feat.

"Can we finish up, Derek. I've got to head to another meeting."

"Sorry, Fred. Something came up and I'm going to have to get back to you."

"What? Are you joking? What games are you playing? We had a deal."

"We had a deal for you to come in and talk to me. Don't

try to twist things." Fred Dundalk was not always nice to people who crossed him. "Tomorrow, I will make my decision, one way or the other."

Fred stared at him for an uncomfortably long time. Derek wasn't going to back down, but he wasn't going to get into a pissing contest either. He stuck out his hand.

"Until tomorrow."

He tried to escort the man out, but their paces didn't quite match. Fred did his usual march, a beat faster. Derek, on the other hand, practically sauntered. He was happy about keeping the boat where he met Toni close at hand.

Chapter 14

Derek's Sunday morning started with a phone call from his mother. He fluffed the pillow under his head so that he could hold the phone between his head and the pillow, close his eyes and occasionally grunt a response.

"Derek, open the door."

Derek blinked. "What?" His words drowned in the huge, erupting yawn.

"We're outside. It's important. Are you still in bed? Boy, it's nine o'clock. Get up!"

Each word screeched through his ear, hit one side of his head and then bounced off to hit the other side. He had worked last night because the insomnia hit like clockwork. At two o'clock in the morning, he came home.

What did she mean by *we?*

"You're outside? Of my house?" *Please say no.*

"Yes. Your father and I are going to the ten a.m. service. I figured that I would swing by because by the time church is over, you'll be hopping around this island. Not that we get to see you anyway."

He felt a lecture coming. Might as well endure it in the privacy of his home, otherwise his neighbors would be able to tell him in detail what his mother had said.

Hurriedly he ran into the bathroom to perform the necessary morning ministrations. He hadn't changed from his T-shirt and shorts. Although wrinkled, they would suffice.

He opened the door in time to stop his mother from completing another call on the phone to him.

"What took you so long?" She pecked him on the cheek and walked in like the woman of the house. And he wasn't about to argue. His father touched his hand to his brow and followed his wife.

"Do you need any coffee or anything?" Derek asked. He sensed that he would need a large mug filled to the brim.

"No. We've had breakfast. The doctor said that your father needs to cut down on the coffee. His nerves and everything that has happened," she offered as an explanation.

"Dad?" Derek looked over at his father. He didn't look sick, but he didn't look…well, there was no other word for it…perky. "What exactly did the doctor say?"

"Your mother is making a big deal out of nothing."

"Big deal, my foot. His heart started beating irregularly. One morning he could barely get out of bed to go to work. The doctor did some tests, but didn't find anything wrong but suggested he adjust his diet. Then I told the doctor about the news. We agreed that it was stress. He ordered him to take a couple weeks off from work and then maybe go back on a relaxed schedule for another couple weeks."

"Good." Derek exhaled, relieved that there wasn't anything physically wrong. All he needed was a little time off.

"There's nothing good about this, Derek. Your father is stressed over a situation that will be there two weeks later, two months later."

"I don't have the time to take him on vacation."

"Stop talking over my head as if I'm the family pet. I'm fine. Sylvia, just drop it."

"Drop what?" Derek looked from one to the other. His father kept his gaze averted, his mouth firmly set. While his mother stood in the dining area where she had stopped her pacing across the room. Her expression was one of irritation.

Derek walked over to his mother, knowing that his father wouldn't talk without major prodding. "Mom?"

"I think that your father should go meet his son."

"Don't make it sound as if I don't want to meet Brad."

"Sorry. I think that it should be done soon because this is eating him up."

His mother wasn't one to get teary-eyed over the story *Old Yeller*. But whenever she was upset or worried about his father, she was like a marshmallow. She wiped the tears welling before they spilled.

"Dad, you go do whatever you have to do. Let me know when you're leaving and I'll help you get whatever you need done." He placed his arm around his father's shoulders to reassure him that he had his support. "Mom, have you started looking into prices? If not, I could do it." He knew this would be tough on them.

"Good. Because I want you to go with your father."

"Huh?"

"This is for your father. *And* you."

"I'll go alone. I am Brad's father. I'm the one that I'm sure he hates."

Derek didn't want to go. Leaving the island was like leaving his comfort zone. That was one thing. But going to Maryland meant more than meeting his brother. He'd secretly hoped that he'd have a second chance to deal with Toni, but not quite so soon.

"Benjamin, you're not going to the States alone. Either Derek goes with you or I go with you." The look she gave Derek was accusatory. "I am the woman that you ended up with after your mother died. I don't think this is the time for me to go traipsing into Brad's life." She paused. "I'm sure one day we will all enjoy each other as a family."

Derek wasn't used to see his mother be so tentative. Yet the present circumstances had everyone on edge. He didn't have much of a choice. "I'll go. Can I have this week to settle a few things?"

"A week is fine."

"Son, I appreciate your company. Maybe you can come with me for the first week and then leave. I'll be fine on my own after that." He laughed, dry and devoid of humor. "I might be sent packing back to the Bahamas within two days." His fingers nervously played with the buttons on his shirt.

"Dad, Mom, come over here." Derek waited until they were sitting near each other. "Listen, we are going to get through this. We are always a family. I want my brother to be a part of this family and his. But if it's not meant to be, we have each other. Dad, if you need me to stay there for longer than a week, I will. As a matter of fact, I can arrange it so that I can conduct some business while I'm there. If I absolutely have to, I'll fly back for a couple days, but I will not leave you alone. No arguing," he urged when his father started to speak.

"All I was going to say was that we can stay in a hotel in that area," Benjamin replied.

When his parents left, Derek didn't climb back into bed. There was no way that he was going to sleep, he told himself.

One week to get his business in order. One week to prepare himself. One week before being near Toni.

The Calverton men were invading the U.S. His father would face his son. And he would face the woman he loved.

He knew that it would take more than a week to prove to Toni that he was worth her time. How many times had he told her how much he admired her determination and focus, especially coming to an island without knowing anyone. But he knew that steely resolve would work against him. The pain and emotional withdrawal that he witnessed that night would not simply fall away without a major effort on his part.

Toni was worth any change on his part that was necessary. Even though he didn't act enthusiastic about accompanying his father, his pulse shot up as they discussed the trip. Would she allow him to at least apologize in person?

Since he only had seven days, he dressed and headed back to the office. Four hours of sleep didn't slow him down as he typed letters to be sent to his clients in the U.S. He had three in Maryland and one in Virginia. Fortified by a mug of steaming coffee at his fingertips, he continued working through the day. Once in a while, he whistled a nameless tune.

Saturday finally arrived without fanfare. The weather was a balmy eighty-five degrees with a cloudless sky. For all purposes, it was a relatively normal day.

Derek sat on his parents' patio waiting for them to stop fussing long enough so they could get to the airport. In the meantime, he enjoyed a cold lemonade packed with lots of ice and admired the beach view.

Once he'd told his secretary that he was going away, she provided him with a checklist. Well, she not only provided it, but kept on him to make sure that he had completed and marked off the items. By Wednesday, he had completed at least half of the items and enjoyed a sense of accomplishment. He couldn't have stayed on top of things and been so calm about his departure if it wasn't for his assistant. He'd ordered a bouquet to be sent to the office on Monday. She'd appreciate the thought.

His father's contacts had come through because he had a choice between staying at a hotel in Baltimore's Inner Harbor or staying in a summer house in Annapolis on the Chesapeake Bay. Derek decided against making a decision. It wasn't for him to decide. He was merely his father's support.

But, he felt as if he was the one who needed support.

"Derek, are you ready? Where are you?"

Derek didn't bother to answer. His mother got herself worked up into a tizzy. And if he wasn't careful, he'd be worked up in the same frenzy. Before too long, everyone would be a big ball of anxiety.

"Ah, there you are. I've got a list of things for you."

"A list? What could I possibly be taking to the States that I can't get there?"

"You have to take gifts to your father's family and your mother's."

"I don't need to go visit anyone, other than Brad, as planned."

His mother looked at her husband. Derek knew that she wanted his father to intercede. He shook his head.

"Sylvia, there is a lot of ground to cover and gaps to fill. Let's take one thing at a time. Even if I go to see my family, I will be the only one going." He touched his wife's face with a gentle pat. "Don't fret, Sylvia. I need a calm head to fly into the unknown."

She kissed him on his lips. They hugged. Derek hoped that they could all get underway before one of them started to bawl. He hoped that he wouldn't be the one to do so.

"I'll drive." Derek took the keys. His mother's driving made him pump imaginary brakes. He didn't need that stress before climbing onto a plane.

He and one of the handymen loaded the suitcases into the SUV. He offered his arm to his father who opted for the backseat. He turned to help his mother, but she was not in sight.

"Where's Mom?"

His father shrugged, avoiding eye contact.

Derek didn't bother to badger his father. He was going straight to the source. He marched into the house. "Mom," he bellowed. Maybe his deep voice would get a reaction.

"Boy, stop yelling in my house."

So it didn't work. "We need to leave. We're supposed to be there two hours before the flight leaves."

"And we're not even twenty minutes from the airport. I have something for you to take. It's for Toni."

"You want me to take something to Toni. I know you are aware that we are not friends. Why would I take something to Toni as if nothing happened between us?"

"This isn't about you. It's my gift to her."

"Mail it."

"You could use it as a way to get close to her."

"Why would I want to do that?"

"Because you're miserable without her. Your father is taking advantage of his second chance. Are you too dense to take advantage of yours?"

"No. But I don't need you manipulating things either." He got himself into this mess. He didn't need his mother to make things worse. "Besides what would I look like showing up out of the blue with a gift from you?"

"Normal. Toni and I have been keeping in touch. She is such a thoughtful person." His mother smiled and fixed the ribbon that was tied around her wrapped gift. "When she left without saying goodbye, I was so sad. I didn't get to know her the way that I thought I would have. But she sent me a thank-you note for my hospitality." His mother looked down at the gift in her hand. "My hospitality wasn't exactly the friendliest. But then I thought that she was only interested in you for a quick fix."

"Mother!"

She waved her hand at him. "When she didn't think I was watching, I'd notice how she would steal glances at you. I thought that she was infatuated with you. I was worried that you'd be hurt. You don't tend to wear your heart on your sleeve." She pulled at his shirt to make a point. "But around her, you were like a pup. I'd hoped that you would have realized that you had someone special. But you pushed her, and what she opened in you, away." She patted his chest. "In here, in your heart."

"I know, Mom. I want to put things right, but I need to do it at my pace."

She sighed. "Take the gift anyway. If your way doesn't work, then you'll have Plan B."

"Thanks for the confidence."

"Prove me wrong."

Finally they headed to the airport. Derek loved his mother, but she was liable to drive him nuts before the plane took off. Each of them had to deal with the reality of the next few days. There was no turning back and bidding a hasty retreat. His mind and body had to react with the same energy and intent.

Even when the flight attendants demonstrated the safety procedures and showed them where the exits were located, he wondered how they would react if he suddenly demanded that they return to the gate. He swallowed a chuckle. In this time of heightened security, he probably would end up being escorted off the plane and directly to the security office.

And so with no distractions to consider, he settled back in his seat. His father flipped through the airplane magazine. Life had taken them to the proverbial fork in the road.

Toni had her job and her condo and not much else. At least while she worked, her mind focused on details. There was no time to wonder what Derek was doing. Those thoughts usually occurred when she was home. The television didn't hold her attention. She'd start reading a book and memories of her vacation would play in a never-ending loop.

She needed a diversion. Donna, Shirley and Nicole were not options. They had blown any possibility of an all-girls night that included her with their silly trick. None of them could understand what she'd gone through and had basically taken Derek's side.

They wanted to make her see it through his eyes. How would she feel if a man had done the same thing to her? Would she be hurt? Would she feel betrayed?

She didn't need them to ask the very questions that she'd asked herself when she'd left. The answers weren't so easy. There were circumstances and expectations that added to the moment when it splintered before falling to pieces. She could spend time trying to reconstruct what used to be, but it would never be the same. It could never be as strong.

Most women on the singles scene would have plans for heading out by ten o'clock for a night of fun and dancing. She'd never seen herself as most women. Although she lived such a life for a brief moment in Nassau, it was too short to say that she'd developed a habit.

Nicole, Donna and Shirley didn't let her doldrums stop them from their Friday night outings. They were sure to tell her that they were going to dinner, then off to play miniature golf. There was a course in Rockville geared to singles or couples on a date. The theme of the course had all kinds of reminders about romance with images of Cupids and love-birds to drive home the point.

Toni knew she was too fragile to act as if her breakup with

Derek did not bother her. It was too soon and her emotions were still raw. She avoided any reminders. Better yet, she would enjoy the solitude. Romance, as far as she was concerned, required a woman to give up too much in this day and age. She didn't plan to be vulnerable anytime soon.

Sitting on her floor with a plate of cookies and a strawberry-kiwi smoothie, Toni spotted the yellow telephone directory. She had an idea for an activity that would satisfy her. She flipped the pages until she spotted the section for martial arts.

The long list of schools and academies was divided into the different martial arts. Toni wasn't sure which one would be ideal, but figured she had nothing to lose in trying a particular style. Her finger scrolled down the page until she found tai chi. There were several in the Annapolis area, one specifically in Glen Knolls. She noted the telephone number and address. Maybe over the upcoming weekend, she'd follow up and try out a few classes.

That task only took an hour. She looked at the empty plate with a few crumbs. The open box sat on the kitchen counter. Another plate of cookies and another smoothie, then she'd go to bed.

Her phone rang. She let it ring until she walked into the kitchen. It was probably her friends calling her to be a pain. Her cookies were more important.

The answering machine clicked on. Her recorded greeting played. She paused with a cookie clenched between her teeth and two more on the plate. A woman said her name. A woman with a familiar Bahamian accent. Toni bit off the cookie and threw the other piece on the plate. It missed. She didn't care. She had sprinted and dived for the wall phone.

"Sylvia," she answered, breathing heavily from the exertion and the way her heartbeat shot into high gear.

"I hope that I didn't get you at a bad time?"

Toni reassured her, going through the usual pleasantries with every nerve ending at attention. Finally there was a break in the conversation.

"Sylvia, did you need something?"

"Oh, almost forgot why I called." She laughed.

Toni didn't believe her for one minute, but did the obligatory laugh.

"I sent you a small gift. Nothing huge, a simple thank-you for your consideration," she said, coughing delicately.

"I'm sorry, Sylvia, but I haven't received anything. I can't believe you did that. How very sweet and thoughtful." Why did she ever believe that Sylvia was a hardnose? "I'll let you know when I do receive it."

"Great. I know that Benjamin may forget, but Derek shouldn't."

"What…I mean, excuse me?" The mere mention of Derek and her thoughts swirled and scrambled into mush. Her tongue didn't cooperate as the questions rolled off like an onrushing tide.

"Benjamin needed closure. He and Derek, what a sweet boy, are coming to meet Brad."

"Does Nicole know?"

"No. Benjamin wanted it that way. He doesn't want to rush into things. He'll call Nicole when he gets there."

The tables had turned and the outcome didn't promise to be any better.

"You know I have to tell her."

"I understand. But don't worry, I have faith in my husband. Plus Brad would love to meet his brother regardless of what he says." She sighed. "Hopefully you and Derek can work through the little bumps that keep you from being more than friends."

Toni changed her mind. Sylvia wasn't hard-nosed. She was a sly instigator, a manipulator. However, the advanced notice was very much appreciated, but a bit on the incredible side.

"I'll let you know when I've received the gift, Sylvia."

"Thank you, Toni. Believe in second chances, sweetheart."

"Bye."

Toni ignored the plate of cookies and grabbed the box. She sat cross-legged on the couch, shoving whole cookies in her mouth. After coming to terms with the reality that she would not see Derek again, fate had interceded.

Sylvia may have wanted to make Benjamin and Derek coming to see Nicole sound like a normal event, but she knew enough about Benjamin to know that this had to be an extremely stressful thing. Her heart went out to this gentle soul. She wished him every bit of luck. Once she got a hold of Nicole, she would do her best to ensure that this time there would be a happy ending between the older man and his younger son.

She couldn't guarantee the same results with Derek. Nor could she guarantee that she would make any effort to ensure a happy ending. The promise of seeing Derek made the butterflies in her stomach flutter. Actually talking to him made the butterflies seem as if they were trying to escape through her chest.

Later that night as she lay in bed, she wondered if he had

changed. Did his eyes still crinkle at the edge when he smiled? Or did he snore when he slept on his back without a pillow? Did he think about their special night on the yacht, the way it filled her thoughts?

Sylvia had mentioned second chances.

Could she erase the steely anger when he'd overheard Nicole's angry remarks. His anger had seared her like a curling iron—no matter how quickly it landed against the skin, a burn was sure to occur. Then when she waited for him to make love, he might as well have performed surgery and plucked out her heart. The pain would have been less intense.

She turned off the bedside lamp and settled between the sheets. Looked like she would be making a visit to Nicole's in the morning. She drifted off to sleep with the whisper of Derek's name on her lips.

Toni sat in Nicole's kitchen inhaling the sweet scent of cinnamon as the French toast cooked in the pan. Nicole had three guests, which meant a hearty breakfast was being served. Brad stood next to his wife making the orange juice using the juicer as their menu advertised.

"What brought you out so early this morning, Toni?" Brad looked at her and chuckled. "Food going low in your bachelorette pad?" He handed her a glass of orange juice. "Don't ever say that you never got a thing from me."

Nicole looked over her shoulder and caught her eye. She remained quiet as she tended to the thick slices frying in the pan. Toni didn't call before showing up at her front door. When Toni raised a finger to her lips after the initial greeting, Nicole caught the signal and refrained from asking any leading questions.

"Brad, you heading out today?"

"Why? Are you taking my lovely wife on another tropical vacation?" He kissed Nicole loudly on her neck. "She came back all chocolatey brown. Good enough to eat." He made a big production of chewing on her neck before planting a wet kiss on her lips. "Don't get jealous, over there."

"Please. I had to bring back your wife because she kept whining for you. She's having a baby and she's turning into a baby."

"Hater. I will look after both my girls."

"Don't listen to him. He's pretending that he wants a girl first." Nicole scooped out the four slices of bread glistening with butter, laced with liberal swirls of cinnamon cooked into them.

"And her name is going to be Bradette," Brad announced with a father's pride.

Toni laughed at his silliness. There was no sign of any strain between her two friends. Something that she was afraid she would have to deal with this morning. Maybe the mini-vacation away from each other helped them in its own way.

Nicole lay four fresh slices of bread dipped in the egg mixture in the pan. Toni heard her stomach growl. She didn't know if she could wait until the guests were fed. Heck, she would pay for a plate of French toast and Canadian bacon if it gave her first dibs.

"Touch any of that food and I will stab your hand with this fork." Nicole didn't turn.

Brad, who hovered over the toast after his task was completed, looked guilty.

"Brad, did you touch that one?" Toni knew that comment was really for her. But why make it easier on Brad.

Nicole swung around and picked up the plate of French toast. She carried the plate back to the stove. "Now I dare either one of you to take it."

Toni tried to make eye contact with Nicole to indicate that they needed to talk. Nicole nodded. Her movements around the kitchen revved up a notch. In a matter of minutes, she had plates of toast, bacon, eggs, fresh tomatoes, a platter of fruit, and muffins sitting in the middle of the large dining table. She usually sat with her guests so that she could answer any questions, assist them with their trip and offer the personal touch that usually brought repeat customers.

This time she delegated that duty to Brad.

"I'll do it because I can see you two need to gossip."

"Why do men think we gossip?"

"Because you wouldn't be out here this early. And you wouldn't be wearing your T-shirt backwards." He grinned at her. That teasing, mischievous expression was identical to Derek's. The image of their faces was mirrored in her mind before she blinked away Derek's face.

She looked down at her clothes. Everything was fine.

"Gotcha!" he said to her.

Once Brad was safely out of the kitchen, Nicole threw down the dish towel. "Okay, spill. You wouldn't come over here unless it was really important. Or unless you've come to apologize about how silly you've been behaving."

"Don't push it, Nicole." She sat back in the chair, displaying a smug smile. "Keep it up and I won't tell you a thing. And you will wish that I had."

Nicole slid into the chair opposite hers. "I have a feeling that I can guess what it's about, but you tell me."

"I talked to Sylvia last night."

"Yes."

"She was giving me a heads-up that Benjamin is arriving today."

"Why?" Nicole held her head in her hands.

"Benjamin wants to meet his son."

"But his son doesn't want to meet him. Good grief, when is this supposed to happen?"

"I don't know. Sounds like it's up to Benjamin."

"Where are they staying?"

"Sylvia didn't know because they were changing their minds about the hotel while they were going to the airport."

"I think that I can handle Benjamin. Sylvia, though, may take some finesse."

"It's not Sylvia who's coming. It's Derek," Toni whispered.

"Benjamin and Derek are coming to see Brad?"

"Who's coming to see me?" Brad stood in the doorway looking back and forth at Toni, then at his wife.

Chapter 15

Toni didn't answer. Her brain froze. Her throat froze. And she would rather have been home at that moment. Her heart pounded against her chest. Maybe passing out could be her saving grace.

"Who is coming to see me, Nicole?"

Nicole looked to Toni for help.

"We met a friend who knew you when you were in college. Small world, huh?" Toni answered.

"What's his name?" Brad directed his question to Nicole.

"I think it was John." She rose and started cleaning the counters. "I gave him our number. He'll probably be calling."

"John. What's his last name?"

Nicole kept wiping at one spot on the counter.

"Don't know. I'm sure he told us, but we had a couple Bahama Mamas during the conversation." Toni shrugged.

Someone from the dining room called Brad's name. He frowned, but left the room to tend to the guest.

Toni felt as if someone had unplugged a hole and the air deflated out of her. She put her elbows on the table and dropped her head into her hands. "What just happened?"

"You know he doesn't believe us. But I couldn't exactly tell him that his father and brother are coming to see him," Nicole whispered.

The phone rang. They stared at it, wondering if it was the beginning of a calamity.

Brad popped into the kitchen. "Nicole, it's for you. Another guest wants to come in tonight. We've got the room, right?"

"Yeah."

"I'll take care of it." Brad left the room.

Nicole smiled, but even Toni could see that she was only barely holding it together.

"I don't know what to do, Toni."

"The good news is that I don't think they are going to get off the plane and come straight here. I also don't think Benjamin will show up at the door to shock anyone. I'll call Sylvia to find out where they are staying. Then I will talk to Benjamin. Maybe you and he can meet somewhere and discuss how you're going to do this."

"But I don't want to do anything. I did all that I'm prepared to do. I just want to go on with my life." She rubbed her tummy.

"I understand. You know that it's no longer up to you or Brad. You presented a gift to Benjamin and now you want to take it away. You're pregnant with your first child. Think about the bond you've created. That bond isn't limited to you, there's a link to Brad as the father."

"Would you meet Benjamin with me?"

"Sure." Toni had no hesitation.

"And I'll go with you to meet Derek."

"No."

"Good. I would be nervous if it was me. But you're strong."

"No, Nicole. I'm not meeting Derek. I know that I will have to deal with him when I meet Benjamin. But there won't be any one-on-one meetings. Derek has his life and his business in the Bahamas. Even if I had any deep feelings for him, this is my home."

Nicole finally finished tending the counter. She hung the dish towel and then turned to face Toni, crossing her arms. "Learn from this, Toni."

Toni returned home. She didn't want to call Sylvia from Nicole's. Brad still looked suspiciously at her. She couldn't tell if he had heard both names, one name, or none. Maybe it was only their guilty, startled looks that made him wary. It didn't matter. She had to leave Nicole's so that she could relax.

Once she got the information from Sylvia, she looked down at the number where Benjamin and Derek could be reached. They had decided on the house. From the address, she could tell that they had friends in sky-high places.

A plan came to mind. She didn't want to examine it too closely. She didn't want to face her motivation behind the decision. Sticking the paper in her pocketbook, Toni grabbed her keys and walked out the door.

The address showed that the house was about fifteen minutes away. She drove past the Naval Academy in Annapolis through the historic district until the city traffic and noise faded. Large mansions and estates could be seen behind enclosed properties or heavily treed landscapes.

She hadn't called Nicole to tell her that she had the number. Something forced her to drive across town to this posh neighborhood. Although she gripped the steering wheel with an iron hold, she wasn't going to change her mind.

To ensure that she wouldn't retreat, she turned down the street that led to a security gate. She didn't realize that she would have to make her presence known. She had wanted to surprise them. Too late now, she gave her name to the guard. She watched him place the call and then when she was cleared, he opened the gate.

Toni admired the magnificent brick facing that resembled an old estate in an English countryside. The landscape had tall evergreens that were planted close together like sentinels to block out prying eyes. Low hedges lined the driveway that forked in front of the house. The six-car garage added to the elegant presentation. She parked her blue sedan in the front.

A short curved stairway started on either side and met at the door. Toni walked up the stairs, looking at the tall windows for any sign of movement. Finally she walked up to the double doors. A lion's head with a large brass ringer through the mouth served as the ornate door knocker. She used it three times, then waited.

The door opened and before she could say anything, Benjamin pulled her into the foyer. He hugged her, laughing with warmth.

"Nice to see you." Toni did miss the older man. She had to admit to feeling pleased that he greeted her with so much enthusiasm.

"Come in, come in. Isn't this place beautiful? I know a judge who loaned me the house. I wish that I could move in here, then Sylvia wouldn't be able to find me." They shared a laugh.

She followed him into the main part of the house. The ceilings were high, crown molding everywhere. She could certainly learn to love a place like this. They went into the vast, formal living room. Large art objects from around the world, she presumed, and busts of various historical figures added to the formality.

She stood until he indicated that it was all right for her to take a seat. Nevertheless she sat on the edge of the large sectional sofa. He stood next to her still beaming. But where was his son? She fought against the urge to ask.

"I don't have to ask you how you knew we were here. Sylvia finally spilled the news that she told you. But that was fine because I'll need some help on this end to make this happen." Benjamin didn't take a seat. He paced, frequently stopping to rub his hands together.

"Benjamin, I told Nicole about your visit."

"It's definite."

Toni restrained herself from arguing the point. It was not her place to do so. "Nicole wants to see you first."

"Why didn't you bring her?"

"I wanted to talk to you before you met with her. Please understand that we all must tread with some delicacy. Nicole was hoping that she would have more time to prepare."

"I may not have that time."

"Are you sick?" she asked, realizing that Benjamin wasn't getting any younger.

"No, no, child, I'm fine."

"No he's not!"

Toni shot up from the couch. She froze in the spot where she stood. The background faded into nothingness. Derek stood before her, angry and imposing. She remained transfixed by his eyes. They were dark pools filled with fiery disapproval, glowering down on her. She swallowed, almost choking on the dryness of her throat.

"The reason why we are here is because he is not well. I want to see my father move on with his life."

"Stop sounding so angry, Derek." Benjamin came over to Toni and took her gently by the shoulder. He walked over to Derek and took his hand. "Here's my promise to you. Let's talk about setting up a meeting with Nicole. Then I will leave you two to talk."

Toni had regained some of her composure. "That won't be necessary Benjamin. I only came to let you know of the difficulty a meeting would cause at this time. Derek and I have nothing further to discuss." She didn't look at him. She had to remind herself that he was no longer important to her life. When she looked at him, her determination to remain strong and committed to their estrangement gave way.

"What is it that you want us to do?" Derek asked, his voice dripping with sarcasm.

"Let me talk to Nicole. She's expecting me to call anyway. Maybe meet with her Monday."

"Monday?" Derek interrupted. "Why not tomorrow. We don't want to be here for a very long time. I mean my father has to go back to work."

"I don't want to rush matters." Benjamin patted her hand. 'I will wait to hear from you."

"I promise that I'll help you, Benjamin." She saw the tiredness in his face. What a mess this was all turning out to be. Benjamin kissed her cheek and left the room.

Toni saw out of the corner of her eye that Derek hadn't moved. After his powerful entrance a few minutes ago, she wasn't sticking around to be blasted by him.

"I will leave now."

Derek warred with himself whether to stop her. He didn't mean to be so angry with her. But he had watched her come into the house, looking so vibrant. She looked unaffected, not pining away. When he heard her voice, it struck a chord that reminded him of what he'd lost. Emotionally charged, he'd come storming into the room.

"Toni?" She didn't pause in her step. Instead her back stiffened as she walked out the door. He ran behind her, chasing her down the stairs. "Toni, please stop."

"Oh, so you can be civil when necessary."

"Yes, I can also apologize." Derek reached for her, but she took a step backward. "I was rude in there. My father isn't as well as he pretends. This stuff is playing havoc with his heart. The doctor has asked him to take it easy."

"I can only imagine." Toni had stopped to listen to him.

He latched on to her sympathy like a man struggling to stay afloat.

"I'm sorry, Toni, for a lot of things." He raked his hand over his head, frustration building. He didn't know how to begin. Under the bright light of the day, he felt exposed, uncomfortable.

"What specifically are you apologizing for?"

"I'm apologizing for the way I treated you. Our last night was so difficult. I couldn't…didn't know how to handle it. I rejected you." He wanted to take a step toward her, but he could see that she was still on edge with him. It hurt that he caused her to mistrust him. "I apologize for snapping at you in there." He pointed with his thumb over his shoulder at the door. "Again the pressure…if you can imagine."

She rattled her keys. "I accept your apology. But I don't accept your reasons. We all have pressure. Maybe we were never meant to be. And since neither of us is interested in a long-term relationship, there should be no bad feelings or regret. We both got what we want—right?"

"I don't like being told what to do," he said, as if talking about the weather and if he cared for rain or sun. "While I'm here, I want us to start on a fresh page."

"Pick up where we left off? Is it that bad, Derek? No dates on the island of love? I know you don't expect me to be your port of call while you're in Maryland. You reminded me that I came to the island with a certain purpose and lustful intent. Now the tables have turned. I'm not interested in being the sequel in your act of revenge."

"You think so little of me."

"Your actions showed how little you thought of me." She rattled her keys again and then walked away down the steps.

Her brutal honesty was a one-two punch to the gut. It left him clutching the canvas for air. She hadn't turned around to gloat at her handiwork. Her head remained focused forward with a clear dismissal of him and anything he'd said. As his brain got to the number eight, he picked up his ego and his determination.

He leaned over the stone balustrade. "Hey, Toni," he bellowed with his second wind.

She looked at him over the top of the car.

"I'm not giving up. What we had was special."

"Everything has an expiration date. Ours has had its time." She waved to him and then got into her car.

Derek didn't run after her. Toni had revealed enough, making him realize that winning her back would not be easy. He didn't know how, but he was confident after seeing her today that it could be done. He wasn't so angry once he saw her pleasure when she saw him. Then, as if she had remembered her purpose, the pleasure turned into irritation and then grim condemnation. He knew that the instant she saw him, she was thinking back to Nassau.

Toni called Nicole later that afternoon, as she'd promised. Nicole agreed to meet them at the house the next day. They had to discuss how they would come to the B&B. Derek took down the details Toni gave and then hung up. She'd expected him to continue his sweet talk to sway her. A little disappointed that he would have given up so easily, she did have whatever few days that she'd see him to convince him to keep trying.

"What's with the smile?" Nicole looked over at her as they drove to Benjamin's.

"I was only thinking how lucky you are."

"Liar, that was a sneaky smile, but I'll accept it for now. Hopefully this mess will be straightened out before the baby comes. I would like to be able to introduce him or her to both grandfathers."

"And uncle," Toni reminded.

"How could I forget the infamous Derek. How did he look?"

"He's elevated to hunk status."

"That's because you are suffering from withdrawal."

"I won't deny that, but I put him on notice that he's not going to pick up where he left off."

"Good move. But don't play the ice queen to the extreme."

"Nicole, come on, what's the purpose of me playing along with Derek when our futures are so far apart."

"He did fly to Maryland, didn't he?"

"With his father. I'm just the side dish, which is why I have to fortify myself against his charm."

"How are you planning to do that?"

Toni drove onto the property after the usual announcement at the security gate. She watched Nicole's reaction, which mirrored hers except Nicole threw in a few expletives for emphasis when the magnificence of the residence came into view.

"I'm not planning anything. I'm going with whatever comes to mind." Toni parked the car. "Come on, let's go."

Nicole shook her head and followed.

This time Benjamin led Toni into the country kitchen. With the chance to visit a second time, Toni's admiration for the house didn't dissipate.

As she stepped onto the tiled floor, her jaw dropped in awe. The kitchen stretched from one side of the house to more than half of its width. The stainless steel against black tile and marble countertops set the room apart from the rest. The kitchen had a professional feel with large industrial appliances. Something she'd expect to see in a small restaurant. Maybe the judge had a large family.

"I've made coffee. Derek bought muffins from a bakery not far from here. By the way, he won't be joining us this morning. He was able to schedule tee time with one of his business partners at a golf course in Rockville."

Toni hid her disappointment and accepted a mug of coffee. With her part in the scheme momentarily on hold, she listened to Nicole and Benjamin chat about the details. If it wasn't so serious, she would have thought that they were overdoing it.

An hour later they left. The plan would unfold later that afternoon. Toni didn't like the way Nicole rubbed her belly. Her face revealed her concern. She worried that the stress of the ordeal wasn't good for her friend.

Toni sat in Nicole's living room in her small apartment in the bed-and-breakfast. With the baby coming, Nicole and Brad had to consider their options. Toni knew that Nicole wanted to build an extension on to the house. She wanted to keep the business, but wanted to make it home.

"First I don't see you and now you won't leave my home," Brad teased.

"I'm only here to eat your food and enjoy hanging out with the rich folks."

"That warped thinking must have come from my wife. It would explain why she shops with the stamina of a marathon runner."

Nicole emerged from the bedroom. "I heard that." She looked tired.

The doorbell rang. Nicole jumped and then mumbled, before going to answer.

"I hope it's not another guest. I don't know how Nicole does it when I leave on business."

Nicole returned with Derek following closely behind her. Toni stood, feeling that it might be necessary to help her friend.

"Brad," Nicole announced, her voice shaking slightly. "I want you to meet your brother, Derek."

Derek walked around Nicole with his hand outstretched toward Brad. From where she sat, Toni looked at the two brothers.

Now that they stood inches apart, she could see the similarities in their profiles. Brad stood slightly taller and wider. Derek was more chiseled. Brad had a more conservative style, while Derek opted for a casual look.

She willed Brad to take Derek's hand, instead of staring at Derek. A sinking feeling swirled in the pit of her stomach. Nicole hadn't talked to Brad. This wasn't good. She walked over to Nicole and grabbed her arm. Nicole shook her head.

"Brad, why don't we take a seat?" Toni couldn't let this spiral into chaos. "Nicole, sit with me."

Everyone sat, except Brad. His shock had turned into a quiet anger. He had yet to shake Derek's hand.

"Derek, you don't know this, but Nicole is pregnant."

"Wonderful. Dad will be so happy to hear the news." Derek patted her shoulder.

Uh-oh, Toni saw the door open to another disaster area. "A baby is such a symbol for renewing goals, dreams, anything positive." She reached into her arsenal for words, anything that would move Brad so that he stopped glowering at them.

"Toni, stop! Nicole, we need to talk, now! Derek, is that it? I don't know what my wife and you planned, but I'm not interested. If anyone bothered to ask me, they would know that there won't be any family reunions."

Derek stood and stuck his hands in his pockets. "Brad, I can't pretend to understand your feelings. But we share genes despite our different backgrounds. When your wife told me about you, I admit that it was a shock. I had feelings that I had to get through with regard to my...our father. Now another generation of Calvertons will be born and I'd like to be part of his or her life."

Toni had to give it to Derek. He had tenacity to take a stand. She liked that in him. To be on the safe side, she'd better get him out of here. She'd never seen Brad resort to violence, but Derek's life story could take him over the edge.

"Where the heck are you from?" Brad pointed at Derek's chest.

"Grew up in Nassau."

"Oh, this keeps getting better and better. Nicole, you didn't go to Nassau to hang out with Toni. You went to dig this up. And you didn't even tell me when you got back?"

"Because I had decided that I wouldn't pursue it."

"Then why is he here?"

"I wanted to meet you."

"Well, we've met." Brad stuck out his hand, which Derek shook. "Now that's done. Everyone back to their own lives."

"Derek and I will leave now. Let things settle." Toni pushed Derek toward the door. "I'll see you outside. Give me a second." She waited until Derek had left before turning back to the unhappy couple with their backs to each other.

"Nicole, I want you to take it easy for that baby. You can't get stressed out about things you can't control." She hugged her friend. She always admired Nicole's courage. When she dealt with her breast cancer in secret, all the girls had been mad. But it was the way Nicole dealt with life. She tended to deal with things alone. Maybe the best thing that could have happened was having a baby that would be dependent on her. "You did the right thing in going to Nassau," Toni reassured her.

"Thanks, Toni. I wish I could turn back the clock." Nicole peeped over Toni's shoulder. "He's so mad."

"You darn right I'm mad. I told you that I didn't want to meet him."

"Why, because he's cuter than you?" Toni prompted.

"This isn't funny."

"I wasn't being funny. I was being truthful. I think he's got you beat with looks and body. Nicole will lie to you and tell you otherwise, but I call it like I see it."

Nicole walked over and hooked her arm through her husband's. "Guess it's time we talk."

"I promise to listen." Brad sighed, a sound filled with exasperation, frustration and his lingering anger.

"Good. Things are under control. I'll check in with you later." Toni clapped her hands.

"Brad, I'm tempted to keep this secret, so let me tell you right now. Your father is here, too," Nicole blurted and immediately shut her eyes.

"I think I hear my cell phone ringing in the car." Toni hurried out of the house. Nicole could never do anything the normal way.

"Is everything under control, now?" Derek approached her.

"It was. Then, Nicole just mentioned your father."

"I didn't realize that she hadn't told him. What was she thinking?"

"Look, Bub. Don't talk about my friend like that." Toni got

into her car. He tapped on her window. Toni pushed the button to ease the window down a few inches. "Yes?"

"Think I could get a ride?"

Toni looked around. "Whoops, I guess you've been left out in the cold." She smiled. "I think this means that I have the upper hand. Hop in."

Derek walked around and got into the car.

Toni put the car in reverse and eased out of the driveway. She was acutely aware of the man next to her. Why was he leaning toward her, getting closer? She couldn't turn her head as she merged into traffic. Then he kissed her bare shoulder.

"You were such a good friend." Another kiss with a slight brush of his tongue on her neck.

"You're going to make me crash." She gulped.

"That's not good. Why don't we swing by your place?" He nibbled on her ear.

All she had to do was hang a right at the next intersection and she'd be home in ten minutes. And he'd have her in bed in two. Her body ached for his attention, missing his focus on details. But she wanted more from Derek than he was willing to give. His tongue trailed a path up her neck.

"Please stop."

He pulled back. The small distance felt like a mile between them. "Am I treading on someone's turf?"

"I'm not anyone's turf." She passed the intersection, relaxing now that she was able to stay strong. She took the direction to the suburb where he was staying.

They didn't say anything until she pulled up to the house. Benjamin must have been looking for them because he came out of the house to wait.

"I'll tell him." Derek restrained her. He squeezed her arm gently before getting out of the car.

Toni placed her hands on the steering wheel. She felt abandoned. Nicole and Brad were having their discussion. Derek and Benjamin shared the moment. All she had was her empty condo.

"Darn it!" She slapped the wheel. She opened the car door and slammed it shut.

Derek looked down at her from the steps.

She shielded her eyes as she gazed up at him.

Chapter 16

Toni felt as if it was the longest walk to the steps. Derek met her halfway with an outstretched hand for assistance. Touching his hand was only one part of his body that she wanted to possess. She stepped closer to him, purposely brushing against his taut frame before heading to the door.

She looked over her shoulder. "I want in."

"And I want you in." He pushed open the door.

She fought to collect her thoughts. *Take it slow. Don't act like your hormones are in a race. As good as he looks, as sexy as he smells, as hypnotic as he sounds, I could easily swoon and commit a few naughty acts with him on the marble-floored foyer.*

"Where's Benjamin going?"

"Benjamin's leaving." Benjamin took the car keys from Derek's hand. "I'm heading out to dinner with some company folk. They wanted me to check out their latest renovations. Will be staying overnight." Benjamin kissed Toni on her cheek.

Toni felt a small ounce of embarrassment, and a ton of appreciation for the older man's tact.

"Dad, don't you need a suitcase?"

"That's what room service is for." He chuckled and walked through the doorway, closing the door with a definitive thud.

Toni stared at the door, knowing that the step she was about to take would set things in motion beyond her ability to cope. Derek touched her shoulder. She leaned her head to the side and brushed his fingers with her cheek. His grip contracted and retracted as she touched his hand.

He pulled her back against his chest.

"Your hair always smells good enough to eat."

"Peaches."

He groaned, running his hands through her hair, from the back to the front. Certain areas of her body were sensitive. Derek could look at her breasts and they reacted like a flower blooming under sunlight. He could place a casual hand on her waist and her stomach muscles tightened to the point that a personal trainer would be proud. But all it took was for him to stroke the back of her neck, going up along her head and she could purr like a lazy cat.

She turned in his arms maintaining contact with his face. Their mouths sought each other's, locking together once they met. Toni had to break away to catch her breath. Derek didn't slow down with his attention, kissing her and playing with the indentations in her neck with his tongue. She felt as if she were in the deep part of the pool—sinking, but certainly not struggling.

His arms wrapped around her in a loving embrace. She held on to his waist to keep grounded, afraid that she would float. He had teased her mouth until she surrendered, inviting him for further exploration. He accepted the offer, plundering and conquering, claiming all that she shared.

Toni returned the favor, wanting to stir his emotions to a fevered pitch. She led her own expedition, bold and daring, moving through familiar terrain. She wanted to feel his skin under her touch. His shirt got in the way. She pulled it up out of his pants and let her fingers close on his flesh.

They pulled apart. The space between them surely had to set off seismic readings. They needed a minute to settle their pulses, steady their breathing, steady themselves in idle mode.

"I don't want you to think that I'm taking you for granted," Derek said.

"I'm not demanding anything of you. All that matters is right here, right now."

He nodded. "But I want you to know, really know in your heart, that I'm here for you, today, tomorrow, and the day after." He repeated "and the day after" until he closed the gap and kissed her deeply.

In a fluid motion, he cradled her to his chest and climbed the stairs. This man always treated her like a princess in a childhood fairy tale. But when he held her in his arms and played havoc with her desires, there was no room for fairy tales. He was a real man with a real woman.

They entered the bedroom where he slept. It took a moment for reality to sink in amid the expansive suite.

"Set me down, please." She couldn't stop staring in amazement at the elegant décor. The room featured a step-down sitting room, a raised floor for the large king-sized bed and the Roman style bathroom that was open except for the toilet area.

"A judge lives here?"

"Only part-time. Isn't it gorgeous?"

"Sinful. I suppose this isn't the master bedroom."

"No, that's off-limits."

"All I can say is wow." Toni looked out the window which offered a wonderful view of the backyard, tennis court, basketball court, and a putting green. "When I grow up I want to marry a man like the judge."

"What about me?"

"I'll treat you like the pool boy. You can stop by Monday and Wednesdays. Fridays you can have off."

"Today is Thursday."

Toni turned the lever, closing the mini-blind. She unbuttoned her shirt, taking her time, enjoying the small tic in Derek's jaw. He took a step forward. She raised a finger, holding him in place. She shrugged out of the shirt, leaving on her lacy underwire bra with its advertised extra support for sexy cleavage. He dutifully bit his lip.

She unsnapped her pants, and pulled down the zipper. Then she squirmed her hips while sliding her pants down, stepping out and then strutting her way to the bed. He grabbed her wrist.

"Not yet." She crawled onto the bed, looking over her shoulder at him. She almost giggled seeing him almost ripping his shirt, popping a few buttons in the process. He pulled off his shirt and tossed it aside. His pants took less time to go flying across the room. Her laughter erupted when he went airborne and landed next to her.

"Playing the superhero, I see."

"Got to do something to beat the judge."

"I can tell you what you need to do." She smiled, sliding under his body.

She loved to look into his eyes. The rich brown color wasn't flat like most brown eyes, but had a hint of gray that made them sexy and alluring. She kissed the tip of his nose, just for the heck of it. She couldn't get enough of him.

"I want you to kiss me right here." She pointed to her neck, raising her chin. "Then here." She tapped her shoulder, sliding off the bra strap to leave the area bare. "How about here." She pointed to the top of her cleavage, looking forward to his warm lips against her skin. Instead of kissing, he traced the center line between her breasts with his tongue until the bra stopped him.

She reached behind her and unsnapped the offending lingerie. He helped her toss it toward his pile of clothes. "I'm going to lose my mind."

"Shh. I'm not done giving instructions."

He groaned. His chest rubbed against her sensitive nipples. She clenched her teeth to keep from crying out.

"You were saying?" he whispered in her ear.

"I want you to kiss me once on each breast." He lowered his head. "But if I don't like the way you kiss, you must do it again. I will grade you."

"I've always been an honor student."

"I don't give As." She pulled a pillow behind her head and braced herself.

He trailed a finger from one breast to another outlining their fullness. She squirmed as he tickled her, pulling on the bedsheets to keep from raking her nails on his back. With her skin tingling from his touch, he then kissed each breast pushing them up with his hands. He avoided her nipples, attending only to the other part of her breast. Her skin tingled, hypersensitive to the tender attention his lips gave. She slapped the mattress, eyes tightly shut, fighting to keep the scream from roaring out of her throat.

"Have I earned my A." He grinned.

"Haven't decided, but some extra credit wouldn't hurt."

"You play dirty," he growled before returning to the business at hand.

Her right breast faced the torture first. His tongue circled the areola, making the skin pucker even tighter. Toni wanted to beg him to stop playing. She couldn't stand it anymore. Deep within she quivered. Her leg wrapped around him. Her body arched, no longer waiting for instructions. Her body responded with primal intent to find pleasure. Right now, she craved his mouth on her nipple.

When he complied, she didn't stop the moan that pealed out of her with slow deliberation. His mouth played havoc while his tongue sent shockwaves of delicious thrills down her spine. He pulled gently, sucking and twirling his tongue.

His cruel intentions became clear when she felt his hand slide down her stomach under the waistband of her panty. He teased the two most sensitive areas of her body, playing one then the other. Bringing her to the edge, then slacking off. He slid on the condom.

By the time he turned his attention to her left breast, she had reached her limit. She pulled off her underwear, not caring for the gentle approach. She wanted him now.

She wrapped her legs around him and pushed him on his side. Then she straddled him, subduing his protests with her mouth. Like a stranded woman in the desert who finally finds an oasis, she mounted him and rocked his senses until he was writhing under her. She wasn't done with him yet. She flexed her muscles, squeezing him, letting him know that the tables had turned and there was no more extra credit.

She leaned over him, enjoying his hands on her hips, guiding and helping her. Their rhythm moved to a hypnotic beat, pulsating against each other. She rocked against him, not rushing anything, simply enjoying their dance.

Staring into each other's eyes, she knew when he couldn't hold back any longer. She let him know that she was also ready. Their bodies timed their releases with natural synchronicity. Arched against each other, muscles taut, in anticipation of the perfect wave that lifted them in unison their bodies collided. They soared with hips interlocked, rolling, dipping, floating, consumed with the feel of each other, skin against skin. Time meant nothing to them. Where they were didn't matter.

The release broke with their frenetic energy. She felt him pulse within her and she answered with her own call. Their bodies went on autopilot finishing the ecstatic ride that had their hearts pumping.

Toni laid her head against Derek's chest using his heartbeat to ease her back from ecstasy. She needed this man like a dose of daily vitamins. Today when she made the conscious decision to get out of her car and tell him that she wanted him, she knew that this was more than a physical relationship. They had great, wonderful, mind-blowing sex filled with a loving respect for each other. But she enjoyed being with him. Lying next to him, listening to his dreams, talking about their families and their quirks added a deeper layer to their relationship.

"Dad wants to go see Brad tomorrow."

"You didn't get a chance to talk to him about today, though."

"It wouldn't matter to him. He says that he knows in his heart that it is time to build that bridge."

"You sound doubtful." She eased up on her elbow to see his face.

"Guess I'm a bit protective. I want to say that he's my father. But that sounds stupid because he's Brad's father, too."

"Are you going with him?"

"Yes. I promised him that I would sit on the sideline."

She kissed him on his cheek. *I love you.* "Call me when you're back home. I want to know how it goes."

"Sure." His lips tightened and he turned to look at her. "You know that once Dad meets Brad, if everything works out, I'm leaving. Dad will stick around for another week, getting to know him. Either way, I'll be gone."

"You say that like there's no discussion. This is the way it is," she mimicked his mannerism.

He got out of the bed and went to the bathroom to clean up. She waited until he was through to take his place in the bathroom. They barely said anything, except for polite "excuse me" and "thank you."

The warm water beat on Toni's upturned face. She enjoyed the feel of rivulets running down her body. This wasn't how she wanted her afterglow to be experienced. She turned off the water, dried off and walked into the room. It was empty.

"Derek?" She walked through the upstairs calling his name.

When he didn't answer, she went downstairs, still calling for him.

"I'm in the kitchen."

Toni heard activity in the kitchen, sounds of pots, silverware and dishes. She also inhaled the wonderful aroma.

"You never cooked for me."

"My father insisted that a man should learn to cook. Women love that stuff."

"Your father didn't say anything like that."

"Ready to think the worst of me?"

"I didn't mean that." She walked to the island situated in the middle of the kitchen. She leaned against the marble counter. "I don't want to argue. I want to remember what we were doing half an hour ago and how wonderful you made me feel."

"Sorry, I'm irritable." He lifted a pot cover and stirred the contents. "Finished. Have a seat."

He spooned out chicken stir fry with broccoli bits, carrots and water chestnuts over fluffy white rice.

"Wow. This smells so good." Toni picked up a fork and hungrily dipped into the small mound. She chewed, groaning with satisfaction. "Didn't think I was hungry until I smelled this. Thank you, baby." She kissed him.

He smiled.

"What's wrong, Derek?"

"Will you come live with me?"

Toni swallowed a piece of broccoli. It scratched its way down her throat. She had to gulp water to help the journey. She coughed, trying to clear the remnants. Her eyes teared.

"Didn't mean to make you choke." He rubbed her back.

"Are you serious? You want me to drop my life and come live with you. Just like that." She waited for him to say more, anything to make the request more emotional. Otherwise his request didn't encourage the kind of commitment that she needed before traipsing off to Nassau.

"We are pretty clear about everything else. Why not about this? We like each other. We want to be together. Do you want me to stay here? I will. Say the words."

Toni dropped the fork. It clattered against the plate.

"You would stay and give up your business?"

He nodded.

This is when she should be doing cartwheels around the kitchen. They would be together. All she had to do was say that she would go live with him or have him stay. If it was so easy, why did it feel like she had to pull teeth?

"This isn't how we should be. I can't go back to living like that. It's not about having a man in my life. Maybe we're pushing ahead too fast." She wiped her mouth on the napkin. "I don't know."

"Are you afraid?"

Toni nodded. Of course, he didn't know that she was resisting something that closely resembled the worst experience in her life. She loved Derek. But it was clear that he didn't, or wasn't prepared to, admit the same. The realization saddened her.

"I wouldn't hurt you. I want to give you whatever you want, whatever you need."

Except your love, her heart cried.

"Derek, would you come to meet my parents?"

"Thought you'd never ask."

She glanced up to see if he was making fun of her. "It's important to me that you meet my mother and father before we can discuss any of this. What you're asking of me is not something I can take lightly."

"I've never asked any woman to live with me or for me to live with her."

"But why ask me?"

His eyes narrowed as he stared at her. Then he shook his head and removed his plate from the table. "What do you want from me, Toni?"

"Not this." She finished eating, although the food had lost its taste. And the aroma no longer tantalized her nose. But she wanted to show him that she didn't run. She had to prove it to herself that she wasn't a coward. Baby steps were all that she could manage.

"Will you give me your answer after I meet your parents?"

"Yes."

Derek drove his father to Nicole's. His mind was elsewhere and this was the last place he wanted to go. After his meeting with Brad, how could he say that he truly wanted a repeat performance? They were both victims of circumstance, but that wasn't an excuse that Brad wanted to hear.

This meeting would decide whether there would be any further contact, whether he could walk away and say that he had a brother.

"Dad, I hope you don't have your hopes too high."

"I only want two things. I want to see my son." He dropped his head, his chin hung low. "And I want to ask for his forgiveness."

Derek touched his father's shoulder. He wanted his love to pour into his father and strengthen him for what he'd have to face. It was not easy for a man to ask forgiveness. But it was doubly hard to accept responsibility for life's misfortunes.

"We'll get through this."

"Yes, we will."

Derek parked the car. Benjamin stepped out and walked to the door. His shoulders back, head up, he reminded Derek of a soldier being court-martialed. Derek followed, his step not quite as upbeat and assured.

Brad opened the door.

Benjamin started talking immediately. Derek paused in midstep coming up the driveway.

There was no traffic. The breeze had stopped. Even the birds stopped chirping. The silence was pregnant, waiting for a sign to release the tension.

Derek saw Brad step aside, allowing his father entry. Then Brad looked at him. Derek moved toward the door, not sure how to greet Brad. His outstretched hand in their previous meeting had initially been ignored. All he could offer was a direct gaze, man to man.

"Derek," Brad said with a curt nod.

"Brad." Derek imitated the head motion, figuring that Nicole must have done some major negotiations to unfreeze Brad's attitude.

"Come in, have a seat. Nicole went shopping. It's the three of us."

"I'm only a driver for my father. I'll sit over here." He took a window seat that was very much in the room. But it was outside of the circle in which the furniture had been arranged.

"Brad, before you begin, let me tell you a few things."

Derek saw Brad's face tighten. He hoped that his father wouldn't launch into one of his long-winded stories. Now was not the time for a story, but it could serve as a breakthrough.

Benjamin began talking. Derek remembered the facts about a young couple, thinking they knew everything they needed to know about life. It struck Derek that the story had taken on a different nuance. His dad described his feelings about the breakup and eventual divorce. What it meant to be able to see his son again. And how he felt knowing that he had another child.

"Only a month ago I thought about how lucky I was to have a productive son and loving wife. I thought about how complete my life had turned out to be, after a rocky childhood and early adulthood." His dad looked over at him, then turned to look at Brad. "When Nicole broke the news, I didn't know how to react. I was shocked. Then the questions started pouring into my head. How could I not know that I had a son? Why didn't my family tell me? Why didn't your mother's family tell me? Was I such a bad father that they thought it best to keep such a secret from me? From you?" He breathed heavily.

Derek grew alarmed over his father's appearance. His movements became agitated. His head drooped as he looked in his lap.

"Shouldn't I have felt some connection, something to tell me that my family wasn't complete? Women have maternal bonds with their children. Why didn't I have paternal feelings?" His voice died away, as if he was simply thinking aloud.

"I grew up thinking that you had abandoned me," Brad said without looking at either of them. "I didn't care that you left me while my grandmother was alive. There were lots of kids in my neighborhood living with their grandmothers. But when she died, it mattered. The first home that I went to had other foster kids with various problems, some emotional, some bordering on criminal. Yet we were all together trying to stay in our own private space. But I told myself every night for the three weeks that I was there that my father would come for me.

"Then I went to an institutional home for boys while the system tried to convince my mother's family to take me. I know that the home tried to talk my family into keeping me, rather than sending me back to them. A cousin came to visit and gave me a lesson in family bonds. She claimed that she was telling it like it was. They had their own problems. I would be fifteen in a couple years and then I'd be a load of trouble. This home wouldn't be too bad because I'd be safe off the streets.

"I don't have any horror stories, thank goodness, to share, but it's an experience that doesn't need to be repeated. And during those years, I learned to…dislike you."

"You can say it—hate me."

"How can I say that I hate you when I look across my living room and see a part of me sitting there? When I look over to the window and see my brother. I can't use that word anymore. It would allow me to hold on to so much bitterness. And that bitterness was getting in the way of my marriage, my family."

Derek couldn't sit back and be a spectator any longer. These men had opened up their hearts to each other. He didn't want the moment to die and fade away, especially as they returned to their respective lives.

"Dad, Brad, I think it's safe to say that we are willing to

come together and talk." He nodded, glad to see that they nodded with him. "I don't want to jump over anyone's concerns or issues that may still need to be handled. But I feel as if we are all open to continuing this new relationship." He paused, again. "Brad, I have to leave and get back to my new business. Dad will stay another week before heading home."

"I would like it if you would stay here." Brad turned to his father.

"I would love to."

"Good. I will tell Nicole when she returns home. She will be ecstatic."

Benjamin stood. "Ah, would you excuse me."

"Oh, sure. It's this way." Brad led his father to the restroom and then returned.

"Look, man. I didn't mean to come into your house without earlier notice. I thought that it had all been worked out," Derek explained.

"I know." Brad offered his hand. "I'm sorry for the way I acted."

"No problem. It's all good."

Brad resumed his seat. Derek followed suit.

"One thing though, what about Toni? That's my girl. I don't want to see her hurt."

Derek had to wonder how Toni had won over the world. Even his mother gave him grief when he called home. Now Brad wanted to play the big brother role.

"I've no intention of hurting Toni."

"But you're leaving."

The accusation grated on his nerves. She'd left him first. Did anyone care?

"I asked her if she wanted me to stay."

"Big mistake." Brad shook his head. "She knows that you're setting her up."

Derek stared at him, baffled by his comment.

"You obviously haven't been around the fearsome four-some—Toni, Nicole, Toni's cousin, and a college friend. They would have told you a thing or two about how you're messing up the relationship."

"What about Toni's part? It's not all about me."

"They'll deal with her, but not in front of you."

Chapter 17

Derek had to admit that he was scared. Not nervous. Not shy. No, he was man enough to know when he felt fear. Meeting Toni's parents wasn't easy for him. Maybe it was the bits and pieces that Toni shared about her father. If he was so judgmental about his daughter, then what would he think of him? Through his eyes, he probably saw a foreigner coming to his house to see his daughter.

"Now you understand how I felt about meeting your mother." Toni fixed his tie before ringing the doorbell.

"I want my father." Derek fiddled with the tie that Toni had just fixed.

"I know you do, you big baby. I think he's enjoying himself with Nicole and Brad."

Derek heard footsteps approach. He fiddled with his clothes, once more.

"Hey, Mom," Toni greeted an older version of herself.

Derek smiled and entered the home. This was the house where Toni grew up and he was fascinated with it, as well as with the framed photos.

"Stop looking at those," Toni groaned.

"Why? I love knowing that you wore braces. Was this the captain of the football team?"

"Basketball."

"But a captain, nevertheless. You aim high."

"So do you with your Miss West Indies."

"I must talk to my mother."

Toni's mother laughed at their teasing.

"Derek, how are you enjoying your stay?"

"Having a good time, Mrs. Kimball."

"Please call me Linda. This is my husband, Wesley." Derek shook their hands. Linda was a perfect hostess who made him comfortable. Wesley, on the other hand, was more formidable, but at least he smiled and shook his hand with a friendly squeeze.

"Dinner is ready. We can go to the lanai. I'll bring out the dishes," Linda said.

"I'll help, Mom."

Great. Now he was left alone with Wesley whose ready smile had vanished when his wife left the room. Derek didn't like the way he examined him, stroking his beard, as if deep in thought. He'd asked Toni about her mother, or maybe it was that Toni talked more about her mother. But this was the man that ruled over his family.

"You're Brad's brother. Heard the story."

Derek nodded. He wasn't sure if his family history would

suffice or whether it wouldn't past muster. His mother's side of the family had toughened him up for the experience of rejection.

"Glad that you got to meet him. Figured that it wouldn't be easy not having roots."

"Toni did her part in getting us together. Toni and Nicole, that is."

"Yeah, they are like Frick and Frack. Can't see one without the other—like twins. No surprise that they dated brothers." He stood. "Let's go. Linda is a good cook. You'll enjoy the meal."

He guessed the first examination was over. Derek supposed that he passed because he was allowed to eat. He let Wesley lead as they headed for the dinner table. What could go wrong with a simple dinner? He breathed a little easier.

Wesley didn't lie. Linda and Toni appeared with dishes that, when uncovered, could feed an army. Fine china was set around the table. Large serving dishes of roasted chicken, scalloped potatoes, spinach, and glazed carrots lined up in the middle of the table. Derek didn't realize how hungry he was until the delicious smell of food wafted through the air and stirred his appetite.

"You're eating like a bird." Wesley's criticism punched its way through the silence and then hung in the air.

"Oh, Wesley, leave Derek alone." Linda turned a concerned face to him. "Are you a vegetarian?"

He had taken the vegetables, but didn't want to take any of the chicken until Wesley or Linda helped themselves. He didn't know whether to acknowledge his role in the traditional sense, since he felt like he'd gone back in time. His concern was now misread as a slight against Linda's cooking. All he wanted to do was eat, not eat and anticipate what question would be thrown at him.

"No, he's not. But look at his physique, does he look like he overeats?" Toni defended.

"And from that comment, I suppose you're saying that I do." Toni's father propped his arm on the table waiting for her answer.

"I'm not about to say anything that will incriminate me." Toni laughed. She leaned over and poked her father in his side. He giggled. Derek's fork dropped. So his daughter was able to transform him into a puddle. He felt better that there were different sides to Wesley Kimball. He piled the chicken on his plate.

Derek enjoyed the easy joking among the family. The scene reminded him of his family. He was thankful that his mother was so adamant that the family stick together, no matter what conflicts they had.

The conversation drifted to several subjects—his childhood, college years, tourism in the Bahamas and the Caribbean, his software business. Derek answered Toni's parents' probing questions. Toni was embarrassed, but that didn't slow down the questions. Her objections were brushed aside with parental indulgence. He had to admit that when they turned to his past relationships, he felt as if he were undergoing a police interrogation, lights and all. He felt the sweat prickle and roll down his back.

"How did you dodge the marriage bullet? You're in your thirties, right?" Wesley waved his fork in the air before stabbing a piece of chicken. "Or are you a ladies' man?"

"Now, Wesley, you're embarrassing your daughter, not to

mention Derek." Linda patted his hand. "You do not have to answer that question.

"Don't encourage him, Derek. If you answer, he won't stop," Linda insisted.

"I'm being attacked for a sensible question, just because I have the guts to ask." Wesley showed no remorse.

"I'll answer you, Mr. Kimball." Derek deliberately used his formal name, to let him know that this was a formal response. "I have dated several women. Some did want to get married. I did not. I believe in getting to know someone. I can't say how long it takes to get to know someone. Sometimes it's purely emotional. But I don't want to compromise."

Wesley chewed his food. His attention focused on the food around the table. "Thank you for being honest.

"I'd like to make a toast." Wesley picked up his wineglass.

"Dad, I think you've had enough."

"Yes, dear. And wine does give you a headache," his wife added.

"Why are they talking to me as if I'm a child?" Wesley looked at Derek for an answer.

Derek shrugged, remaining on neutral ground. Wesley had only had two glasses. Clearly he was not a drinker. At least he wasn't driving later.

"I only want to make a toast. Derek, I'm glad that I met you. I think you're the first man that Toni has brought home. Isn't he, Linda? Can't count any of those other fools as men. Well, I'm glad that she is moving on with her life. So much loss for a young person is unfair, although that husband of hers was a moron."

"Dad!"

"What? Why are you looking at me like that?"

"Wesley, really." Linda threw down her napkin. She got up from the table and removed the bottle of wine from within reach. She tried to get his glass, but he refused to release it until he drained it.

Derek didn't look at Toni, knowing that she suffered under her father's loose tongue. The revelation shocked him, but only as a surprise. It didn't upset him. Didn't make him mad.

But why hadn't she ever told him? Why couldn't she trust him?

Or did he really have to wonder? By keeping this information that revealed her history, she stated her position.

After dinner they returned to the family room. Wesley had been duly admonished and said very little. Derek tried to sit next to Toni, but she remained standing. He tried to hold her hand, but she remained stiff.

Wesley excused himself. Linda was cleaning off the table, refusing their help. He might as well be in the room alone with Toni remaining eerily quiet. She had closed herself off from him.

He placed his hands on her shoulders and turned her to him. "Toni, don't agonize over what your father said. I'm here with you, right now. Let's focus on that."

She nodded. He kissed her forehead.

The setting sun cast a bright glow over the afternoon sky. Toni walked down the neighborhood street to the playground. A few kids played basketball, laughing and talking trash about their court skills. Toni walked over to the swings. She could sit there and still see the game in progress.

She had had to leave and get fresh air. Derek stayed behind

to help her mother. She knew that she should be washing the dishes, but she'd have to apologize later.

To be honest, she needed to work up the courage to talk to Derek. Toni moved her legs enough to get slight movement. Then the momentum picked up and she leaned back and rocked forward picking up the rhythm. She enjoyed the feeling of flying through the air. The breeze washed over her face, blowing her hair in one direction, then another.

Her father's boldness did embarrass her. But he had also turned the key in the lock where she had buried so much and nudged the box open. Her sad history of men wasn't something to be raised like a banner and allowed to flap in the air. Nor was it her first choice for a fireside chat. Her history was ugly, it exposed her gullibility and it brought shame. She'd dated a few men, but rarely beyond a first or second date. Derek had said it was purely emotional. How right he was. She knew in her heart that he was the one. But was she the one for him?

"May I join you?"

Toni opened her eyes, almost losing control of the swing. Derek looked up at her, following the line she created in the air. She allowed herself to slow until she could drag her feet on the ground.

"Everything is cleaned up? Sorry I didn't stick around to help."

"Sure you are." He grinned. "You were trying to get out of scrubbing that roasting pan."

"Mom had you scrubbing pots and pans?"

"Actually, no. I volunteered. Had to woo her somehow." He chuckled. "I'm now her daughter's favorite boyfriend.

When I'm gone back to Nassau, you'll have to find someone to replace me. An impossible task I hope you know." Derek settled his large frame into a swing. His legs awkwardly stuck out to accommodate their length.

"I know," she said softly. "I didn't know how to tell you."

"Figured you would tell me when you're good and ready."

"I'm afraid it will affect the way you may think about me."

"Then you didn't understand how I felt when I showed you my grandfather's house."

Toni heard the hurt that she'd caused. She stopped the swing, walked over and held out her hand. "I'm ready to talk."

"Good. This swing is killing my legs. Let's go for a walk."

They walked along the footpath that wound around a large lake over a mile long. Toni wished that she were strolling with her lover enjoying his sweet love talk, chatting about the future, giddy with love for each other.

While they walked around the paved path, they passed others who jogged, cycled, or skated. She envied being able to throw caution and enjoy the moment with heady abandon. When Derek took her hand and planted a small kiss on it, she wanted to sob against his chest. She wanted to extract a promise from him that he would love her no matter what.

"I was married. Thought that I was in love. More than that, I thought that I could make him love me. I got pregnant." She bit her bottom lip, pushing against the desire to hold selfishly on to her pain. "Still I thought that I could make things better. My father was appalled. My mother felt personally responsible, as if she forgot to tell me something that would have made me make a better choice. I panicked. I wanted to hold onto that image of a perfect family, regardless of the consequences. Would you believe that I asked him to marry me?" She started to cry. Derek led her to a bench. She heard him explain to a few concerned passers-by that she would be all right. She tried to show that she was indeed okay, but ended up blubbering even more.

"I think your runny nose is scaring people, hon."

Toni cried and laughed. When she quieted down, she looked into his face. How strong, open, and honest his eyes were. Why hadn't she met him two years ago?

"He accepted my marriage proposal. Said that he wanted to be responsible. I was elated. I told everyone who was a naysayer." She thought about it. "No one thought he was any good for me. But I can be a stubborn one."

"Tell me about it." He kissed the tip of her nose. "Let's start back. It's getting dark."

She nodded and then turned toward her home. "I lost the baby. I still can't talk about it."

"Don't." Derek placed an arm around her. She enjoyed its warmth and his body firmly next to her. She nestled farther under his arm.

"Once I miscarried, the façade of the marriage fell away revealing the emptiness that had been there all along. I stayed with my parents because I'd fallen into a depression. I filed for a divorce. Sometimes it takes a lot of effort to push forward, but I eventually did."

"I'm proud of you."

"I didn't want to ever be in that vulnerable position again. Losing your heart to someone is a scary thing."

"You're right, but it's not when you lose it to someone you love."

"I thought that I was in love."

"Sounds like you wanted to be in love. But your heart knew that it wasn't."

"Since when are you the expert?"

"Because I was trying to convince myself that I couldn't be in love. But when it's real, you can't walk away from it."

They were back at the playground. The kids at the basketball court were gone. Night had descended and the playground lights lit up the area. They walked down the street back to her home.

"Toni." Derek stopped her in front of the door. "I love you."

Toni stared at his throat. Her mouth got instantly dry. Her heart pounded. Answer him. She wanted to respond, tell him how she felt. But she had to be the sensible one.

"Marry me."

Her story had made him pity her. He didn't reject her as she'd been afraid. His reaction was the opposite.

"There you are. We wondered where you'd gotten to." Her mother opened the door, smiling with the air of someone who didn't know the emotional turmoil she had only missed by a few seconds.

"We went for a walk. I'll get my things together, then we're leaving." Toni walked ahead. She knew that she only postponed a response. Once they were on the road, she would have to tell Derek something.

She heard him chatting with her mother. Then her father entered the room. Her mother excused herself.

"Toni?" Wonderful, her mother was going to talk to her, while her father would talk to Derek.

"Yes, Mom."

"You looked miserable when I opened the door. Can I give you some advice?"

Toni packed a few more items from her room that she wanted to take to her condo. She didn't answer, knowing that her mother would share the advice. She figured it was a mother's prerogative to ignore her daughter's wishes.

"You can't be afraid of life."

"Life has pain and joy, right?" Toni mocked.

Her mother sat on her bed. "There's no ideal in life or love. I don't mean that you shouldn't aspire, but don't build up a skyscraper of standards that no one can meet or overcome."

Toni said nothing. She heard. She listened. Lost in thought, she didn't notice her mother leave the room.

"Derek, I enjoyed talking to you. I'm sorry for being rude."

Derek thanked the older man. How could he be upset by Wesley's questions or by what he said? Toni might never have shared this part of herself if her father hadn't forced the issue.

"Do you love my daughter?"

"Yes." Derek had no more doubts.

"I know that she loves you."

"I hope so." He had never heard those words from her. And that's why he had his doubts.

Chapter 18

Toni arrived in Nassau with one suitcase. Tourists spilled out of the terminals merging into the central path leading to the baggage claim area. Thankfully she had a carry-on for this reason. Without delay, she walked out into the familiar humidity. She hoped that she would see Sylvia soon before she turned around and headed back to the ticket counter.

Sylvia actually believed that Toni could help her son. She didn't feel comfortable with someone having so much faith in her. She'd tried to explain as much to Sylvia, but she was persistent.

Derek was in a state of depression. The guilt weighed on her. The timing of his mood left no doubt that turning down his proposal had done this. Jumping at Sylvia's offer gave her another opportunity to talk to Derek. That's all she wanted to do was talk to him and make him understand that, although she loved him, she was doing what was best.

All she wanted to do was convince him not to sell his business. It had been his dream that he opened and shared with her. They had talked about its impact on the local economy and what it would mean for others who wanted to do something similar. How could he throw it all away?

"Sylvia, over here." Toni spied Sylvia in a bright floral top and white pants walking toward her. Toni hugged Derek's mom. They walked to the car as they traded stories about the plane ride and the congested traffic.

"I couldn't believe it when you called me," Sylvia said. "I was so glad that you changed your mind. I was so thankful. I'm at my wit's end over all this. The next thing was to call a doctor."

Toni stopped in midstride. "It's that bad?" How was she going to pull Derek out of this funk? Maybe she couldn't do this.

"Don't back out on me, now, sweetie. I need you as much as Derek needs you. I'm desperate." Sylvia grabbed her hand, squeezing it in a vise grip. "Nothing scares me much. You should know that about me."

Toni pulled her hand away so the blood could flow. She rubbed it, wondering if it was bruised. "Okay."

"I'm parked over here."

Toni waited for Sylvia to turn the key in the ignition. "How's Benjamin?"

"He's handling this as best as he can. He feels like he can't have any peaceful moments with both sons. I try to keep him calm. He's upset that he can't help Derek." She glanced at Toni. "He didn't want me to call you. Thought I would only make matters worse. But you're pretty level-headed, can keep your emotions in check. You'll be able to help Derek be logical."

"Sylvia, you're putting a lot of faith in me. More than I deserve. I really think you should try a doctor."

"Humor me. If this doesn't work this weekend, then fine, I'll try the doctor."

"And should I expect Benjamin to be mad at me?" Toni hadn't seen him since he and Derek returned to Nassau. She wished that she could explain to the older man why she couldn't be with his son.

"Benjamin is ecstatic that he reconnected with Brad. They are working things out slowly, and at least, they are talking. He's happy. We'll try to get together at year's-end around the holidays. Brad agreed to meet me then." She put her hand over her heart. "I'm so nervous about that. Can you imagine? I have another son."

"This is really good news, Sylvia. All of you deserve every bit of happiness. Benjamin is a devoted father and I know that he will do his best to let Brad know that he loves him."

"Yes, my Benjamin is a keeper."

They zipped through the traffic. Toni recognized the streets that featured various shops. In her two-week stay, Derek had shown her the entire island. Now she no longer felt like a tourist.

"Guess I have to share some news." Sylvia grimaced. "This happened after I called you. And I still think that it's important that you're here."

"What?"

"I have a couple errands. I need to pick up a few things for Derek's wedding."

"Wedding?" Toni instantly wanted to throw up. A ringing clanged in her head. It wasn't the peal of wedding bells.

"Yes. I wanted to tell you. Then you said that you'd promised each other to always remain friends. I need you here as a friend."

"But he's getting married." Derek was getting married? "You begged me to come. You said that he needed to see me. You sent me a ticket." Toni hated to sound so hysterical. But this wasn't easy news to digest and move on. He'd wanted to marry her. He'd pledged his love. How in the heck could he turn around and marry someone else? It had to be on the rebound.

"I wanted you to come and change his mind. Getting married isn't going to get him over you. It's not going to help him with the business."

But he was stable enough to ask another woman to marry him. Her hands curled into fists.

"Before I knew it, he set the wedding date."

"This doesn't sound like a depressed man. And I'm not sure this is a good idea, Sylvia. I came…" *because I love him.*

"Yes, sweetie?" Sylvia prompted. Then she patted her hand. "I'll be right back. I need to pick up his shoes."

Numbness placed its icy fingers along her body, covering her in a chilling embrace despite the tropical heat. She felt it squeeze her gut in a bitter grip. But her heart wouldn't succumb to the despair. She had worked too hard to open her heart and savor every feeling that proved love existed.

Sylvia breezed into the car. She threw the package in the back of the car. "Have another stop."

A few minutes later, they were in front of another store. Toni wished Sylvia wouldn't be so matter-of-fact. How could Derek go from depression to getting married? Who was he marrying? Why was Sylvia playing the errand girl for this event, while taking her to meet Derek? There was a sick element to this.

A tear spilled down her cheek.

"Oh, honey, you're crying. Everything will be okay." Sylvia rubbed her shoulder.

"Was he dating her while we were going out?"

"It's an old flame."

"How could he get married so quickly?"

"He always said that he knows if it is right whether it's one week or one year."

But he'd said those words to her. He couldn't fall in love with her and then turn around and fall in love with an ex-love.

"When is it?" Toni asked, but didn't really want the answer.

"This evening. Would you believe it?"

A coughing fit hit Toni. Sylvia patted her back. Finally her throat stopped tickling. "Sylvia, thanks for the ticket. But I can't stay here while Derek is getting married. I can't pretend that I'm okay with this."

"But you didn't want to marry him. He wanted to get married."

"I do want to marry him."

"Then why did you say no."

"I didn't think that either one of us was being sensible. I was being the rational one."

Sylvia pulled in front of a shop that was painfully familiar. Ginny's shop.

"Got to pick up the bridesmaid and maid of honor dresses."

"Sylvia, are you deliberately being cruel?" Toni shouted. She dabbed at her eyes.

"Cruel? No. I'm a mother doing whatever's necessary for her son's happiness." Sylvia leaned against her door talking through the window. "By the way, I asked Derek if you could attend, he said yes." Sylvia went on with her errand.

"Who cares about what Derek wants!" she shouted in the empty car. "I can't believe that I'm going to my boyfriend's, ex-boyfriend's to be exact, wedding." She wiped her nose and pulled out her cell phone and dialed Nicole.

"Where the heck are you? Brad said you left a message about going out of town." Nicole's tone held disbelief.

"I'm in Nassau."

"What?"

"It's a mess, Nicole. Can you meet me at the airport? I'm coming home tonight. I'll call you once I know the time."

"Why are you in Nassau? Stupid question. Did you see Derek? Did something happen?"

"No, I haven't seen him. Thank goodness. And I don't want to see him." A sob caught in her throat. "Nicole, he's getting married."

"Married! Look, don't stay on this phone crying to me. You had him and you let him go. Now you're there. Make the most of it. Go talk to him."

"And tell him what? Don't get married? Yeah, right."

"We already know that he wants you. The question is do you want him?"

"Yes."

"Listen to me, Toni. I know that you think that it's too late. But this is the man for you. You know that through every inch of your body. Don't screw it up. You love him." The signal faded.

Toni stared at the cell phone in her hand. She wiped her face. In her pocketbook, she searched for makeup. One plum lipstick, black mascara and charcoal eyeliner presented her with slim pickings. They would have to do. She fixed her face, fluffing out her hair around her face. Taking a deep breath to hold off any further tears, she used the mirror in the visor to tame the more stubborn strands of hair.

Sylvia breezed in and laid several full-length dresses in thick plastic cases on the backseat.

Toni pinched her nose. No tears. No tears.

"Are you okay?"

"Yes. Sylvia, where is Derek? I suppose he's home getting ready."

"Probably. Do you want to go see him?"

"Yes."

"Good. You do need to talk and not hold in any anger, or it'll overwhelm your emotions during the wedding."

"I want to talk to him, but I won't be going to the wedding."

"Sure, sweetie."

Ten minutes later they were in front of Derek's house. Toni hopped out and marched to the door. She lied. She was angry enough to sock him in the jaw. She pounded on the door.

"I don't see his car. But I have the key." Sylvia opened the door.

Toni stepped in, looking forward to snooping. Maybe she'd see a framed photograph of the woman who had claimed Derek's heart.

"What's going on?" Toni spun around the room looking at the boxes. "Is he moving?"

"Yeah." Sylvia walked into the kitchen. "Want a Coke?" She popped open a can. "No glasses. Must have packed them." She sipped and then giggled. "Bubbles tickled my nose."

Why was everyone acting as if this was just another day? She wanted to scream. This wasn't normal. Nothing about Derek had been normal. She tried to live her life according to rules. Rules weren't a bad thing. This wasn't part of the rules.

"Did you want to leave him a note?"

Toni shook her head. Leave a note to say what exactly? *Please don't get married!* Or better yet, *You're a dog! Have a happy wedding, break a leg!*

"Toni!" Sylvia stood in the doorway. "Come on. Got to get to the house." She sipped the Coke, tapping her foot happily.

"Where's he moving to?"

"A huge house in the gated community on the north side."

Toni felt the bravado deflate as she got in the car. It was the community where they had gone to look at the celebrity houses.

"Expensive area. He got some major contracts, plus his grandfather had a case of guilt and coughed up some dough. He didn't want it, but I kind of convinced him otherwise."

"I can't do this. I need to make a phone call and get the ticket changed."

"You can do it at the house. I'd hoped you changed your mind, though."

Toni turned in the seat. "Sylvia, would you go to Benjamin's wedding if it was to another woman?"

"No."

"See!"

"But that's because I would make sure he only married one person—me."

"What if you'd turned him down?"

"Then there's nothing to lose. You were prepared to live your life without him when you said no. Now you're asking for a second chance and why not?"

"But we don't know where he is?"

Sylvia pulled into her driveway. She honked her horn. When the servants came out, she had them take the packages in the house. Toni saw her suitcase being carried in. She didn't object. The decision had poured into her like cement and hardened into determination.

She walked into the house. The familiar rooms welcomed her. Toni visibly relaxed. This had to be a sign that she treated Derek's childhood home as if it were hers. She had come to love this family.

"Toni?" Derek came in from the patio. "I thought that was you." He came over and hugged her, kissing her on her cheek—like a friend. "What are you doing here?"

Toni backed away from him, flustered by his effusiveness. Before she could answer, he pulled her into the living room. "Dad, it's Toni."

Benjamin hugged her. He did look brighter since visiting Maryland. She hugged him back, genuinely glad to see him.

"Did you come for Derek's wedding?"

"I came because Sylvia asked me." She couldn't mention the word wedding. She looked at Derek, hoping he would deny this ludicrous thing that she'd heard when they finally talked.

"Good. I would have hated for you to miss it."

"Benjamin, would you excuse us?" No sense in dragging it out. She looked deep into Derek's eyes to see if there was any sign that he was in turmoil. Maybe he felt pressured to get married, have someone commit to him because she had turned him down. There was nothing staring back from the chocolate-brown eyes, except a benign friendliness.

"Could we sit?" she asked after Benjamin left the room.

"Sure. Would you like something to drink?"

She shook her head. His polite attention drove her crazy. Where was the passion that was just below the surface? Where was his teasing and inappropriate kissing on her neck?

"Derek, I don't know how to say this. How to begin."

"Take your time." He laughed, slapping his knee. "At least I don't have to get ready for another couple hours. Then it's down the aisle for me."

"Shut up!" Her hand shot up to her mouth. She gasped behind her fingers. Then she lowered her trembling hand and took a breath. "Who are you marrying?"

"You don't know her."

"Entertain me. Maybe I want to write her name in the card."

"I'll do better than that, I'll introduce you. She'll be here soon."

Toni looked around, expecting a supermodel-type to walk through the door. She had to recall Sylvia's advice to get her through this. At this moment, her thoughts were filled with mayhem.

"Before she comes, I want to ask you something."

Derek didn't respond.

"Would you please reconsider marrying?"

Derek didn't respond.

"I know that I sound crazy." She looked up to the ceiling, squeezing her eyes shut for the courage to continue. "I have been hiding for a long time. I've been keeping a part of my feelings in reserve for that day when I may have to tap into them for help."

Derek still didn't respond.

"You could help here," Toni prompted.

"I've already said what was in my heart. I meant it then."

"And what about now? I want you in my life. I know that I said no. I like saying no." She tried to laugh at her own joke. "I love you, Derek." There, she saw a reaction. Maybe he had a twitch, but she was accepting that as a breakthrough. "I have loved you since day three after we met."

"Why not day one?"

"Because I was in the state of liking in day one."

"Day two?"

"I was in a state of lust."

"I kind of liked the lust, though." He smiled, slow and very sexy.

"I can do lust. Give me a second chance."

"On one condition." His lips claimed hers, bold and daring. She surrendered, opening herself, inviting him. His tongue began a slow dance, leading in its mating ritual with her tongue. Slow, deep exploration stirred her passion locked deep in the core of her being. He sucked on her lips and she sighed as she floated in a cloud of love that was infused in a glorious ray of colors. He was making her lose her mind. She wrapped her arms around him and arched against him with a need that was full of wanton lust.

"I want you until it hurts." Toni gasped for air.

"On one condition," Derek whispered.

"Anything."

"I want you to marry me." He pulled a ring from his pocket and held it up.

Toni looked at the diamond. It was a rock sparkling in the light. She held out her left hand. She had to place it on his knee to keep it steady. "What about your wedding today—two wives?"

"No, only one wife. It's always been one wife—you." He kissed her again and slid the ring on her finger.

"Congratulations!" The roar of voices startled her.

Toni saw her parents come into the room. Her mother was crying. Her father's chest was puffed out like a proud peacock while he shook everyone's hand. Then Benjamin hugged them both. Toni looked at Sylvia. "Somehow, I know this has you written all over it."

"You were taking too long to come to your senses. Obviously Derek couldn't close the deal. As a former real estate agent, one thing I did learn was how to close the deal."

"I'd say that I closed this one just fine."

"I was about to slap a 'Rated X' sticker on both of your foreheads," Linda teased.

Toni's face grew hot at the realization that they'd heard everything.

"Don't worry, sweetie. I'm the only one who witnessed. And I won't tell. But a few more seconds and I would have had to go find my husband."

Toni giggled and hugged Sylvia. "The clothes from Ginny?"

"They're down the hall. Might as well get dressed. The

guests are here. The judge will be here soon. All the required paperwork was handled."

Toni went down the hall. Excitement bubbled within her soaring to a delirious state. She walked into the room and saw the dress, her wedding dress, hanging on the closet door. Tears streamed down her face and she wept softly. Ginny had kept her dress. She looked down at the ballerina-style slippers. She touched them, blinking away the blinding tears. "How did she know my size?"

"Because I told her." Nicole stepped out of the shadows in the room.

Then Toni noticed Shirley and Donna. "Oh my gosh. I can't believe all of you are here?"

"We had to make sure that you didn't screw this up *again*. We were all prepared to yell at you until you had no other choice. So we're glad that you did it with only a little nudge."

"You guys are the greatest."

"Okay, hurry up and get dressed. Our clothes are in Linda's room. Your father will come and get you when it's time. I'll stop by to help you with the finishing touches," Nicole offered.

Toni had to sit on the bed before she could dress. This was the time that her fear would get the best of her. She would consider everything that could go wrong. The doubts that she'd held on to would emerge creating havoc. Her pattern had always been to take the path that looked straight and flat. She didn't like surprises.

Today was the best surprise of her life. She had to throw caution, doubts and insecurities that she used as her crutch to the wind. When she saw Derek, she knew the only way to conquer and claim him for herself was to trust him.

She went to the adjoining bathroom and started her preparation. In an hour, she would be a bride. Her future husband stood several feet away, waiting for her. Finally she could say with honesty that she had put the past firmly behind her. She didn't need it to live. Its imprint would be a part of her past. But she had found focus with a strong, loving man and she wanted to spend the rest of her life with him.

She slipped the dress over her head. She had dubbed this dress her magic dress. It transformed her and she felt like a princess going to meet her prince. A soft knock at the door sounded.

"You look beautiful, my friend." Nicole stepped in the room in a rose spaghetti-strapped dress fashioned after the wedding dress. Her bodice hugged her frame and the skirt billowed out in a soft, lightweight material.

"I hope that dress is not squeezing my niece's head."

"It's pretty comfortable. Believe me, I thought the same thing when I saw the style. And your *nephew* is doing fine. But enough about me, I want you to know how beautiful you look. Your face is so radiant that I don't know how you could have doubted being with this man. You are the best thing that came into his life. When I first saw you together, I recognized what I had experienced with Brad. Both of you were glowing, but too blinded to see what was right in front of your faces. Derek understood a little before you, but boy, what an outcome!"

Her father popped his head in. "It's time."

Toni opened the door wider to see her father standing in

ront of her in a black tuxedo. His face was tight as he fought
o keep his emotions in check. She tiptoed and kissed his
heek.

"You look so beautiful. I knew from the first time that I
met Derek that he would be the man you deserved to have at
our side. I was afraid that you didn't believe yourself
worthy."

"Everyone is telling me the same thing. I was afraid, but
m not anymore."

The music sounded. She saw her friends walk up the
allway and disappear around the corner. She didn't even
now where to walk, what to do. The reality of how crazy this
was tickled her and she giggled.

"Are you okay?" Her father stopped walking.

"Yes, Dad. This is a little over the top, don't you think?"

"Since when did you do anything without a little pizzazz."

They walked down the hallway and emerged in the center
f the house. Toni saw the layout for the outdoor wedding.
here were flowers everywhere. She saw her friends and
amily and a few of the people whom she'd met when she
went to the reception with Derek. Of course, there were
eople who were Sylvia's friends. But that didn't matter. At
he front, in an all-white tuxedo, her man stood waiting for
er.

She walked onto the patio, wishing that she could pick up
he dress and run into his arms.

"Oh, Dad," Toni whispered through clenched teeth, "no
vine, please."

"You don't have to worry. Your mother has already
hreatened me."

Toni grinned. Everything would be all right.

She took her place next to Derek. She looked at his handsome profile. He stared straight ahead. "I love you," she whispered.

He answered with a squeeze of her hand.

The first words of the official ceremony were spoken. Toni tried to focus on each sentence. Memorize it. Ponder its meaning. All she could clearly hear as it registered through the swirl of excitement were the words "you may now kiss the bride."

Then her husband's lips obeyed and extracted her promise *to love and cherish him*. She wasn't to be denied and extracted his pledge *until death do us part*.

Derek looked at his wife. He drew in a satisfied breath. Their journey toward love had been eventful, but he was sure that it was their destiny to meet and complete the circle of love. As he surveyed the families that had come together with a common purpose to celebrate their love and commitment, their well wishes overwhelmed him.

He admired Toni in her beautiful dress. She looked regal, yet delicate in a fashion, but with courage and strength that he valued and honored. She was his woman. His wife. His soul mate. He leaned over and whispered in her ear. "I will always love you, Toni Calverton."

Dear Reader,

Here's the second installment of the story about the ladies in Glen Knolls, Maryland. *Island Rendezvous* is the sequel to *Romantic Times BOOKclub* Top Pick—*Finders Keepers,* in which Nicole and Brad Montgomery fell in love.

Brad's story wasn't complete until he resolved the anger and bitterness he felt toward his father, and to some degree toward his brother. In *Island Rendezvous,* reconciliation and hope are the messages of love. The spotlight shines on the unlikely match between Toni Kimball and Derek Calverton, Brad's brother, in the wonderful, tropical setting of Nassau, Bahamas.

I'd love to hear your thoughts about the story, which gave me a great sense of satisfaction to write. You may contact me at michellemonkou@aol.com, or write to P.O. Box 2904, Laurel, Maryland 20709. Visit my Web site atwww.michellemonkou.com.

Only Shirley and Donna are left. Whose story will be next?

Stay tuned.

Michelle Monkou